BLOOD QUEEN

BLOOD QUEEN

THE BLOOD BOUND SERIES
BOOK 4

SABRINA VOERMAN

Blood Queen: The Blood Bound Series, Book Four
By Sabrina Voerman
Published by Quill & Crow Publishing House

Cover Design by Fay Lane

Edited by Tiffany Putenis, Lisa Morris

Interior by Cassandra L. Thompson

Printed in the United States of America

ISBN (ebook) 978-1-958228-95-1

ISBN (print) 978-1-958228-96-8

Publisher's Website: quillandcrowpublishinghouse.com

THE BLOOD BOUND SERIES
BY SABRINA VOERMAN

Weaving the real world with fantasy, The Blood Bound Series features four books inspired by history and brimming with magic. Witches, werewolves, vampires, and sirens are at the helm of the series, featuring an overarching story that expands over centuries.

This is the fourth book in The Blood Bound Series. Blood Coven is the first book, Ashen Heart is the second book, and Song of the Sea is the third. All three of those books can be read in any order, but they do have some minor connections that cross over. The preferred order is the publication order.

For Kate.
xoxo

A NOTE FROM THE PUBLISHER

Please consult the back of the book for content warnings. Index A is a helpful guide to understand the Blood Bound Series timeline. Index B includes a list of potential triggers.

A BRIEF HISTORY OF WITCHES
AN EXCERPT

~

The Year of the Curse

...an ancient power drawn from the blood of virgins. Some believed lathering oneself in animal blood was good for the skin. To go one step further may warrant far more powerful side effects. It has spread through the witch community that this is the key to immortality. With the right incantation, it is suggested one may absorb the youth of each sacrifice into their own skin to remain young.

Whether a witch has succeeded at this is undetermined. How doth one record such things, when it takes years to reveal whether or not such trials prove successful?

On such a note, how can one live with oneself, bathing in the blood of young virgin girls?

Such things will be tried—of that I have no doubt—but for the sake of girls all over the world, especially those who may themselves be witches...

I hope it never does.

1

TATIANA

The Year of the Moon
Silvania

Blood-stained.

Four young women stood in the forest just outside of Silvania. They could not go back to the town where whole families had been slain overnight. Should they return, they would be torn apart or burned at the stake. They could not remain inside the house where their friend—witch, sister—had been murdered. They had nowhere to go.

Tatiana Floarea came to her senses as a raven quorked in the trees above them. As she jerked her head toward the sound, she noticed snow beginning to fall. Slowly, the bloodstained earth around them disappeared under its perfection.

Making the world new again.

Tatiana sighed and did what she always did—she rolled up her sleeves and dealt with the mess. She walked past her sister Lilianna, who was quietly consoling Alina. They didn't need to speak to offer solace.

Sorin turned to look at Tatiana, her brown curls matted with blood and gore. Her dark eyes focused on the eldest Floarea sister. "Where are you going?"

"We cannot leave so many bodies in the open," Tatiana said. "They'll find my father—if they haven't already—but it will take them days, maybe weeks, before they come this far. No one checked on Heather Luca."

"Except Red," Lilianna said, earning a sharp glare from her sister. It was too soon to be talking about Red, especially in front of Alina. Though Tatiana had never felt that kind of love, her heart sank when she thought of Alina having lost Red so soon. She wondered if her friend would ever love again—it might be easier if she didn't. Loving someone could lead to a lot of pain.

Tatiana continued toward the house where it all happened. Her body rebelled, shying away from the site, but she forced herself to do what needed to be done. Sorin followed Tatiana's lead.

The pungent scent of death hit them as they entered. Though it had only been a few hours, the house reeked as though it was made of death and decay. She wondered if a building could hold things like that. The earth gave witches their power—perhaps this house could give death.

Bones and feathers hung from the ceilings, and blood and candles were strewn over the floor next to Blaez's body. He was the only person who died willingly that night. Tatiana's heart ached for him—his suffering lasted centuries, and his only relief was death.

"We should bury him," Sorin said.

"It took us hours to dig Red's grave..." Tatiana replied cautiously. Perhaps the Wolf of Silvania deserved to be buried. But with their hands frozen, blisters ripped and weeping, and snow falling, it was not possible. "I think we should bring the others...Red's father and the huntsman—into the house."

"And then?"

"We burn it," Tatiana replied. "A fitting way for the final Luca to go." She walked to the fireplace and stoked the embers, brilliant red inside the black. After putting another log on, she watched as the fire took hold. Turning to Sorin, she waited for a response.

"Very well," Sorin agreed.

They emerged from the house, taking a few blankets to drape over a shocked Alina. Tatiana took a bundle while Sorin beckoned Lilianna to help her bring the bodies back in.

"His arms are so stiff," Lilianna said to Sorin. She was too young to be learning about death and the horrors of the world, yet she knew them well. It was no surprise to Tatiana that her little sister found humor in it—after all, it was either that or end up like Alina.

Alina Nastaca, her eyes cold and dead, shivered violently without warming up. Tatiana approached with the blanket, draping it over Alina's icy shoulders. The woman jerked away, letting the blanket fall to the freshly dug grave. She slumped back down, her dress in the dirt and snow, her hands torn to shreds.

"Alina..." Tatiana said, using the same soft voice she used whenever Lilianna clammed up. "Come on," she said while offering her hand. "You still have us."

Alina looked up but did not extend her hand. Tatiana reached down and hoisted Alina to her feet. Her body was cold to the touch, as if she had died that night. Alina didn't resist Tatiana and leaned into her friend. Rubbing her hands over Alina's arms, Tatiana brought her to the front of the house.

Then she remembered there was another house out there—Blaez's home.

They had somewhere to go. Somewhere to hide until they decided what to do next.

A distant howl made Tatiana's skin crawl. There were no wolves in Silvania—not the regular kind.

Sorin and Lilianna emerged from the house; Sorin grasped a stick with knots in it. It looked like a walking stick, only too small, even for someone hunched over. Recalling the bruises on Red's whole body, she suspected what it might have been used for. A small sob escaped her, but she reeled it back in before anyone could notice.

Alina softened in her grasp. A shared loss was easier to bear.

On top of the stick, Sorin had placed a burning cloth dipped in oil. She stood in the doorway, raising her palm to the frame. None of those left alive had ever been here before tonight, and Tatiana saw no sentimental value in the house of horrors.

Sorin used the stick to catch the curtains on fire, then tossed it into the house. Lilianna and Sorin walked toward Tatiana and Alina as it slowly burned, and smoke began to billow out the door.

Tatiana reached for her sister, pulling her close. With Alina on one side and Liliana on the other, she longed for Sorin to join. They were stronger together, but the older woman always kept herself just distant enough that she could leave if she had to. Only now, there was nowhere for them to go. As the house began to fall apart, Tatiana realized how much they needed Sorin. She was the only one who had been to other places.

The house crumbled, along with the Luca legacy.

"Well, well," a velvet voice behind them called out. "What have we here?"

2

TORENIA

The air smelled sour.

One by one, the four young women turned to face Torenia Luca. Three of them were huddled together, a wraith-like blonde girl and two brunettes who appeared to be sisters. A dark-skinned woman, a few years older than the others, stood separate from them. She looked like the leader—not because of her age, but because of the authority with which she held herself.

Torenia saw herself in that stance. It was obvious to her that this was the coven she was looking for.

Next to them, the home Adam built after Torenia left him for dead was a smoldering heap. Torenia knew the sourness came from the house—the horrors that occurred inside dispersing into the air.

But it was not the home she was here for. She came for the four wide-eyed women who turned to look at her when she spoke.

"Who are you?" the taller brunette asked. She looked like the youngest, with similar round eyes and a button nose.

Torenia's red-painted lips twitched.

The blonde one quickly replied, "She's the Vampire whor—"

"Is that what they call me here?" Torenia cut her off. "It's not a very kind thing to say about another woman, now is it?"

"No," the blonde replied.

"My name is Torenia Luca."

A pregnant pause filled the air between them, broken by the youngest. She cocked her head to the side, studying Torenia with curious eyes. "You're Red's aunt!"

"Red?" Torenia raised a black eyebrow, its darkness a stark contrast to her pale skin. She had not seen sunlight in over a hundred years.

"Rose Luca," the blonde said.

"Ah, yes," Torenia replied with a gentle nod. Her hair fell from where it was tucked under her cloak. She removed the hood, letting it rest against her back, and cast a tight-lipped, sympathetic smile at the girls. "You appear to be mourning her."

"Why are you here?" The fourth girl—the one with dark hair and even darker eyes—spoke for the first time. A plump rat perched on her shoulder. She did not ask the question with malice or distrust but rather with curiosity.

"My dearest Rahella summoned me," Torenia said as she raised an arm. Her familiar flew down from a branch and landed on the leather bracer.

"Where did you come from?"

Torenia just smiled. "We have much to discuss, but it is best done somewhere warm. You must be freezing—come; let us find somewhere to collect yourselves."

"We cannot go back," the youngest said.

"What's your name?" Torenia stepped closer as she asked, already feeling the warmth of this young one. She only momentarily reminisced about being that young, though she would never wish to return to such a vulnerable age again.

Vulnerable and naïve.

"Lilianna, and this is my sister Tatiana," Lilianna said. Tatiana's expression was pinched, as though she didn't want her name revealed to this stranger. "And Sorin and Alina."

Torenia grinned, her lips still closed. She did not know what they were aware of, and it was best to allow some secrets to reveal themselves only when the time was right. When she lived here—so long ago now—she knew little of the world and what other paths she could take.

Torenia envied that these girls had one another. That had not been an option for her, and she wondered if her life would be vastly different if she'd had a coven to call her sisters rather than Aster. As she surveyed the dirty, bloodstained faces before her, she realized that things hadn't changed. If she'd had a coven, she would have been killed, just like Madame Scarlett.

"It's such an honor to meet you all. I only wish I could have met Rose as well." Torenia furrowed her brow. "How did it happen?"

"A man," Lilianna said quietly.

The chill in the air was not due to the snow. Torenia knew all too well how much damage men could do, and it was evident these young women did as well.

"Is this man dead?" Torenia inquired. Rahella pushed off her arm and flew to a branch. She laced her gloved fingers together in front of her.

"They're all dead," Alina said, voice devoid of emotion.

"All?"

"Her father, grandmother, the huntsman, and the Wolf," Lilianna explained.

Torenia's jaw clenched. The Wolf was dead. It was not as though she would have been able to use him for his purpose—not without a daughter to sacrifice—but she had not expected these women to have accomplished what they did. When Rahella summoned Torenia, she knew something big had happened in the town she was exiled from, but she never would have guessed this.

The wolves would come soon.

She glanced at the burning house. Walking toward the fire with boots crunching in the snow, she waved her hands over the flames and it sputtered, then died. Controlling fire was one of the most difficult areas of magic, and Torenia felt a sharp pain in her chest. Her body remained rigid for a moment, and she hoped none of the girls noticed. She could not risk appearing weak in front of them. When the smoldering embers went cold, she walked into the heap of debris. It did not take long before she felt the crunch of bones beneath her feet.

They had a telltale snap.

Kneeling, she rifled through the ashes until she found what she was looking for. Still hot to the touch, she pulled out the skulls one by one and lined them up on the snow. She polished each one of their black stains and studied them. Then, she removed her glove and placed her hand on them, one at a time. She could feel the essence of who they belonged to before.

The first one felt like tar burning through her veins. The Wolf, and all the agony he suffered.

The second one held very little, and she discarded it. The huntsman.

The final two were both Lucas—she could feel it deep in the marrow of her own bones. Her lip raised in disgust.

"I thought you were supposed to respect the dead," Alina said, her eyes pits of sorrow.

Torenia scowled. "I do not respect most of the living. Why should I respect them once they are dead?"

She rose, stuffing three of the skulls into the bag at her hip before emerging from the pit of ashes. The women were watching her every move, clearly unsure what to make of her. "We respect those who earn it—no one else."

It was their first lesson.

"Come. Let's get you all cleaned up," Torenia said, beckoning them to follow her. Though it was dark, she could see everything. She heard them muttering under their breath, wondering if they should follow her, before she heard the crunch of their footsteps in the snow.

Torenia paused at the town line, staring at it with a scowl. Oh, how she loathed this place. She crossed over it and shuddered. Nearly one hundred years had passed since Torenia Luca last stepped foot in Silvania.

It still smelled bitter.

"Where are we going?" Sorin asked. "They will drive us out or kill us for what we did here."

Torenia grinned at Sorin. "Well then, you must have done something right. Much blood has been spilled tonight, but not quite enough."

"What are you planning?" Lilianna asked, glancing up at Torenia with big green eyes. A little duckling seeking a mother to imprint upon.

"I cannot let this town forget I exist. They drove me out when I was practically a child," Torenia explained. "I should eat all their children."

"What?" Tatiana snapped, pulling her sister away from Torenia.

"I am joking!" Torenia drew out the final word. "The children here face enough hardship, which is why they become such insufferable adults."

"So, what are you going to do?" Sorin asked now.

"Tell me—did Rose Luca's mother treat her well?"

"No," Alina said.

"Well, perhaps we should pay Mother Dearest a visit. I'm utterly famished," she said. As they waltzed through the town, Torenia knew exactly where to find the Luca home—the same place it had always been.

There was a light on. Mother was waiting up all night for Father, but did she know what happened to Daughter?

She would soon find out.

3

SORIN

Sorin Nabita watched as Torenia Luca waltzed toward the Lucas' front door. Her gloved fingers wrapped around the brass knocker, sending it clattering against the thick oak door. Red's mother opened the door, bedraggled in her wrinkled nightgown. She looked little like Red—her hair fairer than her daughter's, her face more angled. Her pinched brows betrayed her confusion, then fear.

Before she could speak, Torenia pushed into the house, kicking the door shut behind her and muffling the woman's screams. Sorin felt no sympathy for the woman who was supposed to protect Red but never did.

Without a word, she followed the footsteps in the snow.

"Wait," Tatiana shouted. "You don't need to see. We've seen enough bloodshed."

Sorin raised her head a little higher, keeping her shoulders back. It was she who kept this coven together, and though their newest recruit was dead, she was determined to keep it intact. The other girls had never seen anything beyond this place—they had not explored the world as she had. Maybe they couldn't see it yet, but Torenia Luca was their best chance to get out of this horrid town, to offer them safety.

Why else would she have come?

Leaving the trio outside in the cold, Sorin shut the door behind her. A splash of blood adorned the walls, and a streak in the hallway lead to the family room. The shadows on the walls amplified the horror she found there. Torenia's cloak lay over the bricks at the hearth, and she towered over Red's mother, who was bent at a painful angle.

The black-haired witch had her teeth sunk into the woman's throat. She watched with fascination as the dying woman's brown eyes darted frantically, landing on Sorin. When Sorin did not flinch under her begging gaze, tears leaked from her eyes as her life disappeared from her body.

Torenia tossed her aside, wiping her mouth on her glove.

Reflecting, Sorin searched for any sense of empathy for the woman. It startled her to think she was immune to seeing another life fade, but she had been driven from her home at a young age, forced to seek safety over and over again. Only her arrival in Silvania brought her a moment of reprieve. With Alina and the others beside her, she felt protected. She knew it was folly to think such things could come so easily—the cost of protection was high.

Sorin came back to her senses when someone brushed against her. Lilianna stood there, wide-eyed. Sorin blinked in surprise—she had snuck up on her, something very few were able to do. Normally, Lucien would alert her, but he was asleep in her pocket.

Tatiana followed her sister and gasped, pulling Lilianna into her chest, forcing her to look away from the scene. The longer Tatiana treated Lilianna like a child, the quicker she would break their bond.

A ghost-like figure walked down the hall, not bothering to glance at the slaughter in the family room—Alina.

"My work here is almost finished," Torenia said, a drop of blood upon her cheek. The stark contrast enhanced her icy blue eyes.

"Will they know it was you?" Sorin asked. "They may think it was the Wolf."

"Let them," Torenia said. "Let them dwell on it. Let them fear what might come for them next. The Wolf is gone, but they don't know that yet. Let them lose sleep, fearing the things that go bump in the night —the witches, the lycans, the vampires." She paused. "The Blood Queen."

"Dawn is coming," Sorin pointed out as if Torenia was not always aware of the rising sun.

"Just one more stop. You four should rest up here. Eat, pack warm clothing, and rest." Torenia's voice fluctuated between manic and motherly as she directed them. She gathered her skirts and stepped over the body, pausing only to wait for the girls to move out of her way. When they parted, Sorin watched her waltz out into the snow.

She wanted to follow. She had so many questions for this mysterious woman. Connected to the town, yet clearly not welcome, she reeked of power—it dripped like the blood she drank. She knew Torenia was a witch and a vampire. She called herself the Blood Queen, but she didn't yet know the true weight of that title.

Lilianna stepped over Red's mother and grabbed Torenia's discarded cloak. She draped it around her body and smiled as the velvet fabric pooled around her feet—Torenia was tall and slender, while Lilianna was short. Tatiana appeared torn between pulling her sister away from the carnage and following Alina.

Quiet weeping came from the room in the back. Alina had found Red's room.

She licked her lips, then followed Torenia. Her footsteps in the snow were already beginning to fill, but Sorin could follow them with ease. They led her to the cemetery. There, near the edges, where the snow was slowly devouring a rickety old fence, was Torenia. With a shovel in hand, she began to dig, peeling off another layer of clothing as she began to sweat from the exertion.

Sorin walked through the headstones, weaving around them, avoiding walking on the graves. The earth was sour here—there was no magic in the treeless void where corpses reigned. Most of the graves were shallow.

Apparently, so was the one Torenia was digging up. It took her scarcely any time to reach what she came for.

Who she came for.

Torenia had a wild look on her face. She tossed the shovel down and dropped to her knees, uncaring that the sun brightened the black clouds to gray. Reaching her hand into the dirt, she pulled up a skull. She rubbed the dirt from it with her sleeve, then rose to her full height, staring into the eye sockets.

"Perfectly intact," Torenia said quietly. "I always wanted to drink from the skulls of my enemies, and who was a greater enemy than you?"

"Who is it?" Sorin asked.

Torenia turned, unsurprised that Sorin was there. She hadn't done anything to try and sneak up on Torenia, and she did not think it would be easy to surprise her.

Torenia looked Sorin dead in the eyes. "My sister."

Something about the way she said it told Sorin that this was to remain between them. Had the others been there, she might not have said anything about enemies, and she definitely wouldn't have admitted the skull belonged to her sister.

"What did she do to you?"

"That is water under the bridge," Torenia said. Then she put the skull in the bag, where it rattled against the others. "Where I am from, we look to the future."

"Then why collect the skulls?"

"They make mighty fine goblets," Torenia said with a grin. She patted the skulls. "We look to the future, but we never forget the past. Something tells me you understand that."

Sorin nodded slowly. Inside her pocket, Lucien turned. Torenia's eyes went to the movement. "My familiar, Lucien."

"Do the others have familiars?"

"No," Sorin said.

"They have so much to learn," Torenia said, glancing at the sky. "And while I can stop time, I cannot stop the sun."

Side by side, they returned to the Luca house.

Torenia shut all the blinds tight and retired to the master bedroom without a word. Sorin stood in the doorway of the house, wondering what was next. The sun was rising, and while most townsfolk minded their own business, someone may have discovered Mr. Floarea.

They would leave by nightfall.

Sorin went to the family room where the body had been covered with a blanket. With the blinds shut, no one would come to the Luca home right away. She stoked the fire to make it appear that someone was there and to keep the heat in. Alina and Torenia might not feel the cold, but she was from somewhere much warmer than Silvania.

"Sorin," Lilianna said behind her.

Sorin spun around to face the youngest witch.

"Alina and Tati want to talk," she said. She looked at the covered body and smiled. "Isn't Torenia amazing?"

Sorin blinked, stunned. This was a pivotal moment. She knew she wanted to go with Torenia, wherever that took her. She suspected Tatiana and Alina did not trust Torenia, but Lilianna's agreement would be needed for the coven to stay together. She quickly smiled. "Yes, I believe she can offer us more than we've ever had."

Lilianna's eyes filled with light. She always managed to find the good in all things for someone who suffered so much.

"Come. Let's see what they want to discuss," Sorin said.

Perhaps it was time for greater things.

4

ALINA

Alina Nastaca did not trust the new witch in their midst—this interloper.

While Sorin and Red's aunt were out of the house, Alina sat in the room of the girl she loved, the bareness of it breaking her heart even more. The drab curtains hung limp against the window, and the neatly made bed suggested that Red had made it the morning before she was sacrificed. A candle, its wax melted in a brass holder, sat atop the bedside table. Nothing was under the bed except for dust.

Kneeling, she opened the bedside drawer and pulled out a match to light the candle. The wick caught fire, the orange glow illuminating the wall. The shadows inside the drawer deepened. Alina pulled out a handful of pressed flowers, salve Alina had given Red after their first night in the woods, and a few pebbles that were smooth and cool to the touch.

That was all that was left of Red.

Alina began to cry. During her moment of vulnerability, Tatiana came in and comforted her with hollow words that she couldn't comprehend. Only the melting tallow candles and the light from the window revealed how much time passed. As the last threads of Alina's heart snapped, she cursed herself for allowing it to control her.

For years she had longed for Red, but their time together was scarcely a fortnight, a few stolen kisses, and a bond of blood. With Red gone, Alina could feel that bond, a throbbing pain in the scar on her palm. She would be with her forever, but all she could feel was the profound agony of losing her.

The front door of the house slammed shut and a sense of dread wafted in.

She was back.

Tatiana whispered, "She wants us to go with her, back to wherever she is from."

Alina wiped her tears with enough force to leave a redness upon her cheeks.

"We need to speak with the others," Alina croaked. "We need to decide what to do."

Tatiana looked sideways at Alina, pursing her lips together. They were both thinking the same thing—what would they do now? Having remained in town this long posed a threat to their lives. Any longer, the bodies may be found; the town would want villains for the crimes.

They would want the witches to burn.

It felt wrong to think about leaving the place she grew up. She always imagined herself growing old, living at home, eventually being declared unfit for marriage and labeled a spinster. She looked forward to that moment when she would be safe from being stuck with a man. Alina had hoped she could live at home with her father and go unnoticed; Red had given her hope that she could have more than that.

Hope had been snuffed out, though, and she could not live in Silvania anymore. Even if the others fled and took the blame of the murders with them, Alina couldn't be where Red had once been. Not now, after seeing Red reduced to dried flowers and collected rocks. Watching the town forget about her would be a cruelty she could not withstand.

Alina hadn't noticed Lilianna in the room with them. She and Tatiana spoke quietly to one another.

"Torenia's even more beautiful than Mama was," Lilianna said to Tatiana.

"Don't say that," Tatiana scolded. "Go see if Sorin has returned— we must speak with her."

"Are we going to go with Torenia?" Lilianna asked as she walked to the doorway.

"That is what we must discuss." Tatiana then gestured with her hand, urging Lilianna to do as she was told. Tatiana was only seventeen and a mother to her younger sister. When Lilianna left the room, Tatiana's face dropped. Alina could see why she was scared. Torenia might take over that role Tatiana was forced to accept with grace—better a sister for a mother than a stranger.

Before Sorin and Lilianna came in, Alina knew what they wanted. The two of them fawned over Torenia already; they would go hand in hand with the woman. And Tatiana would follow Lilianna anywhere she went.

"She'll come around," Alina said. "We do not need to go with Torenia."

Tatiana said nothing more as the others walked in.

Sorin was the first to speak. She did not sit—she did not even enter the room, instead standing in the doorway. "We must gather our wits. We leave at dusk."

"So, you have decided for all of us, then?" Alina asked, feeling small and seated on the floor with tear-stained cheeks. With shaky legs, she stood up, facing Sorin head-on.

"I have always done what I thought best for the safety of the coven," Sorin responded curtly.

Alina cocked her head to the side. She wanted to ask Sorin if she did everything to protect Red, but stopped herself before she said something she would regret—something that could break them apart even further. They had all done everything they could to protect Red; the blame could not be put on Sorin. If anyone was guilty, it was Alina who lured Red into the coven in the first place. Had she curbed her feelings for Red, she would have been sacrificed, and Blaez would have sent her somewhere safe to live out her life.

She would have lived a peaceful life instead of a life in pieces.

Sorin softened. "We cannot stay. We all understand the dangers of remaining here any longer."

"What about the dangers of going with a nightwalker?" Alina inquired.

"She offers us safety, protection from the people who want us dead. Or at least muzzled."

The statement hung in the air for a moment. The suffocation that Alina felt being in Red's home suddenly crashed down on her. She wanted to go home and hide away in her room with her tonics, with moonbeams pouring in through her windows. That life was over.

"Oh, Tati, can we please?" Lilianna asked, her voice dripping with desperation and adoration.

"I'm not sure, Lili," Tatiana replied tentatively. She flinched when Lilianna grabbed her hands and stared up at her with her big doe eyes. Tatiana looked around, searching for help that no one in the room could offer. "Perhaps if she only ran a coven...But I agree with Alina, trusting a vampire seems dangerous."

"We trusted our lives to a deranged werewolf," Lilianna retorted.

"That was different—we had no choice."

"We have no choice now," Sorin said.

Lilianna detached from her sister and stepped over to Sorin. "I'm going, Tati."

Alina knew it was settled. Just as she imagined this would go—Sorin stood her ground and used her authority to make the decision, and all she needed was for vulnerable, naïve Lilianna to agree with her. From there, Tatiana would follow. Alina was in no shape to be alone.

"I suppose," Tatiana began, "since we have no place here, Torenia is our only option."

"I do not trust her," Alina said. She already knew she would go with them, but she needed to make her feelings on the subject clear. That she would leave if given the chance. "After what she did to those bodies, to Red's mother..."

"Everyone who died last night deserved it except Red," Sorin stated. "Torenia has been just as hurt by the hands of men in this town."

Alina didn't doubt that. She dipped her head and nodded. "We'll go with her then."

The moment the words left her lips, she felt as though she had given up a part of herself.

5

LILIANNA

The moment Lilianna Floarea heard movement from the master bedroom at the end of the hall, she hopped to her feet. She wanted to be the first one Torenia saw. The others spent the remainder of the day scouring what they could from Red's clothes—not all of them fit. They were too big on Lilianna, and Sorin was too tall. But Alina and Tatiana fit into them. But Alina refused to wear them until Tatiana convinced her it would allow her to be closer to Red.

That was when Lilianna slipped out of Red's room and stood at Torenia's door. Soft shuffling inside, a quork of a raven, and the soft music of her laugh. Her laugh was like magic, like a siren's song luring Lilianna in. Unable to resist, she knocked on the door.

"Come, child," Torenia said.

Lilianna's heart lurched into her throat when she heard her honeyed voice. She had called her *child*—was it in jest because she was so young, or was it carefully chosen because Torenia saw her as kin? She entered the room. Torenia sat upon the nook in the window, wide enough for two people to sit side by side. Torenia patted the spot beside her.

"Good evening, Lilianna," Torenia said, her head cocking to the side. Her perfect black hair fell in a cascading curtain around her face, and she brushed it back with regal grace. "How are you feeling?"

"Oh..." Lilianna was surprised by the question. "I'm all right, all things considered."

"All things considered, indeed. You have proven very resilient." Torenia turned to kiss her raven upon its head, and the bird took off. She gestured to the window. "Familiars are like children in many ways. Loved by their mothers, resilient to their mistakes."

Lilianna realized she was only inches away, and she sat in the nook beside Torenia—this beautiful queen before her who dripped with splendor and beauty. She tucked her dirty feet under her dress, embarrassed that she hadn't spent much time pulling herself together. Torenia undoubtedly noticed. Did she still have some of her father's blood on her skin? The thought made her hair raise.

"Tell me about your mother," Torenia suggested. "Did she treat you well?"

"Oh, yes," Lilianna said with a nod. "When she got sick...Tatiana and I knew what would happen."

"Do you possess the gift of foresight, or simply an unfortunate understanding of men?"

"The second one," Lilianna mumbled, looking at her hands where they kneaded her dress, wrinkling it.

Torenia placed her hand on Lilianna's cheek. "I cannot bring your mother back, but I can promise you one thing."

Lilianna followed the gentle guide of Torenia's hand, lifting her eyes to meet her blue stare.

"I can keep you safe from men."

"How?" Lilianna realized her voice was naught but a whisper, dull and shallow.

Torenia leaned in close and whispered, "I will show you how to take everything from them. Just as I once did."

Lilianna looked up, mouth agape. She embraced Torenia without thinking. The nightwalker, however, did not recoil or stiffen. Instead, she wrapped her long arms around Lilianna's body and allowed her to sink into her motherly embrace. Suddenly Lilianna felt like a child again, young and naïve. She felt as though so long as she was with Torenia, she would never be harmed again—she would be protected for all her life.

Lilianna Floarea remembered what it felt like to have a mother when Torenia kissed her forehead.

~

Lilianna was overjoyed when they packed up food and water. Sorin and Torenia had stolen some horses in the night, but not enough for them to each have their own. Torenia had her own, Sorin and Alina were to share, but neither Tatiana nor Lilianna knew how to ride.

"You can ride with me," Torenia said, reaching down.

Lilianna saw Tati lurch from the corner of her eye. Before her sister could protest, she took Torenia's hand and was hoisted upon the creature. She sat snug in front of Torenia, who wrapped protective arms around her to grab hold of the reins.

Sorin then got her own, and Tatiana joined Alina.

They departed with only the moon to guide them. With a steady pace and the sound of horse's hooves crunching through the icy snow, Lilianna felt the excitement of leaving Silvania behind her. All the horrors she faced there could be forgotten. Putting distance between that place, Lilianna settled into the ride, leaning back against Torenia for warmth.

"Tell me about my great-niece," Torenia suggested.

Lilianna looked up over her shoulder at Torenia. A blush crept over Lilianna's cold cheeks, and she looked ahead quickly. She spoke quietly. "We sensed she was like us, so we promised her safety with us...but..."

"We cannot fulfill every promise, even with the best of intentions," Torenia replied to ease the guilt. "Let me guess...pig's heart, carrion, and lavender?"

Lilianna nodded.

"Were you successful?"

"No," Alina said, startling Lilianna. Torenia did not flinch. "We were obviously not."

Sorin added her thoughts to the mix. "We made mistakes. Certain possibilities were overlooked. The Wolf never harmed Red."

Lilianna looked up at Torenia again, assessing her facial features. It was as if she was made from marble, for she gave away nothing. Every pause and every word was carefully selected.

Lilianna aspired to be as calculated as her one day.

Torenia let the quiet pass for a few moments before saying, "Tell me what happened to the Wolf. How did you undo what Azalea Luca started?"

"A daughter sacrificing a parent. The roles were reversed, and we had three generations of Luca blood," Sorin told her. "Earth, blood, and moon magic were used to create the Wolf, but lineage played a key role. Using those same magics, we turned the curse inward on itself."

"Very impressive," Torenia said, and Lilianna could tell she meant it. Only there was an edge to her tone. Perhaps she wanted the Wolf to be able to use him.

Lilianna wondered if Torenia had any children.

Silence permeated between them once again. The horses trotted on as snow continued to fall, and a chill seeped into Lilianna's bones. She pitied Sorin, who was from a much warmer place than Silvania. But Sorin did not look as cold or exhausted as the rest of them did. She looked strong, in complete control, as if in leaving Silvania and their mistakes behind, she took with her a new confidence. Perhaps she found comfort in moving on.

"Why did you decide to become a vampire?" Lilianna asked.

"I was promised eternal beauty, endless power," Torenia said.

"But vampires don't live forever," Sorin countered.

"That is correct. I was...lied to. In a sense. I was promised these things when I was at my lowest. I was young and wanted to believe. I put my trust into someone who saw potential in me."

"How is it that you have remained young, then, if vampires do not live forever?" Tatiana asked.

Torenia stiffened ever so slightly. Only Lilianna would notice because she was flush against her. "Roman Sokolov promised me things, but he lied to me about how to achieve them. However, I still obtained them. Now, what does that tell you?"

"That you are smarter than him?" Lilianna asked.

Torenia laughed, and the sound warmed Lilianna. To have made her laugh...it was a good feeling. "Oh Lilianna, you are so right. I was smarter than him and his dog of a brother, Ivan. They wanted grandiose power, yet they had a narrow vision. Focused so much on one small thing that troubled them, they didn't see me weave their power into my own web until they were caught in it. Oh, Roman promised me power, and I did have to fight for it. I had to do a lot for it." Torenia let out a sigh. "We cannot rise from the top if we have not known the bottom. That is why you four are so important for my cause."

Lilianna looked over at her sister, the gleam of the moonlight making her face glow white. They met eyes, wondering what her cause might be. Alina, riding behind Tatiana, remained stony-faced. Sorin, her eyes wide, appeared interested, a small smile on her lips.

6

TORENIA

Upon arriving at the inn where they would rest through the day, Torenia sensed a shift in the woods—they were not alone. Rahella swooped in and landed on Torenia's shoulder, digging in her talons. When the stable came into sight, Torenia steered the horses toward it.

The young women looked tired and achy as they slid from the horses. Unused to long journeys, they would be exhausted by sunrise tomorrow. However, Torenia sensed that they stayed up late into the night, so adjusting to her restricted hours would not be too troublesome.

A bleary-eyed stable boy came to tend to them, taking the horses and guiding them to the stables after she tossed him some coin.

"Treat them as you would your own child, boy," she said, flashing a close-lipped smile at him. He stammered over his words, but Torenia was already ushering the girls inside.

The tavern was a familiar sight—places like this reminded her of her youth. All the strange folk she met in small town taverns and inns —people seeking love potions, tonics to stop pregnancy, a helping hand to murder a man. She even met the youngest Sokolov brother in a tavern like this one. Torenia wasn't one to fantasize about lost opportunities, but she sometimes wondered how different her life would have been if she had met Nikolai first instead of Roman. As much as she hated to admit it, she was glad to have met Ivan—she missed the way he obeyed her.

Once inside, Torenia approached the innkeeper. She fished a small handful of coin from her velvet pouch and placed them on the counter. "Three rooms for the day. We will depart at nightfall. Two doubles, one single."

The innkeeper looked up with knitted brows. His beady eyes focused on her, assessing. To help him understand, she flashed a grin, her fangs on display. With only the slightest of recoils, he pushed the coin back to her. "Free of charge."

"I insist on paying my dues," Torenia replied. She closed the coin purse and tucked it into the pockets in her skirts, leaving the pile of coins on the counter. "A queen who does not is a queen who ends up with her head on a silver platter."

The man accepted the coin and handed her three keys.

Torenia grabbed them in one swift motion, then headed toward the coven. Other than Sorin, none of them had ever left Silvania. A long night of travel and sleeping in an unfamiliar bed would be strange to them, but their lives would certainly never go back to normal. She suspected that their normal had never been pleasant—whatever life Torenia brought them to would be infinitely better than what they left behind.

"You can all share a room or split between the two. Choose which-ever option is most comfortable for you. I paid more than enough for hot baths and meals, so please indulge. We leave at nightfall," Torenia said as they arrived outside their rooms. She handed Sorin the two keys. "Our journey will take many weeks."

"Where are you taking us?" Alina asked.

"Osleka," Torenia told them.

"What is in Osleka?" Tatiana studied Torenia, her eyebrows raised.

"My Sisterhood." Torenia unlocked her room and entered, leaving them to ponder her response in the hall.

She overheard Lilianna mentioning something about Torenia being a queen and listened as the others debated if they could believe that. A smile dusted her lips—she liked that one. Full of resilience and just enough spark.

The first thing she did when she entered the room was to open the window to allow Rahella access. The essence of dawn revealed itself in muted orange at the horizon's edge. The clouds lifted ever so slightly, the snowflakes hardly visible. The further north they went, however, the harsher the journey would be. It was tiresome having to travel rather than transferring her consciousness through living beings to arrive where she wished.

During her time as the ruler of the Sisterhood and the most powerful witch in history, Torenia had learned how to travel through other beings. Her mind slipped into her familiar's, or any other bird, mammal—even a tree. She could slip through time and space to any destination she wanted. It was exhausting and took its toll on her, but it was easier than riding for weeks on end, restricted to the night.

Rahella swooped into the window. Torenia listened—she knew someone was waiting for her just at the edges of the woods. Someone had been following them since their departure from Silvania. There was naught but a quarter hour of darkness left—this could not be put off any longer. She donned her cloak and hurried down the steps, slowing her pace while outside. Letting them see she was rushing and worried made her appear weak, like she feared the sun.

It told the she-wolf exactly how much time Torenia would give her.

From the edge of the forest, a figure appeared—tall in stature but hunched slightly. Daciana's hair was a mess, tangled and wild, her deep-featured face etched with lines. She was not old, but the hardness in her face showed what she endured every full moon. A scar was carved down the length of her jaw on one side. She had one eye; the other had been ripped out long before Torenia knew her. A woodsy pine scent followed her.

"Good evening, Daciana," Torenia said, her voice filling the morning air.

The other woman grimaced. Anyone unfamiliar with Daciana might assume she was going to attack. Instead, a throaty growl emitted from her, escaping from her bared teeth. They were far from perfect— the opposite of Torenia's. Daciana snapped her teeth, shut her eyes, and tilted her head.

Finally, as Torenia's patience grew thin, Daciana said, "Wolf... is...dead...?"

"Yes," Torenia said with a nod. Though it was not she who had done the task, the wolves didn't need to know that. "Silvania is ripe for the taking."

"You...have...delivered."

Daciana slinked back into the woods, and Torenia retired to the safety of the inn. But not before noticing the lithe, blonde figure in the window above. Alina was looking down, head cocked to the side, wearing a stoic face that did not betray her thoughts. Torenia, however, knew she was trying to find something wrong with her, to give her friends a reason to leave. But it would be the death of them all if they tried to make it on their own.

Torenia silently ascended the stairs. At the top, she glanced between her room and the other two. Part of her wished to speak to Alina and deal with their issues head-on, but the other part felt it best to let this run its course. The girl would either come around, or she would choose a life alone, with no one to support her. That would be a very hard life for someone with a heart as soft as Alina's.

Lingering outside her room, she fumbled with the key just long enough for the door beside her to creak open. Though Alina stepped out, both Tatiana and Lilianna were in the room, peering out of the doorway. Sorin must have taken the other room. This came as no surprise to Torenia—Sorin was much older than the others. Pausing, Torenia raised an eyebrow toward the blonde.

"Yes?"

"Who was that?" Alina asked, closing the door behind her.

Weighing the benefits, Torenia decided some honesty would go a long way. She turned to face the younger woman, folding her thumb over the key in her hand. "Her name is Daciana. She is the leader of a pack. Wolves."

She let the word dangle—a word that meant so much to those who were raised in Silvania. Her tone was soft though, suggesting that Alina could dig deeper should she have more questions. Every smart witch did.

"Werewolves? Like him?" Alina cocked her head to the side, staring into Torenia's eyes.

"Like him and yet not," Torenia explained. She paused to glance around, making sure there was no one on the steps listening. The further they moved away from Silvania, the less any common person would know of Azalea Luca, but it never hurt to be cautious. "Over the centuries since Azalea Luca created Blaez Köiv and he came to Silvania, the packs surrounding the area have been very unhappy."

"That is a long time to be unhappy," Alina said thoughtfully. It was clear that she understood the implications of using blood magic—how it lingered, rippling out like a rock dropped in a lake. Azalea's curse did just that.

Torenia knew that Alina was not talking about the wolves any longer. "You are hurting."

Alina looked up with glassy eyes.

"It took me many years to truly let someone in. Someone I could... love, I suppose," Torenia explained, thinking back to Anja. "She taught me many things: trust, cunning, the powers of observation, patience. Watching her grow old was horrible."

Alina cut her off. "If you are about to say that watching a loved one age and die is worse than watching them get ripped apart, I will stop you there."

"I wasn't," Torenia retorted sharply, their camaraderie dissipating. "I was going to say that the strongest move on. Only the weak dwell on things that cannot be undone."

Alina recoiled slightly. The words bit into her already aching heart. It was clear that they would never understand one another. She turned and gripped the doorknob to her room. With a slow turn of her head, she asked Torenia, "Could you not have allowed yourself to age with her? If you loved her so much..."

Torenia flashed an unfriendly smile. "I loved my empire more."

7

ALINA

Alina crept back into the room where Tatiana and Lilianna now slept. Lilianna was asleep, and Tatiana had her eyes closed, stroking her sister's hair slowly. None of the coven complained about adjusting to sleeping during the day. Exhausted from the onslaught of death followed by the forcefulness of their fleeing, they caught sleep wherever they could.

Alina slid under the blanket but was unable to find rest. Instead, she replayed her conversation with Torenia over and over in her head.

Just because Red's death shattered her, that did not make her weak. That was where Torenia was wrong. It made her so strong that she continued on after losing her love.

Alina wondered, as she lay in her bed, if she ever really had Red? Certainly not, for she could not control another being. But what would they even call the fleeting desire they shared? Infatuation, destroyed by the Lucas' need for power? Maybe Red and Torenia were not so different after all—they were both of Azalea Luca's blood.

She rolled onto her back and stared at the ceiling, feeling the weight of a thousand pounds crushing her chest. The agony of losing Red was unbearable, and she worried about who else she might lose. Closing herself off to all she might love seemed the most viable option, but it had not worked when she tried with Red.

She once asked for protection from love, but now all she wanted was a chance at love offered to her again. A voice quietly cooed in the back of her mind—*be careful what you wish for.*

∼

In the following weeks, travel became more gruelling and some nights it snowed so hard that the roads were impassable. And yet, with persistence and perhaps a little bit of magical influence, they made it. The winter in Osleka was violent; though the snow seemed to melt where their horses stepped, as though there was a globe of warmth around them. The further north they traveled, the evergreens changed color, from rich green, to rust, to deep red. Alina had never seen anything like it.

She urged her horse along to bring herself beside Torenia. "What happened to the trees?"

Torenia looked at the crimson trees bordering the road. "The soil here has been soaked in the blood of thousands over the centuries. It began some time ago, though more recently this coloring has become more prominent."

Alina wondered what could have happened recently that could change nature so strikingly. How much blood had to be spilled for the very earth to alter like that? "What happened recently?" she asked.

"Nothing that concerns you." Torenia picked up her pace, putting distance between them.

Alina slowed her horse and fell back in with the others, her eyes narrowed at the vampire leading them deeper into her territory. She shuddered, glancing once more at the blood-soaked trees, the unease settling into her bones.

"How long has it been night?" Sorin asked in a muted whisper. Lilianna was riding with Tatiana, who learned over the last few weeks how to ride. Animals took to her, just as children did. A true matriarch.

"I heard that if you go far enough north, the sun doesn't come out in the winter," Tatiana explained. She yanked up her jacket collar up higher and pulled her sister closer to keep warm. Torenia's magic helped, but it did not make winter disappear. The night sky was clouded, but a dull light from the fortress up ahead cast a glow. They all bustled with quiet excitement—until now, they could see nothing but an outline of the witch ahead of them.

"A fitting place for a nightwalker," Alina commented, looking at the woman in front of them seated casually on her horse, as though she was one with the beast.

"It must be a sacred time for rituals," Sorin replied, looking up at the dark skies.

"What the earth gives, she too must take back," Tatiana reminded them. "A moon cycle of night means a similar cycle of daylight. So this becomes a most perilous place for a vampire."

Lilianna grinned. "To live dangerously—it shows her power, does it not?"

Sorin nodded in agreement, but Alina scowled. "It sounds foolish."

Lilianna gasped, pointing her gloved hand ahead of them toward the massive fortress. The castle was monstrous to Alina, who had only seen small, modest houses her whole life. The windows were aglow with firelight, and a winding path sheltered on either side with massive hedges, perfectly trimmed, made its way from the road all the way to the entrance. The hedges were covered in a layer of snow six inches deep, and as they neared them, they realized red flowers bloomed within. A miracle in this cold—or rather, witchcraft.

They passed a large statue of a woman, her hand reaching up to the skies, that had partially crumbled long ago. When they reached the haunting building, Torenia elegantly dismounted from her horse, stroking the animal's velvet nose and whispering to it. The beast shuddered, a dusting of snow falling from its mane and tail. She turned to look at each of the girls. One by one, they hopped off their horses and joined her on the walkway.

Alina watched from the corner of her eye as Lilianna mimicked Torenia, petting the horse and whispering a quiet thank you. Alina was unsure if Torenia thanked her horse or whispered something more sinister—the way her familiar lurked, she would not trust any animal in this place. She wondered if a witch could have more than one familiar.

She was out of her depth. She felt like a child being tossed into a pit of wolves, defenseless and with no comparable survival skills. Her mind drifted to the wolves Torenia spoke with, her heart beating fast at the thought of the town she left behind, defenseless against a pack of wolves.

She shut her eyes, refusing to think of her parents.

Without any acknowledgement, Torenia walked through the hedge-shrouded pathway. The others quickly fell in line, following along like ducklings. Alina picked up the rear, glancing behind her as the vegetation obstructed her view. It was not a labyrinth, yet she felt as though she left herself behind, that she was simply a shell of who she used to be. Or perhaps she left herself behind with Red. Silvania once threatened her, making her feel like an outcast. Now it beckoned her to return home, something in the air pulling her back.

Two giant black doors closed behind Alina, sealing her inside the monstrous castle. Pillars lined the sides of the massive throne room, and the granite floors were enough to take her breath away. Everything was black and white, including the throne standing at the back of the giant room amongst the rubble of two other thrones. The two seats that once flanked the middle had crumbled and were torn down.

Alina wondered why they were destroyed and why they were left that way. She suspected the queen herself desecrated the thrones.

Who threatened Torenia so badly that she did such damage?

I loved my empire more.

"*Koroleva*, your safe return is well received," a woman said, snapping Alina from her thoughts. This woman could have been any of the girls' mothers, with crow's feet around her eyes and frown lines at her mouth, except she had dark purple scars upon her cheeks, as though a dagger had been drawn down the length of them with haste.

"What does *K-Koroleva* mean?" Lilianna asked, struggling with the pronunciation of the foreign word.

"It means *queen*. With your permission, I'll grant all of you the ability to understand all tongues. I would suggest you learn the language, however," Torenia told them, removing her cloak and handing it to the woman. "Thank you, Vera."

Vera offered to take the rest of their bundles of clothing, but none of them were ready to part with their warm outer garments just yet. The lingering effects of the Oslekan winter clung to them.

"Do you consent?" Torenia asked.

Alina stiffened as the others agreed without delay. Alina wanted to be able to understand what anyone said in her presence, but she didn't want to let this woman cast any magic upon her. Torenia waited, her eyes on Alina.

"There is no trickery?" Alina inquired. "The spell you cast will allow us only to understand other tongues, nothing more?"

"Yes," Torenia replied. "I will not do anything to any of you without your consent."

"Very well," Alina said, feeling like she was losing more of herself by allowing this. She kept her eyes firmly on Torenia as she began to mutter the incantation.

"Loquimini omnes linguas. Audi omnes linguas. Novimus omnes linguas." Torenia repeated the words thrice before pulling a glowing white thread from her mouth. She brought it to Lilianna first, who parted her lips. One by one, she gave this thread of language to each member of the coven.

Alina listened for any trickery or deceit in the spell but heard nothing. When it was her turn, she felt the fine thread weave its way back and forth over her tongue, granting her the ability to understand and speak any language she came across. Torenia's power was immeasurable and terrifying. But knowing what was being spoken and knowing nothing could be said behind her back that she wouldn't understand gave her a sliver of relief.

"Vera, this is Alina, Lilianna, Tatiana, and Sorin. Please show them to their rooms and the bathhouse. Give them the full tour when they have settled in and gotten comfortable," Torenia commanded in a tone that revealed she would not accept defiance.

Vera gave a respectful nod, then looked at the bundled-up girls. Beckoning for them to follow, she led them through the grand foyer. The white granite had black running through it, reminding Alina of veins through a body. Thick pillars reached the ceilings, which were domed and painted with vampires in battle. Their feet pattered against the stone floors. Nothing about the castle was warm or welcoming.

The throne room funneled into an antechamber, which led to a large foyer with stairs wrapping around either side. Leading from the foyer were many doors to unknown places. Vera quickly explained, "The upper levels contain the bedrooms. This door leads to the west wing where the conference room, dining area, ballroom, and scullery are located."

The stairs were dimly lit with evenly spaced lanterns and wide enough for three to walk side by side comfortably. The rich red carpet lining the steps silenced their footsteps.

"Down this hallway, you will find the guest bedrooms. Each has its own bed and bath chambers; however, there is also a bathhouse on the lowest level. Should any of you desire a bath in your personal chamber, all you need to do is ask. The bathhouse is always ready for use, as it has direct connections to the hot springs nearby," Vera finished with a deep breath.

"Can we sleep together?" Tatiana asked. "For a few nights at least... until we get comfortable."

Vera smiled, her scarred cheeks pinched tight like morbid dimples. "Of course. Torenia has informed me that this is to be your home as much as hers."

"What happened to your cheeks?" Alina inquired, her voice flat.

Vera's smile disappeared as a stern look overtook her features. "Nothing to concern yourself with. I do not ask about your scars, do I?"

Alina stared Vera down, unspoken words hanging in the air; she suspected Torenia had mutilated her face. Sorin grabbed Alina's bicep before the situation escalated. "Come, let's wash up and get comfortable."

Ushered into a room, Alina looked around. There were two giant arched windows overlooking the castle grounds. A giant hedge maze was lost in the snow. It went on forever, much further than she could see in the dark. Inside the room was a bed large enough to fit three or four of them comfortably.

From single straw-filled beds to this.

Yet Alina didn't feel she was moving up—she worried she would forget who she was in a place like this.

Kneeling before the fireplace, she worked quickly, getting her hands dirty to make the perfect balance of wood and straw to start the fire. When the wood shavings and straw caught, she blew gently, coaxing it to grow. Behind her, she could hear the sisters exploring the room, looking at everything, opening drawers and closets. She should have smiled for them, pleased that they could experience this joy after everything they endured.

"Look at these clothes!" Lilianna exclaimed. There was a shuffle of feet, the soft sound of fabric between fingers.

Alina looked over her shoulder, her lips pressed tight together. The sisters were pulling out gowns and cloaks, hats made of furs, and holding them up to their bodies to guess what they would look like, but not committing to a single one. Movement in the doorway grabbed Alina's attention.

Sorin joined them at last, having lingered outside of the room for the duration it took Alina to get the fire started. "Alina." Sorin's voice was low, her words only for Alina. "You must speak your thoughts."

"She's trying to buy us," Alina said bluntly. She turned back to the fire and felt the heat against her cheeks.

"Or perhaps she is just being generous," Sorin countered, her voice softer now.

"We are going to the bathhouse," Lilianna exclaimed. "Join us!"

The youngest's delight was hard to brush off. A bathhouse sounded wonderful, like everything Alina's tired, aching body needed. So many nights riding on horseback combined with sleeping in different beds everyday made the thought of these luxuries more than welcoming. It was like a succubus beckoning her with hungry eyes.

"We will meet you down there," Sorin said. When the younger girls left the room, Tatiana shot a glance between Sorin and Alina. Only when they were gone did Sorin address her again. "Promise me you will give this a chance. We may thrive here."

"She wanted to take back the town," Alina said, her eyes watering now. "We could have done that. We could still do that..." she trailed off, remembering the wolves. Her lower lip quivered. "What have we done?"

"Pardon?" Sorin cocked her head to the side.

"She sent a pack of wolves right into Silvania..." Alina whimpered.

"Wolves?"

"H-his presence kept them out, and we killed him. We let this happen."

Sorin crossed her arms over her chest. "We do not know what the wolves will do. It is best not to dwell on it, Alina. Come; let us bathe, and I will ask Torenia what she can do about it."

Alina snapped her head up. As if Torenia, who ushered the wolves in and beckoned them into the town, would be able to do anything about it. Sorin trusted the vampire too much. The other woman offered her hand, but Alina got to her shaking feet on her own. She brushed past Sorin and out of the bedroom, wiping tears from her eyes as she thought about the innocents in Silvania being torn to shreds by a pack of bloodthirsty werewolves.

8

SORIN

On the third night after their arrival at the Sisterhood, Sorin stood admiring a horrific painting on the wall. It depicted a great battle under a starless sky—nothing but endless black, a familiar castle hidden within its depths. The base of the piece was a perfect contrast—pure, untouched white snow. The middle, though, was what caught Sorin's attention. Hundreds of vampires clad in gray slaughtered each other, many without their heads, jaws ripped off, limbs missing. The white snow turned red in the middle of the work.

It was not a depiction of good versus evil.

"Deliciously macabre, is it not?" Torenia asked. She would have startled Sorin had Lucien not wriggled within her pocket to notify her of another presence.

"Were you there?" Sorin asked, still looking at the artwork.

"No, I was fighting my own battles in that wretched town," Torenia replied. She hooked her arm into Sorin's and slowly guided her down the hall. "I did not show up here until long after the Brotherhood was established. By then, it was crumbling at the hands of its leader."

"Who were they?" Sorin and Torenia turned down another hall. It would take weeks before Sorin knew this place, but like everywhere she had ever lived, she would know it inside and out. She had no doubt that she may have to flee one day.

"Roman Sokolov and his brother, Ivan." Torenia chuckled lightly. "They came from nothing, like us, and they strove for and achieved greatness. But men are often uncertain what to do with power. They get tangled up in revenge and lose their grip. They say women are too emotional." She scoffed. "I would beg to differ."

"I only ever saw men burning witches—and women—at the stake," Sorin agreed. Lucien wriggled, reaching his paws out of her pocket and clambering up to her shoulder. His whiskers tickled her neck.

"How long have you and your familiar been connected?" Torenia asked.

"Since I was a child. I needed one to survive," Sorin explained. "To be my eyes and ears."

"A familiar is the most important friend for a young witch," she agreed. They stopped outside a set of large doors. The knobs were black onyx, and the keyhole large enough for someone to see through. "You mentioned before that the others do not have familiars yet?"

"Correct."

"Perhaps they should."

Sorin lifted Lucien from her shoulder. He was large for his kind, as most familiars tended to be. His pink tail curled around Sorin's wrist. "No. You must earn their trust before they have eyes and ears here."

"Well said." Torenia smiled. "Tell me about them."

Sorin turned to the balcony overlooking the throne room with its smashed thrones. They were two floors up, but heights never bothered her. Lucien detached from her and scurried along the railing, hopping down onto the floor with a near-silent plop when he reached the corner. He wasn't needed there anymore—he was needed to ensure none of the others were listening. "You have Lilianna wrapped around your finger. Tatiana will follow her to the ends of the earth, whatever she chooses, or she will do what is in Lilianna's best interest."

"And Alina?"

"She has lost the ability to trust, I think. Or, if she can, you will have to earn it, and it will not be an easy task. Silvania failed her. She believes this place will fail her too and wants to return home with her tail between her legs. If you want her trust, you must give her something to believe in."

"I can work with that," Torenia told her. "Thank you for being honest with me, Sorin."

Sorin turned to Torenia. "As I said before, I want you to teach me."

Torenia grinned, her teeth glimmering against the glow of the torch. "I think you are ready."

The Vampire Queen extended her hand. There was no hesitation in Sorin's actions as she did just that. Torenia's hands were surprisingly warm, and any prior thought that a nightwalker's skin might be cold and dead was cast out of Sorin's mind. Torenia pushed open the doors to reveal the stunning room within.

Pillars stood on either side, with gargoyles carved into the marble holding them up. They were crude depictions of what some lore suggested vampires to look like, but Sorin knew they were beautiful like Torenia. In the middle of the room stood a massive table made of a single slab of wood—the tree must have been ancient to be so large. Sorin's heartstrings tugged ever so slightly—the earth gave life to those trees, and the earth gave life to witchcraft. A great fire burned in a hearth at the end of the room, and lanterns hung all around them, giving the room the feel of daylight.

A man and a woman waited in the room. He was tall and lean, with graying hair. The woman had long black hair pinned back regally. Her gown was a floor-length material that shimmered in the light—a rich crimson adorned with gold fringe, buttons, and filigree.

She smiled at Sorin, her hands clasped in front of her hips. She felt warmth toward her, for she looked more like Sorin with her dark skin.

The man was the first to speak, and he did not address Torenia with deference like Vera had. He did not call her *Koroleva*. "Your departure was most untimely," he stated.

"My departure was necessary, Alexei. This will be the last time family business interferes with our goals," Torenia stated, not lacing her words with venom as Sorin thought she might. These were the two people Torenia trusted most—she did not need to dangle her superiority over them. Sorin wondered what that meant about her position.

"Sorin." Torenia turned her attention back to her. "I would like to introduce you to Alexei, my counsellor of war and strategy, and Zaina, my most trusted advisor."

They both nodded at Sorin. She dipped her head in kind, returning the gesture.

"Your family business is attended to, then," Zaina said, pulling out a heavy chair. It groaned against the floor.

Torenia sat at the head of the table with Zaina on her right and Alexei on her left. Sorin sat beside Zaina, quietly observing.

"Yes, it is. I brought back with me a handful of witches in whom I see great potential, as well. The more witches we have here, the safer and stronger we are. It is high time that we bring more of us here. Too long has this castle been devoid of the Craft."

An uncomfortable quiet filled the room when Torenia finished speaking.

"The Old Bloods may perceive this as you building an army," Zaina said.

"I already have an army." Torenia cocked her head to the side, eying Zaina, then looking at Alexei. Sorin presumed that as war advisor, he was also in control of the army.

"I have also brought peace between the lycans who roam and my former home. For centuries there were disputes of territory among the lycans. I..." Torenia paused and looked at Sorin. "The witches I speak of have opened a door that had been shuttered for four hundred years. Because of what Sorin and her friends have done, I was able to give territory back to a clan I believe we can trust."

Alexei leapt to his feet. "The lycans are not a stable ally, Torenia. What were you thinking?"

"I need allies."

"There are better ways to seek allies," Alexei said. He crossed his arms over his broad chest. "You're not thinking about the consequences of this foolish plan."

"Do I wish to get into bed with the wolves? No. However, I understand that there is a war coming, and I may need their support." Torenia argued.

Sorin thought of Alina and her fear of the wolves terrorizing the town they left behind.

"The Old Bloods will see this as a power play. You're expanding your territory much farther than expected. They are being forced back on two sides now," Alexi pointed out.

Torenia raised her lip in disgust. "I fought for so long for the rights of Half Bloods. These Old Bloods—these inbred monstrosities—cannot win. They cannot tear down what we have built."

"What are Old Bloods?" Sorin asked. If she wanted to sit at this table, to be an equal, she needed to know what Zaina and Alexei knew. Knowledge was power.

It was Zaina who answered. "Old Blood vampires are those of the purest blood. Dating back to the very first recorded nightwalkers, they were determined to keep their blood pure. They saw themselves as royalty—"

"They still do," Torenia added. "Nicholas Lebedev is the last of the Old Bloods. Him, his sister, and their monster children."

"Many Pure Bloods think this way, as well. However, to an Old Blood, even a Pure Blood with Half Blooded lineage would not be considered worthy, since their ancestors were once man. For many years, the few remaining Old Bloods took a quiet backseat in Krovberg. Many speculate that their health issues began to take a toll when they receded into the shadows to live out their days.

"For many decades after Roman solidified the Brotherhood, and after Torenia became his successor with the Sisterhood, they remained quiet. Now, however, they have sprung up again. To everyone's surprise, they made an alliance with the armies of man to destroy the Pure and Half Bloods."

"What is the benefit for man?" Sorin inquired.

Torenia was still scowling, so Alexei answered. "There are few Old Bloods left. To rid the world of all other vampires would mean peace for man. The Old Bloods would eventually die out; it will not be long before they can no longer breed."

"And yet this newest batch of brats is a new kind of nightwalker," Torenia snapped. "A more carnal, ruthless nightwalker that cannot be reasoned with. They have no morals, and they feed on everything."

Sorin shuddered. So many generations of vampires, piling on the violence and hunger for blood, must amount to something closer to beast than man. She knew of vampires, witches, lycans, and sirens, but she had never heard of this grotesque hierarchy within the night-walkers.

"If there are so few Old Bloods, why not take them out now?" Sorin asked. "Before they learn of your alliance with the wolves?"

"Maksim Chernov. Nicholas's most powerful piece on the board." Torenia grimaced. "He's a warlock. And they are already well protected by man. They quietly gathered their forces; we did not see it."

An eerie silence filled the room. Sorin glanced between the counselor and advisor, who did not make eye contact. They knew something that Sorin did not. Something about Torenia they were not sharing. What could have distracted Torenia and her people while the Old Bloods allied with man?

"In a century of ruling, I have never faced war. If this is where we must go, so be it," Torenia stated.

"War is not the only option," Zaina said.

"What do you think, Sorin?" Torenia asked, ignoring Zaina.

Sorin saw the look in Torenia's eyes. She knew what she was asking. "I've seen people drowned, burned, and hanged, despite their innocence. If not fighting back means the death of innocents, then war must be faced. However, suppose you could get past the army, past man, and straight into the heart of the Old Bloods. Cut off the head from the inside."

Torenia raised an eyebrow.

Alexei looked wary. "That sounds like an excellent way to start a war, not end one."

"They have children," Torenia said, seeing what Sorin was thinking. "Brats rampant with illness. We send someone to aid them. A nanny."

Sorin immediately thought of Tatiana.

"And the wolves," Torenia added. "We will need someone to build an alliance with Daciana and her pack."

Alina, Sorin thought. Her coven was dispersing as the meeting wrapped up, even though she had not voiced her thoughts aloud. Tasks were given; messages would be relayed. Sorin stopped listening, thinking about the young women she spent so much time protecting. Before she knew it, she was alone with Torenia again.

"I need to gain their trust, all of them. I do believe I know just how to do that," Torenia said, placing her hand on Sorin's shoulder. "There is a Blue Moon coming. I will call a gathering."

"A gathering of what?"
"Witches."

9

LILIANNA

A Witches Feast—that was what Torenia called it.

Lilianna, though excited to meet other witches, was more excited to explore every nook and cranny in the castle. The expansive building was cavernous, with all sorts of entrances, exits, hallways, and trick doors. Often void of people, Lilianna found it easy to spend her days trying on all the pretty gowns—many of which weren't in Lilianna's size—and making sure she knew every last twist and turn of the place. It was best to know how to escape, not that Lilianna ever wanted to leave. She wouldn't dream of it.

Only select areas remained unvisited. She reminded herself that she had all the time in the world, but this was the prime opportunity to go to some places Vera said were off-limits. The wretch often caught Lilianna trying to get through a door with a heavy iron bolt closing it off, always sending her off with a scolding. This merely piqued her interest and furthered a need to discover what lay behind the door.

She knew this behavior would certainly get her in trouble, but Lilianna was free of worry for the first time. Her father was dead. Her sister, alive and well. Nothing could ail her. Nothing could hinder the elation she felt.

Now was the perfect time, as Vera was busy ensuring everything was in order for the Witches' Feast. Torenia had left, not telling anyone where she went—just that she would return before the guests arrived. She told the girls to wear whatever their hearts desired. While she was eager to wear a gown for the splendor of the feast, she felt most comfortable in her daywear: a skirt, blouse, and bare feet. Her mother had called it her troublemaking attire.

Her bare feet pitter-pattered along the cold stone floors as she passed the throne room. The massive, desecrated dais beckoned her. There were a few steps that led to the only remaining seat. Glancing over her shoulder, Lilianna smirked, then proceeded to clamber up the stairs to sit upon the remaining throne.

Playfully, because she was alone, she stuck out her hand, one finger extended as though there were a big, gaudy ring on it for a peasant to kiss. "Bow before your queen," she whispered, then repeated it louder when no one came to tell her to get off the throne. She was low blood —she would never sit on a throne.

When no one came around to scold her, the fun ebbed. She slipped off the throne, bored. The others were always occupied and didn't want to explore. Since they had arrived, things were different. Alina was always sad. Sorin was hardly around, and Tatiana was suddenly too mature for the pranks they used to play on the townsfolk of Silvania.

Continuing her intended task, she slipped unnoticed through corridors and hallways, her fingertips touching the ornate frames surrounding the portraits. Soon, the iron-bolted door was within her sights, and she hurried on silent feet.

Despite the bolt, the knob turned with ease. It was unlocked, like every other door in the castle, begging her to enter. Lilianna couldn't understand why Vera always sent her away. Leaving the doors unlocked meant that she was supposed to enter, to discover, to explore. Though Vera always caught her, Torenia had not once made mention of Lilianna's need for discovery. Either Vera never told Torenia, or Torenia wanted her to explore.

Closing the door quietly, Lilianna saw a winding stairwell before her. The steps were made of stone and made no noise, unlike her home back in Silvania where she could hear as her father approached the bedroom she shared with Tati. The sound of creaking floors always brought a lump into her throat, disgust forming like a ball of black tar in the pit of her stomach. Once in the safety behind that closed door,

Lilianna rushed down the steps, her fingertips trailing along the rock walls cocooning the spiraling staircase.

She was hit abruptly by a powerful, rank smell. It reminded her of the graveyard back home when bodies piled up in the winter as cold and illness killed the villagers. They would remain frozen and not smell too bad, but as the winter turned into spring, the bodies warmed and rot kicked in before the ground was soft enough to dig. That pit of bodies on the edge of the town always smelled sour and sickly sweet. The smell made Lilianna pause—did she dare go further? Was there a mass grave underneath the castle? Was this why Vera did not want her to enter?

"Surely not," Lilianna whispered to herself. "Why would Torenia keep dead bodies in her home?"

Telling herself it was simply an old castle, Lilianna continued. There was a light ahead, a flickering glow beckoning Lilianna further, but the sounds of ragged, raspy breaths and moans of pain made her slow again. Curiosity ate away at her, though, and she pressed on despite her fear. Her heart beat so hard she could hear nothing but the rush of blood through her veins.

The sight as she came around the corner sent a chill up her spine, rooting her to the spot. Down a long, dark hallway lit by two torches on either wall, there were cages. Not for dogs or for other animals, but humans. Lilianna gagged. Was it the scent of unclean bodies and their excrement or the fact that there were humans in cages that made her head spin?

It was so much worse than dead bodies.

A hand reached out, appearing skeletal in the flickering light. It grabbed at her dress. Lilianna recoiled quickly, turning to head back up the stairs. Someone called for her, begging for her help—she wasn't even sure if it was an adult or child, the voice was so distorted. A cry arose from all of the caged people, the sound following her as she flew up the stairs as fast as her feet could carry her. Tripping over an uneven stair, Lilianna slammed down on the stone step, her shins splitting open and blood smearing her dress. Her hands reacted fast enough that she didn't hit her face, but she suddenly lacked the energy to pull herself back to her feet. She huddled against the wall and clutched her knees to her chest, covering her ears with her hands.

They cried and shouted for her.

Their smell clung to her white dress.

Light flooded the stairwell—she was only five steps away from the exit. She glanced up, unsure if she should flee or hide. Would she be put in one of those cages? She whimpered and scooted away from whoever was at the door as they walked toward her carrying an oil lamp.

Torenia appeared, dressed in a blood-red gown.

"Ah, Lili, my sweet girl," Torenia said. "Come; let me explain."

"Who are they?"

Torenia crouched down, placing the lantern on the step above them. It made the shadows dance, a theatrical show to pair with the uneven and desperate shouts from below. Lilianna realized then that the screams had stopped, but she still heard them in her brain.

"A long time ago, three brothers created this place—the harvest, they called it," Torenia explained. "They had the poor, the homeless, the needy. They saw it as a way to clean up the cities and keep ourselves well-fed. However, down there, there are no more poor and needy. Instead, I have collected the worst of humanity. Lilianna, your father hurt you, didn't he?"

She nodded hastily.

"People like him get away with what they do unless people like us do what must be done. Men who hurt their daughters, their wives, strangers even... They get away with all their heinous crimes. But, over time, people learned to send me letters and confide in me about who hurt them. I round up the accused and bring them here to harvest as my food source. It may seem evil, but it is justice. If you had a choice, would you have asked me to bring your father here? To drain him of his dignity and his selfish pride? To drain him of his life as he tried to do to you and your sister?"

Lilianna processed Torenia's words, glancing back down the stairs. Though she could no longer see the caged people, she remembered it clearly. It was etched into her memory forever. She nodded. "Mhm..."

"Down there are the worst people in existence. The ones who prey upon the weak. I do not stand for that in my region. If I could extend my justice to the whole world and protect all the abused, I would. My influence does not go that far, though I have friends in the far reaches who do the same. We will be discussing many things this evening, including whether or not to remind the world of our power. You see, they have forgotten we exist—they no longer fear witches because we have been forced into hiding. Many of us oppose the idea of remaining hidden. Being hidden is the same as remaining silent when there is injustice.

"Tonight, you will meet some of those women. Would you like to meet those who share similar stories? Women who took back what was theirs, just as you and Tatiana did?"

Torenia touched her hand to Lilianna's cheek, a warmth radiating through her.

Lilianna did want to meet others. Such warmth came from this nightwalker—more than even Lilianna's mother had done. Lilianna's mother had been unable to protect her daughters from their father, but Torenia kept them safe. She was keeping all those who were abused safe.

"Yes," Lilianna replied, almost adding "Mama" but catching herself just in time.

10

ALINA

Alina tried on another dress, but it didn't feel right. No matter what Lilianna and Tatiana said about her looking amazing, she felt wrong in these glamorous dresses, these over-the-top ball gowns. Rifling through the closet, she found something else, something that she didn't know existed—at least not for women. She had found a pair of leather trousers, smooth but crisp from lack of use. While the other girls were dressing and trying on anything and everything, she pulled out the trousers. They looked to be fitted for someone her size.

Looking around suspiciously, she wondered if someone put them there by accident. Accident or not, if there was any place for her to try them on, it was here. The leather clung to her legs as she stepped into them, and she stumbled slightly. Despite this, they offered enough room that she didn't feel horribly constricted; after taking a few steps, she realized how freeing it felt to be wearing something she had only seen men wear. Tucking in her white blouse, she glanced at her reflection in the window.

"Those are silly," Lilianna said with a laugh, tearing Alina from her thoughts.

As Alina blushed red, Tatiana pinched her sister's arm. "I think they look splendid, Alina."

"They're too much, aren't they?" Alina sighed, glancing at herself.

They framed her legs and hips nicely, which had filled out since she arrived here. With the blouse tucked in, she looked like she could take on the world, the silk clinging to her skin like moth kisses.

"No," Tatiana said as she rose to a stand. She placed her hand gently on Alina's shoulder. "It feels like a statement."

"Where is Sorin?" Alina changed the topic from her attire to the missing witch. The longer they had been here, the less they saw of her. In Silvania, they had spent nearly every night out in the woods together. Now, they scarcely saw Sorin.

Lilianna seemed to know all the gossip in the castle. "I saw her with Torenia this afternoon. She said she would meet us at supper."

"Do you think we'll have to watch Torenia drink blood?" Tatiana asked.

Her younger sister blanched, and her bottom lip shook ever so slightly as she played with the ends of her mousey brown hair. Her eyes locked on the window where snow built up around the edges. Her words didn't come tumbling out as Alina expected.

Vera knocked on the door and opened it simultaneously, not giving the girls a chance to answer it themselves and stopping Alina from asking Lilianna what she wanted to say. "The *Koroleva* calls."

The three exchanged glances before following Vera down the hallway to the dining room. Until now, the girls had eaten in their room or the kitchen. This was the first time they were to eat in the dining room. The room ran thirty feet long and twenty feet wide, with a massive table in the center. A white lace runner was spread over the center of the table and piled high platters of all sorts of decadent foods —from fresh breads to warm aromatic soups filling the room with wisps of steam to foreign-looking fruits and spiced meats, there was anything and everything the girls could imagine. Accustomed to under-cooked meat from animals they raised and only what vegetables were in season, this was the grandest feast they had ever seen.

The food, however, was the least remarkable thing. What caught Alina's eye were those present. Aside from Sorin, there were five other women at the table. Trying not to stare, yet too intrigued to look away, she tried to glance at all of them without making it obvious she was staring.

The one who had called the Witches' Feast was not yet present.

Tatiana and Lilianna sat on the opposite side of the table, a bit further down, and immediately submerged themselves in conversation with the other witches. Alina took a seat beside Sorin, pulling out the hefty chair that weighed nearly as much as she did. Leaning in, she whispered, "Where is Torenia?"

Sorin pressed her lips into a tight line. "She is very busy, but she will be here soon."

Alina's cheeks flushed. There used to be no secrets between them, but now Sorin had tossed her away as though she wasn't worthy of knowledge. What made her better than Alina? Because she trusted Torenia, a vampire who liked to torment the living and desecrate corpses?

Sorin knew what Torenia was up to and chose to hide it from her. Something constricted around Alina's heart. Across from her, a woman with hair like fire smiled. Crow's feet appeared at the corners of her blue eyes—not ice blue like Torenia's, but a soft cornflower blue bordering on purple. Her hair was pulled back into masterfully done braids, crowning her head, though much of it remained loose.

"I am Gyda, and this is Helga."

The woman beside Gyda nodded sternly, then contorted her hands in strange positions.

"Helga had her tongue cut out; the people in her town didn't like what she uttered. She cannot speak with her voice. Do you know sign-speak?"

Alina blinked, then shook her head. "I...I'm afraid I don't."

Helga signed something to Gyda, who laughed, deep and rumbly. "She said she never considered herself a witch until they took her tongue—they created what they feared her to be. Now she has a penchant for using tongues in her potions."

Alina's lips twitched into a smile. "I have never heard of tongue magic."

Helga and Gyda both let out hearty cackles. "You have heard of Blood Magic, yes?"

Alina nodded.

Helga signed something, and when Alina looked to Gyda for a translation, the red-haired woman sighed. "She said to be wary of the Blood Queen."

The Blood Queen.

Torenia.

Before either Gyda or Helga could say anything else, the host arrived. Torenia stepped through the doors, a black silk gown trailing behind her and her corset cinched tight. Even though Alina distrusted and disliked Torenia, there was no denying that she was the most beautiful person she ever laid eyes on. At least on the outside.

"I offer my sincerest apologies for the delay," Torenia said, pulling the chair at the head of the table back with a ring-clad hand. She stepped in front of it but did not sit down. "You have all come tonight in support of ending the Old Bloods, who pose not only a threat to vampires, but to all humanity. I thank all of you for your unyielding support, but I will not speak of Old Bloods and strategy tonight. I have other, more important things to discuss.

"Tonight the Witches Feast falls upon a full moon—a powerful moon that incites the horrors of the lycans and enhances the potions and poisons created. It also turns the tides of the world, something I know we are all striving to do as the turn of the century comes upon us."

Torenia sat down, placing her hands in her lap. "Thank you all for coming to meet our newest Sisters. Sorin, Alina, Tatiana, and Lilianna are survivors of what could have been another witch burning in a town that refused to grow, refused to understand that which is different. Different, like us."

Alina swallowed. She once told Red that she loved differently than other people.

Glasses were raised as words were uttered in tongues Alina only knew because of Torenia's spell. Her drink tasted bitter.

"I see you have all begun to mingle. It deeply pleases me to see such power in one room. To the newest of our Sisters," Torenia looked at the four youngest in the room. "These are some of the few people who are trying to prevent witch burnings around the world. After a dark time, we worked for many years to make people forget about witches so we may be left in peace. We believed we could only achieve safety with secrecy."

There was a pause, and Alina knew Torenia was about to change the world these other witches fought for. Her stomach roiled. Why was it Torenia's decision?

"We are entering a frightening new century, one where man will rule again with an iron fist. As we all know—as we all feel in the marrow of our bones—man does not like that which he does not understand. We must make them understand."

Murmurs picked up among those at the table. No longer worried about staring, Alina surveyed the faces. Helga and Gyda spoke with their hands, faces giving nothing away. The others spoke different languages. The newest Sisters—Alina and the others—did not know what to make of all this. She had never followed the politics of the tiny village she was raised in; how could she ever hope to grasp the politics of witches around the whole world?

Torenia cleared her throat to gather attention again. The others went quiet, and Vera silently placed a pitcher of crimson blood upon the table before disappearing again.

"I brought you here today for a vote—a vote for witches around the world and how we must proceed. Do we strip ourselves of our pride and continue to disappear underground? Do we allow the new generations to forget what they are capable of? Or do we take a stand? We are here, and we should not hide from man." Torenia leaned over the arm of her chair to pull something from a bag. Out came a perfectly white skull. A human skull. She filled it with blood from a pitcher beside her. "Please, feast—do not hesitate to mingle. There are no formalities here. We all want the same thing—for witches to thrive. Chat amongst yourselves and let us decide what is best for all of us."

She sipped from the skull and stared at Alina while she did.

Alina worried the cuticle at the edge of her nail. She wanted to tear it off and make it bleed, to ache with that flayed agony. Chatter rose again, and everyone began to eat as though hunger consumed them. The thought of eating while Torenia drank blood made her stomach turn. Over the din, Alina asked Torenia, "Where were you?"

Torenia eyed her with a stoic expression. Her lips were deeper red with the blood that stained them. "I had some unfinished family business to attend to."

She brought the skull to her lips again, never taking her eyes off of Alina. Her fingers were stained with dirt.

Alina knew whose skull it was. She rose from her chair, the sound of it skittering along the marble floor, shocking everyone into silence. As she stormed out of the room, despair clawed at her chest like an animal trapped inside a cage, desperate to escape. When she made it down the hall and away from the feast, a sob burst from her.

~

It was Gyda who found Alina after her outburst, sitting outside in the snowy courtyard. Her trousers did less to keep her warm than layered skirts would have, but she felt little except sorrow and rage.

"I can see you have suffered greatly," the woman said, her northern accent making her words harsh and guttural. "And that you suffer still."

Alina said nothing. She would trust no one who aligned with Torenia.

"You are right to distrust her."

Now Alina looked at Gyda with hard eyes lined with tears.

Gyda went on. "Be wary. Keep one eye open, and look out for your Sisters. Torenia is not what she seems. The vote tonight went against what she wanted, and there comes a time when all empires fall."

"What are you suggesting?" Alina asked, her voice a scratchy croak. "Why do they call her the Blood Queen?"

"Never let your guard down." Those were Gyda's parting words before she disappeared back into the castle.

With this knowledge tucked away, she let herself wallow in sadness a moment longer, then got to her feet and entered the warmth of the castle. Red was dead—there was no sense in thinking about it now. The others were alive. Even if she could no longer trust Sorin, it was her duty to keep Lilianna and Tatiana safe.

By the time she made it back to their shared room, both had returned from the feast. Wherever Sorin was, Alina didn't care. Both the sisters looked up at her, but it was Tatiana who approached.

"Your hands are freezing," Tatiana exclaimed. She held them between her smooth palms, warming them. "Where were you?"

"I must tell you something—both of you," Alina announced, though she left her hands in Tatiana's. It felt too pleasant to withdraw. "One of the witches, Gyda, told me to be wary of Torenia."

Lilianna was attentive now, narrowing her eyes. "Then we must be wary of Gyda."

"Torenia brought them all here to convince us she was a good person, and they warned us against her behind her back. What does that tell you?" Alina implored.

"That tells you that Gy-da," Lilianna said, mocking her name, "is afraid of what Torenia is capable of. Rather than supporting her, they lie about her behind her back. It's shameful, and you should be ashamed, Alina. Torenia took us in, gave us everything and more!"

"She has a point," Tatiana said. Her brows pinched with betrayal when Alina yanked her hands away. "I think we should be careful, yes. There is never harm in caution. Perhaps Torenia has done some bad things—everyone in power has regrets. However, we must consider that she is trying to be different, to be better, and we must offer her that opportunity."

"Maybe they don't trust her because she is a nightwalker," Lilianna suggested.

"Nor should we," Alina said. "We are nothing but food."

"She won't eat us!" Lilianna growled.

"They call her the Blood Queen!" Alina shouted, raising her voice more than intended. She was certain Torenia had spies all over.

The door to the bedroom opened wide, revealing Sorin, stone-faced. The silence that permeated the room was like the quiet that followed the first snowfall, only it didn't come with elation and joy—it came dripping with dread.

"Now, don't go quiet on me. We have much to discuss, and it won't resolve itself. We will fix this tonight," Sorin said. No one needed to ask what needed fixing. The gap between the four of them was getting bigger every day. Alina bit her tongue to hold back a retort—Sorin was the one who held the hammer that drove the wedge. "You are forgetting your ancestors. Hatred was the reason behind the Wolf. Distrust and malice are clouding your judgment."

"They were *her* ancestors—Torenia's. What does that tell you?" Alina asked.

"They were Red's, as well," Sorin replied. She shut the door behind her, sealing them in with a silent promise that they would not emerge until everything was sorted out.

"Sorin is right," Tatiana said quietly. She always remained as neutral as possible, and Alina admired that. Though Tatiana doubted herself sometimes, Alina knew her power was stronger than she would admit. The power to calm and nurture was as valid as a power to curse or lift curses. "Our ancestors might not have been related to the Lucas, but they all cowered in fear of their neighbor. Surely, such deeply ingrained hatred fueled the curse. They lived in terror that another would unleash the Wolf upon their family. We must be better than that—we cannot be fearful of one another. And we certainly cannot conspire behind each other's backs. We must be a united force."

"I stand with Torenia," Sorin said, as though they didn't already know.

"Oh, I do too!" Lilianna chimed in, moving to stand beside Sorin.

Tatiana pressed her lips tight. "I do not feel threatened by Torenia and chose to remain in her care. I may not trust her, but trust is hard to come by after..."

Alina looked up, hair hanging limp around her face. In the month they had been there, her hair had grown but was thinning. She was somewhere she did not belong. Her body, or perhaps her mind, was giving up after the loss of Red, leaving all traces of her behind.

"I cannot live here," Alina mumbled. Too quietly. "I cannot live here!" It came out carnal and animalistic. "She reminds me of *her*, some warped version of her. The version of her that she would have become if...if her plan had worked." She spoke her mind. "I saw her growing colder that night. I watched her turn wicked, and I thought... I thought if we were beside her, we would simply reclaim the town, put things right. But now that I've seen who she is related to, I know that she would have turned out the same or worse."

Tatiana touched her shoulder. "What are you talking about?"

"I mean Red! She was dark inside! After she ordered the Wolf to murder her grandmother and killed her father the way she did... We all understood why she had to do it, just as we did with your father." She looked pointedly at Lilianna and Tatiana. "Except him. Blaez. He knew what the Lucas were capable of, the evil they harnessed, and he didn't want to help. They were corrupt, all of them, and Torenia is no different."

A moment of silence passed before Sorin spoke. "I believe you should return home, Alina."

"I can't," Alina cried, dropping to her knees and cradling her head. "I cannot bear to see what the wolves did to it. I will have nothing to return to."

"Perhaps it is better there now," Lilianna suggested quietly—a thought Alina had never considered.

Could Lilianna be right?

A BRIEF HISTORY OF WITCHES
AN EXCERPT

~

Upon studying the infamous case of Azalea Luca, it was clear that her quest for power would stop at nothing. One must try to determine whether or not she was lucid or suffered extreme hysteria. What level of insanity must take hold of the mind to possess someone to murder their own child in cold blood, simply to gain power?

Her quest for power was futile from the beginning. While looking back at the evidence—though there is very little, simply rumors and what was left from the scene—I have made it of utmost importance to get to the real reason behind the massacre of the previous winter, whatever it takes.

Azalea Luca was a witch many in Ocleau sought out, whether for her ability to create tonics for ailments or poisons for abusers. She was never considered a good person, nor did she want to be seen as such. She was simply necessary, like many of us who hide in the darkest corners, dealing in crooked things. There have always been the prostitutes, the witches, the assassins—people seek out some manner of that which is banished.

This is the very reason why Azalea Luca was able to continue to operate as the town's witch: the people needed her for reasons they dared not share in public.

It is my understanding that Azalea Luca killed her daughter Juniper in an effort to control a lycan.

Such power would have earned her the title of most powerful person in Ocleau. It is unclear whether or not her son, Matthias, was in on it as well. Once accused of drowning his beloved—a young woman named Rüna—Matthias returned nearly a decade later. From the moment of his return, the once calm and content town of Ocleau was thrown into upheaval.

It is my belief that Matthias Luca wished to have the power of the Moon Curse. Such power, combined with his mother's extensive knowledge and expertise in witchcraft, would have made the Luca family not only the most powerful but also the most feared.

It is my belief, though I cannot confirm such theories, that Azalea went behind Matthias's back to try and control the lycan—for he had left once before, and she refused to let this new level of power slip from her grasp. Azalea knew that Matthias would be more powerful than her—at least with brute force—if he had any control of the lycan Blaez Kõiv.

From what I found in Azalea Luca's abandoned home after the execution, an untested possession theory had a hand in all this bloodshed. Azalea Luca discovered that one's consciousness could be placed within the body of an animal. This is not new knowledge, by any means — familiars were traditionally the consciousness of a human put into an animal, until witches later discovered that animals possess their own consciousness, and most began bonding with their beasts.

The study I read revealed a way to control the human and animal combination—unlike a familiar who will do these things willingly, this particular method of control is beyond simple magic. A seasoned witch can control every decision of the human-animal for eternity, but it requires a sacrifice.

That of a daughter.

It is my belief that Azalea Luca chose to murder her daughter in order to control the lycan in their midst. How Blaez Kõiv got mixed up in all of this, I have yet to discover.

In conclusion, Azalea Luca, or perhaps all of the Lucas, have an insatiable need for power. The more they get, the more they need. They will stop at nothing for that power, whether it be advancing in witchcraft, controlling beasts that should be permitted to run free, or even remaining youthful for eternity (evidence found in Azalea Luca's home suggested she was considering blood bathing to remain youthful). I fear for the world should the Luca family continue to produce witches.

Matthias Luca fled after the trial, and Blaez Kõiv disappeared after his banishment.

Only time will tell what might happen should Matthias Luca use the wolf he inadvertently inherited. Only time will tell what will happen to Blaez Kõiv.

11

TORENIA

Torenia ran her finger over her bottom lip, staring up from between the woman's legs with lust dripping from her gaze. Her hands ran up the supple thighs and around the curves of her hips. The woman groaned and jerked ever so slightly, the aftermath of pleasure still vibrating through her. Torenia was far from done with her—even though dawn was nearing, it didn't mean Torenia had to lock herself inside a coffin until nightfall. She had other means to pass the time.

Until a knock echoed through the bed chambers.

Under any other circumstance, Torenia would have cursed the person on the other side of the door. She swore if it were Alexei or Zaina, she would have their heads—they knew better. It was likely one of the young ones. Rising from her position, she cast a sympathetic glance at the woman in her bed.

"Duty calls," she told her. Gracefully, she stepped down from the bed and reached for her robe, slipping it on and loosely cinching the belt. It left little to the imagination, but then, so did most of her wardrobe.

Opening the door, Torenia was unsurprised to see Sorin standing there. They stood nearly eye to eye, though Torenia was slightly taller. "It is nearly dawn."

"This could not wait," Sorin said sternly. "It's Alina."

"So be it," Torenia said with a sigh. She shut the bedroom door behind her and slipped an arm through Sorin's. They walked down the dimly lit hall, following the stairs and heading toward the throne room. Torenia thought fondly of the memories there, particularly when she ripped out Svetlana's heart. That was the moment she learned that ruthlessness and the need for power were within her very lifeblood, in her namesake, not because of what she was taught. It was not Roman Sokolov who made her that way, though she could not deny that he laid the path for her to find her true self. It was she who fought for the rights of people like her. People who had not been born with his privilege. Yes, he fought his way through poverty, but he was still one step ahead of where she started.

"Alina fears your bloodline is cursed," Sorin said as they walked.

The slow saunter of a pace was pleasant, though Torenia was still sour, wishing that she was back in bed. "She is correct to assume this. And to fear it."

"The curse was broken, was it not?" Sorin asked, not slowing her walk.

Torenia stopped her now, studying her face. Sorin's dark eyes had seen much in their time on this earth—a blink of an eye to Torenia, but likely just as many horrors, or at least near to it. Not many had suffered what Torenia had.

She banished the thoughts of that dark time and focused on the present. "Blaez Kõiv's curse was broken, but not the Lucas'. There were two curses at hand that fateful day, all those years ago. Azalea Luca caused a ripple when she murdered her daughter, one that continued for three hundred years before it faded."

Sorin did the math. "So, Red was not afflicted?"

Torenia offered a wry smile. "She was. Because of me."

Sorin narrowed her eyes and cocked her head to the side.

Torenia sighed. "It was not my *finest* moment. When I learned the curse was lifted, I returned to my home and did some unspeakable things." The words would have shuddered out of her had she been a weaker person. What she had done was vile—at the time, it hadn't bothered her conscience. But since...

"You started it again," Sorin realized. "The massacre..."

Torenia nodded. "There are many reasons why they call me the

Blood Queen. Alas, they call me something far worse in Silvania, and for good reason."

Sorin's expression was pinched. The truth was presented to her. Torenia would not lie to Sorin—she merely hoped it wouldn't scare her away. Suspecting it wouldn't, Torenia waited a beat before she said, "If you would like to leave, all of you are welcome to go at any time."

Snapping back to the present, Sorin shook her head gently. A curl fell from where it had been tucked behind her ear. "She wishes to go home. She fears what has happened there since the wolves took over, and guilt haunts her. Alina had a family there, a family who cared for her."

"I would have no qualms with her departure." Torenia leaned against the banister overlooking the throne room. "What is stopping her?"

"She doesn't trust you. Leaving the others behind would also haunt her."

"Then I will make a deal with her. The witches voiced their thoughts on reminding the world we exist, much to my dismay, but I cannot afford to lose their strength and numbers. At this time, my focus is on wiping out the Old Bloods before the incestuous monsters lose their grip on humanity and are unleashed. If I make a pact with the wolves—and I have already gained their favor—then Alina may return there with the knowledge she will be safe. She may return to be with her family, and she can live among the wolves. How they plan on ruling, I know not, but I will need them when the war shows up at my door."

"Alina does not trust you."

"She does not have to," Torenia said. "I have no intent to harm her. She bonded with Gyda at the Witches Feast, did she not? I will send her with Gyda to ensure safe travel, a pact with the wolves, and the promise to never show my face in Silvania unless I've requested permission. Would Alina agree to this?"

Sorin looked over the banister, staring down at the throne. Once a beautiful piece of art, it was now a mockery. It served as a painful reminder to a time Torenia wished never to think back on—a time when she lost her head. A time when she lost her heart.

"It would be a start," Sorin decided.

"Then that is where we shall begin. My predecessor died for no good reason, all because his desire for vengeance upon his brother consumed him. Part of me believes he knew his time was coming, and he wanted his little brother to go down with him. This is not the path I wish to follow, though it is a path I have trodden once before. I am not Roman, but I know I have enemies. They will come for me if I attack the Old Bloods. Alternately, the Old Bloods will come for me if they suspect I made a deal with a wolf pack. This is why I need to send Alina in my stead."

It was not the only reason Torenia wished Alina to be out of her hair.

She placed a hand on Sorin's shoulder and gave it a gentle squeeze to show their camaraderie. Sorin was the one whom Torenia needed more than the rest of them; however, they came as a foursome. With Sorin at the helm, the others would see that Torenia could be trusted. Lilianna was wrapped around Torenia's finger and would be easy to manipulate when necessary. Tatiana had her guard up, for good reason, but it encouraged the divide Torenia needed to snuff out. Sending Alina away would clear the air enough to encourage Tatiana to do what Torenia needed. Each had their role—Torenia just had to play the board until they were in their places.

"You wish to send Alina to form an alliance with the wolves. You wish to send another of us to Krovberg, to the Old Bloods—Tatiana, correct?" Sorin's words shocked Torenia.

She hadn't planned on telling Sorin. She had planned for the pieces to fall in place and for it to appear as natural—the slow divide that occurred when adolescents became adults.

Sorin, as perceptive as a seer, saw through it all. Torenia would not be surprised if she had some seer blood in her.

"The thought crossed my mind," Torenia admitted. She decided it would be best to speak somewhere private. Lilianna had been known to wander the castle, getting into all sorts of places she shouldn't. Though the other girls had no familiars, Torenia wouldn't put it past them to lurk and linger to listen. Information was more valuable than any currency.

She guided Sorin to her study, which had once been Roman's. Very little had changed since the *Korol* had died. The walls were still lined with books, many containing the lore of sirens and snow maidens, foolish tales that the eldest Sokolov believed in. Now they were for looks, though most of the books Torenia had replaced with valuable ones: books on the Craft, books on lycanthropy, books on history, and Azalea Luca's book, a detailed grimoire with many witches' voices within.

Someone had stolen that one many years ago, when Torenia was most vulnerable. She would never allow herself to be that weak again. Nothing could replace what she had lost.

After lighting the lanterns in the room, Torenia leaned against the desk. She looked Sorin in the eyes. "At the Witches' Feast, they spoke of hiding, did they not? Becoming cave-dwellers as the dawn of man begins. What do you think of this, Sorin?"

"It sounds safe, yet suffocating."

Good. She understood.

"And what does the dawn of man sound like?"

"Death to all others."

"Precisely," Torenia said with a sigh. "Man has partnered with the Old Bloods—they see it as their ticket to slaughtering the few of us who remain out of the shadows. Where would it stop, though? Man would have my head on a silver platter, I have no doubt. But they will never stop. They will hunt down every vampire, every witch, every lycan, every siren, until there are none left. You said you saw innocents die. This would be no different.

"The witches wish for the Old Bloods to be removed from the world. They are an aberration. A stain. Then they wish to hide away, to let magic die. Tell me, Sorin, will you hide when it is over? Or will you stand up for the rights of those who are not man?"

Sorin looked at Torenia. "I am no coward."

12

TATIANA

Tatiana's best friend was leaving today.

She watched the sun rise over the glistening mounds of snow. Every tree branch was dusted in white, occasional droplets of water falling from them like crystals in the warmth of the sun. Only a glimmer of their strange redness showed through. It was still early in the year—not warm enough to feel comfortable—but Tatiana felt very little. It was nothing new, that numbness she felt as she sat upon the roof of the castle just outside her window. The steep roof offered little for her to cling to, and her toes were curling and uncurling just to keep her in place. A massive fur blanket draped around her shoulders, dwarfing her completely.

The sun rose high enough over the next half hour, reaching Tatiana at last. Its golden light surged through her, making her feel alive. Ever since her mother died, Tatiana would hide on the roof after chores because she knew her father would never find her up there. Still, at suppertime, she would drop off the edge into the hay bales, slither into the open bedroom window, and be ready to prepare their meals. She wished she could trade places with every chicken she killed for dinner. A swift death after a long life of being completely free—untouched, unharmed. The irony was that Tatiana's father protected the chickens, killing them only when needed. He cared for his poultry more than he cared for his daughters.

Tatiana spat off the edge of the castle. Her spittle did not go far and seemed to freeze the moment it left her lips. With a sigh, she heaved the fur around her and pulled it tighter to her chest. Glancing at the sun again, she realized that she would never choose to deny herself this pleasure. She got very little in life, but the sunshine meant the night was over, that she and Lilianna survived another night.

She would never give up the sunshine.

With that decision and feeling proud of it, Tatiana headed back down the peak and slipped into a window just like she used to at home. Alina was leaving today—or perhaps, she thought, returning. When Tatiana chopped her father into pieces, she also severed her ties to the town. She also decided she would never step foot in Silvania again.

Yet she did not feel quite at home here, either.

The small coven that used to sizzle pig's hearts in flames and spread herbal concoctions into their open flesh wounds was falling apart. One dead. One leaving, perhaps forever. One seeing herself as above them now that she had greater, stronger company. Tatiana was left with only her sister, and a growing crevasse stretched between them, too.

Only a fool would think that girlish friendships would last forever. Though young, she had endured enough in her lifetime to know that there was no such thing as a happy ending. But she hoped that there would be a chance that the life she lived could bring her happiness. She needed purpose—one that was bigger than protecting her sister. Her sister had Torenia now—she saw that. She accepted it.

In the empty bedroom, Tatiana embraced the extended silence and peace she had to herself. She selected a rather mundane dress and pinafore and stockings that were thick and warm. She had not yet gotten used to the bitter cold of Osleka, but she knew one day she would adapt and adjust. Draping a thick wool scarf around her neck and a fur hat over her wavy brown hair, Tatiana looked at herself in the mirror. She looked older and realized that she had not looked at herself since her mother died. Only seventeen, yet she had aged so much in the past few months.

"Perhaps I will be able to stay beautiful like Torenia," she whispered, then immediately shied away from herself in the mirror. She wondered how Torenia did it. What kind of magic could allow her to live forever?

Never one to be late, Tatiana left the room and made her way to the throne room. It had the highest ceilings of any building that she had ever seen. It seemed to reach to the skies, with great pillars on either side holding it all up. In the center of the back wall was the single throne. Where three once sat in regal splendor, only one still stood. Tatiana eyed it with mild curiosity every time, but she was content with her knowledge and did not wish to dig further. When one dug deep enough, they would find skeletons they didn't mean to exhume.

The roaring fire crackled, beckoning her. She went to it, placing her hands a few inches from the mantel and letting the warmth spread through her. Sweat beaded under her arms and along the small of her back.

The white walls of the throne room, upon closer inspection, were peppered with black. The marble floors were almost flawless, save for an ancient crack from a lifetime ago. It was a beautiful hall, and Tatiana knew Torenia suited that throne. She had not seen her there, and she wondered if the idea of thrones and queens was an ancient and dwindling system.

Tatiana wondered if the single throne and the two broken ones were kept as a reminder. If thrones and royalty were a thing of the past, what was the future?

Tatiana already knew.

Man.

It left a bitter taste in her mouth. She knew that Torenia, despite her flaws, had reason to oppose the idea of hiding. Hiding wouldn't keep them safe; it would suffocate them.

"I'm going to miss you," Alina said, her silent approach startling Tatiana. Alina was always like a ghost in her movements, lithe and silent.

"We will meet again," Tatiana replied firmly.

"Gyda and I are beginning the journey home, and I fear what I may find there," Alina said. "I thought I had nothing to lose when Red died, but I was wrong. The town may have been a wretched place, but things are different now. The Luca curse is gone."

"Do you think…" Tatiana's voice trailed off.

"That Torenia could bring him back? No. I believe that the Wolf is gone, but…I think there is something more. Something isn't right with Torenia. Last night, I was at the library to see why they called her the Blood Queen. There was not much, but… There were suggestions of something truly evil."

"And?" Tatiana inquired.

"I discovered that bathing in the blood of virgins can keep one youthful."

Tatiana's hands balled into fists, and her nails dug into her soft palms. "She's still so beautiful after all these years. Alina, you don't think—?"

Before Alina could answer, Torenia entered with Sorin and Lilianna flanking her. Tatiana's chest tightened—though she knew Lilianna had found a replacement for their mother, it still hurt her to see her little sister replacing her, too. She looked away and whispered to Alina. "My purpose here is dwindling."

Alina spared her a look of sympathy. After all her sadness and despair, she still had a soft spot for her oldest friend. They had played when they were children, before their parents scolded them for making friends. For fraternizing with the enemy—all neighbors in Silvania were the enemy.

"Find a way out of this place," Alina whispered back. "Promise me."

Tatiana didn't get a chance to answer.

"Though you have not been with us long," Torenia said to Alina, "your presence has made an impact. Alina Nastaca, it was you who brought these women together. You who united them and made them strong despite adversity and abuse." Torenia glanced sympathetically at Tatiana, her hand placed warmly on Lilianna's shoulder. She carried on after a brief pause. "You are a beacon of light among the darkness— know that I truly believe that. As one who has seen the dark and perhaps even been the dark itself, I envy you for what you are capable of. Your decision to return to your home to ensure the safety of your family is a brave and selfless one.

"I have sent ahead a voice to speak on my behalf, to let Daciana know you are to return and that you are to be accepted, as well as your family untouched. Do not let this fool you—they are wolves and perhaps cannot be trusted. But I have done this with the hope of protecting what you have left. Make peace with that place—something I could not do even after a hundred years. You are stronger than me, Alina."

Her words surprised Tatiana, but she could feel the tension radiating from Alina. She didn't believe them.

"Thank you," Alina said quietly.

"Gyda will meet you in three days at the inn I've marked on your map and will join you on your travels. She has business with the pack, and she is one of my most trusted acquaintances," Torenia said. Alina kept her face an unreadable blank slate. Torenia's painted red lip twitched. "You will need to travel on your own at first. I trust you will be able to find the way?"

Alina nodded sternly. "Yes, I will find it." She turned to Tatiana then, embracing her and whispering, "Promise me."

Tatiana knew she was asking her to leave this place. Though Tatiana did not know how, or where she might go, or how she could possibly leave her little sister behind, she agreed. "I promise."

Alina then turned to Lilianna, who rushed ahead and slammed into her. The hug was childish and heartfelt, but Alina was extremely petite, and Lilianna's forcefulness nearly knocked them both down. She stumbled, then laughed lightly. The laughter sprinkled through the air, warming it more than the fire could. Tatiana looked at the ground and smiled—Lilianna was a beacon of light too.

Finally, Alina approached Sorin, gripping both of her hands. "May the choices you make be the right ones, Sorin."

Sorin did not reply. Alina's final words were sharp and accusatory, hidden within advice. Instead, Sorin simply nodded once, lips pressed tight. There it was, Tatiana noted, the divide between them stemming from Sorin choosing Torenia over Alina.

Alina went to the massive double doors, which opened with a wave of Torenia's hand. She glanced back once through her long blonde hair, knotted and ratty. Sunshine flooded the room, not quite reaching Torenia.

Torenia stood at the edge of the stream of light, knowing how dangerous it was, yet flaunting her lack of fear. As Alina stepped out onto the great steps, Torenia said, "Don't stray from the path, dear. Dangerous things lurk along the edges."

13

ALINA

Only when the mammoth castle was out of sight did Alina feel she could breathe again. That horrible place was behind her now. Though she had not suffered within its walls, she could feel the suffering of so many others. It was a place of war and torture—not a place for someone like her. Despite the fires in every hearth, the Blood Queen's castle was always cold.

Finally free of the Blood Queen, Alina felt a warmth creep out from her heart, as though it dared to reach out again, brave enough to show itself. She was alone, and she'd never felt safer. Torenia had gifted her a nameless horse that she had struggled to mount earlier, but she grew more comfortable in its presence with each sturdy step.

A few months had gone by since Red's death. The pain still lingered, but she carefully constructed walls around her heart. Dwelling on the past, on the dead, would do her no good. She knew she would never forget Red, but she could honor her by returning to the town and trying to fix it. That was what Red always wanted, deep down. It wasn't to rule with an iron fist or to massacre anyone who looked at them wrong. It was to fix what was wrong in that crooked place.

At least, that's what she told herself.

On the third day, Alina found the inn Torenia had marked on her map. As she neared it, she wondered if this was the right choice. To join up with someone who supported Torenia did not fit into Alina's plan. Gyda had said not to trust Torenia, but for all she knew, it could be a ruse. She did not need a chaperone—though she did not know the way home, she was a capable woman who could figure it out. Nibbling her lip, Alina decided she wanted nothing to do with Torenia. Pulling back and using her heels to dig into the horse's muscular sides, she began to back up the horse.

"Change your mind?" A vaguely familiar voice echoed through the surrounding woods. She looked down, and beside her stood a familiar red-haired woman. Multiple variations of meticulous braids pulled her hair from her face, revealing eyes filled with knowledge. Helga stood next to her, a soft smile on her lips, her wheat-colored hair loose and free.

"Helga and I will claim not to have seen you pass through if you wish it. Alas, I am supposed to escort you to the parlay, but—" Her thick Northern accent was hard for Alina to understand, yet she leaned toward Gyda with the need to hear more.

"Say what you wish, but I am aware that Torenia does not trust me and has sent you to watch over me. I have no doubt she sent her familiar as well," Alina countered, surprised by the harshness in her words. Gyda fascinated her—she had an air of leadership about her. And yet she knew she could trust no one under the spell of the Blood Queen.

"Say what *you* wish, but know that Torenia trusts me to carry out what she has tasked me with, as I have carried out her other tasks. However, I am an individual with my own interests to consider, and Torenia is unaware of a few changes coming her way."

"What sort of changes?" Alina whispered.

Helga signed something to Gyda, who raised her hand in a motion for her to stop. Alina scowled internally. She wanted to know what Helga had to say. She looked to the blonde, sending a soft smile her way. Perhaps Helga would teach her how to do that.

Gyda looked up, searching for something within the darkening skies among the shadowed treetops. Though no raven was in sight, a witch as powerful and old as Torenia would surely have more than one set of eyes.

"Let's rest here for the night," Gyda suggested, signing to Helga as she spoke and gesturing to the inn.

Alina swung down from the horse. The earth below her was muddy from the spring rains and horses trampling through. Traveling through an Oslekan winter once had been enough for her, even with Torenia's magical influence making the journey easier.

Once inside, the warmth of the fire hit them full blast, forcing Alina to peel off layers before she began to sweat. A tavern was attached to the inn, the front door leading right into the cozy dining room. A few patrons were already sipping ale from massive mugs, and in no time at all, Helga and Gyda carried three, guiding Alina to seats in the back. The crackling wood stove was next to them, making Alina crave that frothy ale to cool her down.

Helga signed something and Gyda nodded, then translated. "It would be much safer to speak without words; alas, you have not yet learned. I urge you to speak quietly—we are too close to the Blood Queen's home to trust that we are out of her clutches." Gyda set the volume of their conversation, which was a decibel above a whisper. "Why are you returning to a place where you are not welcome?"

Alina eyed Gyda skeptically. "I am more welcome there than here."

Gyda nodded. She glanced around the room. The walls were dark and lined with paintings and oil lamps. The windows at the front let in the remnants of late-afternoon light, which was scarce. Gyda took a sip of ale, leaving a line of froth on her upper lip.

"How can I trust you?" Alina asked. Alina left behind the people she trusted when she left the castle. Once she had trusted Sorin, Tatiana, Lilianna, and Red. Now Red was gone, Sorin was under Torenia's spell, Lilianna too... The last person she could truly, deeply trust was Tatiana, and she feared she would never see her again. Having someone else she might be able to confide in...that was worth all the gold in the world. She looked at Helga, sensing the warmth coming from her—she reminded Alina of her mother.

"Many years ago, what was once the Brotherhood—an organization that strived for equality but was built on blood—became the Sisterhood," Gyda began. "At first, it was a huge change, one that was very much needed among those who are...different. Torenia pulled people from around the world, seeking out leaders like herself to make a pact.

Like one giant coven. She had Half Bloods, Pure Bloods, and she had more witches in her counsel.

"Her efforts were noticed because we were stronger as a collective. And yet she still needed more, though she did not show it at first. From stories I have heard, she governed us because she was the one who created the earth-spanning coven. But she could not, not from so far away, trapped in the northern edges of Osleka, restricted to the night. She assumed those who feared her would always remain loyal—she never considered the possibility that they would rebel."

Alina realized she was leaning so close to Gyda that she could smell her ale-scented breath. Her hands were clutching her thighs, her knuckles gone white. Leaning back, Alina took a deep breath and awaited the rest of the story.

"I have heard that there is a branch of witches who seek order and attain it secretly. They make certain...events occur to keep the peace among witches. Order must be kept to protect us from man. Torenia wishes to expose us all and to rise up against man. But we do not have the numbers or the power. We must accept that the secrecy of our kind is the only way to survive. However, the nightwalker sees them as food, and so she is blind to our reasoning."

"But the vote at the Witches' Feast..."

"She was outnumbered, but that can change." Gyda scowled. "I stand beside her decision to remove the Old Bloods—that I will assist with. However, afterwards, something must change."

Helga signed something, her eyes downcast, a frown on her lips.

Gyda sighed, sipped her ale, then translated. "Our power is weakening. The earth is being soiled, tarnished, torn apart. Moon and blood magic are as strong as ever, but the main source of the Craft... It is dwindling."

Alina blinked, stunned. Helga nodded solemnly.

Gyda said slowly, "During my time on this earth, I was there to witness Torenia's Dark Years."

"Dark Years?"

"You saw her throne room—there used to be three thrones. A century ago, they were meant for a king, queen, and their heir. The castle was then taken over by Roman Sokolov and his brothers, who named it the Brotherhood. They governed the vampires, and I will admit, history says they did well, if you ignore the slaughter and the pile of nightwalker bodies that carried them up the steps to the throne. Torenia was mentored by Roman, the worst of them, though that is debatable. I believe this is part of the reason why she snapped."

"Is the other part in her blood?"

"Alina, I deeply appreciate your understanding. This is why we chose you."

Alina considered these words, then said, "Tell me about the Dark Years."

14

SORIN

There was something peculiar about the air in the castle. Something sour permeated the air that normally smelled like the crisp outdoors, thanks to the earthy scent of wood burning in all the fireplaces around the glamorous building. The sourness did not come from food left out to rot or some animal that died and went unnoticed by the maids. It was malicious. Sorin could feel it vibrating through her bones.

She found herself deep in the library, in the crevices filled with forgotten, dusty books. Books on witchcraft throughout the ages, across the world—it was a plethora of information. Already she had stored away new tricks and spells, curses and potions.

All thoughts of those spells and potions disappeared when that sourness wafted into the room. Sorin looked up from the book she was reading and whispered, "Lucien."

The rat crawled through the bookshelf where Sorin had removed a book earlier that evening. Long whiskers tested the space before he wriggled through. Any other animal would have made the delicately balanced books cascade like dominoes, but Lucien was graceful. Crawling up Sorin's extended hand and arm, she lifted him to meet her eyes.

"What do you sense, love?" she asked him.

A pulsing sensation rippled through her from Lucien. It formed into a heartbeat, but not one she recognized. Not one from the castle —it was a man's heartbeat. The castle only held women, with the exception of Torenia's war counsellor, Alexei—but this was not his heartbeat. This was too quick. He was nervous.

Sorin gasped, rising to her feet so quickly that her head spun. Not waiting for her mind to clear, she ran, hitting her shoulder against the bookshelf. A book fell from its shelves, landing with a thud that filled the library, but quickly faded.

As she ran, she brandished the knife she kept in her boot. Lucien clung to the cloth of her shirt, climbing down before plopping to the ground. His nimble body scurried ahead of her, leading the way. Up the stairs he went, running along the banister as Sorin ran alongside him. He leapt down from atop the stairwell, racing to Lilianna and Tatiana's bedroom.

Sorin's heart hammered hard. *No, not them.*

She saw a scuff of dirt outside the door—a boot print exiting the room. Turning around, she debated going back, but she had to ensure that Lilianna and Tatiana were not in the room. She opened the door with bated breath. The window was open; a grappling hook dug into the plaster. Sorin was relieved to find it empty with no sign of struggle —whenever the intruder entered, Lilianna and Tatiana were not present.

She turned and ran as fast as she could. Lucien was out of sight, but the sourness in the air led her way. She could smell his nervous sweat, thick and putrid. He was near, and he was terrified. Blood pulsed in her ears, deafening her as she flew down the steps.

Her eyes scanned desperately for another trace of the man. Standing in the throne room, Sorin had too many options. Doorways surrounded her, giving her unlimited options, but only one would be correct. She realized this man was not here for her friends but for Torenia. Powerful people came with enemies—Sorin had been told this by the Blood Queen herself.

She had to make a choice. A flash of darkness caught her attention. Standing at the base of the broken throne stood a man, his hand on the great seat. He was taller than Sorin, but lanky despite his thick clothing. He appeared to have traveled a long way.

Sorin approached him silently; his attention remained on the throne until she was just out of arm's length. Her palms were so sweaty that the dagger nearly slipped from her grasp.

He stumbled down the few steps of the throne, pulling out a small, slender sword. Sorin recoiled; his reach and weapon were longer, and she had to be smart.

"Don't try to stop me!" he shouted, his voice as nervous as Sorin was.

"Stop you from what, boy?" she asked, cocking her head to the side.

Regaining some of his confidence, he stood taller, stepping closer to her. His words didn't quiver when he spoke this time. "Down with the Blood Queen."

He lunged at Sorin, the sword grazing her arm. Vulgar words in her native tongue slipped out as she spun to attack the man. Perhaps he was no more than a boy—scarcely twenty, if that—but this did not change her plan of action. His youth meant nothing. He stumbled after his weapon grazed her, having braced himself for the sword to hit its mark.

With his side exposed, he turned to try again, but Sorin closed the gap between them. She plunged the dagger into his ribs, pressing her other hand against his bony chest. His shock froze him, allowing her to twist the dagger. He cried out and collapsed to his knees, and Sorin dropped with him, keeping the blade in her grasp.

The commotion brought the others, with Torenia at the head of the pack, and her advisor, Zaina, and Lilianna at her heels. Torenia's lip raised in a snarl, but the dead expression in her blue eyes didn't falter. She knelt beside Sorin and the boy, looking at the witch, then the attempted assassin.

"Who sent you?" Torenia spat.

He gurgled blood in response.

Torenia hissed, gripping his cheeks and forcing him to look at her. "Was it the Old Bloods?"

The boy spat blood at her. Torenia did not flinch when the spray of saliva and blood dotted her cheeks and forehead. Her demeanor changed in a split second, as though someone inside her came out, crawled through her flesh, and took over.

"My dear, I can stop the hurt," she said. "If you tell me who sent you, I can make it go away."

Torenia gently pushed Sorin away from the boy. She released the dagger, but she left the blade inside him.

Torenia had the situation under control now. The Blood Queen pulled out the dagger as the boy whimpered. Placing her hand over the wound, she whispered something in a deep voice that could sedate or destroy all at once.

The pain must have ebbed, for the boy breathed out in relief.

"Tell me who sent you, my love," she whispered, her dark voice long gone. "And I will stop the pain. Was it the Old Bloods? Was it Lebedev and Maksim?"

"Y-Yes," he croaked. With pleading eyes, he begged. "Make it go away, p-please."

Torenia's softness disappeared in a snap. Her upper lip twitched as she brought her lips to his cheek. She planted a stain the shape of her lips there, a mark of death. She dug her fingers into the wound at his side, and he shrieked. He threw his head back, trying to wriggle away from her, but she clamped her teeth down on his throat. For the first time, Lilianna and Sorin had a real look at the vampire.

Her ferocity as she fed was unlike anything Sorin had ever seen before. She remained steady, but her stomach roiled as she watched. The hair on the back of her neck and her arms stood on end. She glanced at her young friend—Lilianna grinned from ear to ear.

Drained of blood, Torenia shoved the boy to the ground and rose. Her teeth glittered red, and she wiped her mouth with the back of her hand. Her lipstick smeared into the blood spray, combined into a strange hue against her nearly translucent skin.

"Send his head to the Old Bloods," Torenia snapped. "This blatant attack will not go without repercussions."

"This is what they wanted," Zaina suggested carefully. "For you to react. They know how you respond to things. The Old Bloods knew you would take it personally."

"They wanted me dead," Torenia snarled.

"No," Sorin said. "Zaina is right. They sent an unskilled boy. They wanted you to react. They must know you sent someone to speak with the wolves, so they are trying to rattle you."

Torenia's features tightened. Then she breathed out and smiled, and everyone in the room relaxed except Lilianna, who hadn't been tense to begin with. Sorin watched how fascinated she was with Torenia. It was only a matter of time.

"Then burn the body. They'll never know what happened to their little puppet." She turned to Sorin. "I need you in the library. Now."

15

LILIANNA

The groans and pleading used to make Lilianna's skin crawl. Now, she admired the durability of the human race—how much pain and agony they could survive. Some lasted longer than others, and some had their minds break before their bodies began to fail. The stronger ones spoke to her in gravelly voices, as though the pain was etched into their throats. Each word they spoke, each breath they took, made their veins bulge where the needle was inserted. Their blood was slowly drained from them, their bodies growing weaker.

Some didn't touch the food, but some ate fervently each time it was brought to them. Lilianna once tried some of their food before it was handed to them. It was watery soup with chunks of what might have been human meat—she didn't let herself think about this too much. The bread was always fresh, though, perhaps because Torenia wanted her own food to have some nourishment. The fresher the fodder, the fresher the blood.

Every few hours, someone would come down and clear out the ones drained that day. Torenia didn't need much—one full-grown person's worth of blood a day. Sometimes, she drank a mixture to keep the fodder alive longer. At the end of the hallway of pain—as Lilianna started calling it— were canisters filled with blood featuring spiles at their bases, allowing them to release their contents.

Since Alina left two weeks ago, Lilianna felt free. She felt as though the pressure of being what Alina wanted them to be was gone. She could be herself.

Today, she brought a cup with her.

"Just a taste," she told herself as she lifted the nozzle, and the crimson blood gushed free. It came out slow and thick at first, and something about the semi-coagulated blood made her nose wrinkle. Swirling the cup, she tried to thin its consistency, but that only revealed how much like molasses the blood was. She gagged, unsure if she could bring herself to drink it.

After seeing Torenia feed so viciously on the boy who tried to kill her, Lilianna had thought of nothing else. She wanted that kind of power.

"I should warm it up," she decided, and turned to walk back through the hallway. People reached through their cages at her, and she glared at them. In her eyes, they were all her father. If what Torenia told her was true, if none of them were any better than her father, then they all deserved this. She clutched the cup a little tighter and hustled up the steps. When she reached the top of the big oak door, it opened right as she reached for the handle.

The cup fell out of her hand, the blood spilling over her pinafore.

"Ack!" Lilianna shouted as she staggered backward, bumping against the rock wall behind her. The light that flooded the hallway from the main room revealed a silhouette. When Lilianna's eyes adjusted, she saw her sister and sighed in relief. Then her skin grew clammy. What would Tatiana think when she realized what was down here? And how could Lilianna hide it now that she was covered in blood, holding a cup of what was left of it?

"I've been looking all over for you, Lili," Tatiana scolded, but her words were too soft to take the scolding seriously. Then she saw the blood. Her eyes widened, and her mouth opened in a panic. "Lilianna, are you hurt?"

Her hands were now all over Lilianna, looking for the wound. When she gathered her bearings, Lilianna pushed her sister off her and skirted toward the steps, blocking Tatiana's way should she decide to go down the stairs. A part of Lilianna said that Tatiana didn't need to know. Perhaps she could understand, but Lilianna didn't want her to see.

It was something she shared with Torenia.

It was then she wished her sister were gone, out of the castle, out of Osleka. Far away, so she didn't have to lie to her or listen to her rational thoughts. At that moment, Lilianna knew she wanted to be like Torenia, no matter the cost. She would not let her sister stand in her way.

"You're not hurt," Tatiana said with relief. "Whose... Whose blood is that?"

Lilianna shrugged.

"Lili, please answer me." Tatiana sounded so much like their mother when she was alive. With her somber, soft way of asking what sort of trouble the girls got into, it was impossible to lie to her.

"You know Torenia is a nightwalker. I was bringing her a goblet from her stores," she said. It was easier to tell a lie that was close to the truth. "You startled me, and I spilled it."

Tatiana nodded, lips pressed tight together. "Lili, may I ask you something?"

"Here?" she hissed.

"Outside."

Tatiana and Lilianna went to the garden in the back of the castle, to its labyrinth of hedges, massive rose bushes, and ancient, dried-up vines. Inside were various seats made of stone and intricate carvings of gargoyles holding glass orbs and leering at them from above. A fountain in the center trickled cold water, algae and grime staining the once-white stones with greens and blacks.

The soft spring sun could almost be considered warm, but there was a bite to the air. Lilianna wrapped her stained hands around her stomach, trying to keep her fingertips warm against the cloth of her dress.

"You like it here, right?" Tatiana asked, placing a hand on her sister's arm.

Lilianna looked at the hand that rested there, then at her sister's solemn yet sturdy expression. "Yes. I finally feel safe and free."

Tatiana nodded. "I'm glad you have finally found a place that offers you those things."

Silence filled the space between them. Lilianna wasn't sure how to reply. She knew her sister had something prepared before she came looking for her, and Lilianna wanted to know what it was. She had a feeling she knew.

"I feel...I have yet to find my place in this world. Sorin's is here with Torenia. Alina's may be Silvania. I think yours is here, too, Lilianna, surrounded by women who will keep you safe. Surrounded by witches who will be better sisters to you than I can be. But, Lili...my place is not here. Do you understand?"

Lilianna did and she didn't. She understood that the grandiose castle, with so much death permeating its walls, could never be a place where Tatiana Floarea could live. Not when she had seen so many horrors. Lili heard her sister's whimpers at night as she slept, knowing she could feel the evil that occurred on these grounds. The ghosts of the dead haunted her dreams. That's why she could not go back to Silvania, where the ghost of their father would haunt her, too. Where would Tatiana go?

"Having met the other witches, I understand there is a whole world out there, and I would like to see more of it. At the end of the month, I will be leaving. I do not know where, and I do not know if I will return. What I do know is that I'll miss you deeply, and I'll never forget you." She placed her hand on Lilianna's cheek, now wet with streaks of tears. "I think, deep down, I'll know if you need me. I will always find you if you do."

"There is one other thing," Tatiana continued. "I know what you want from Torenia."

Lilianna couldn't bring herself to meet her sister's gaze.

"I want you to know—though I wish you wouldn't—you do have my blessing."

Her head snapped up, and she looked lovingly at her sister. Her sister, who always tried to protect her from their father, who wielded an ax to end it, who traveled all this way to stay by her side. Her sister, whom she no longer needed, not now that she had Torenia. A swell of love filled her chest, hurting her heart, and she embraced Tatiana in a sloppy hug. Cheek against shoulder, arms trapped against sides. Eventually, they sorted it out, and the hug deepened.

"How did you know?" Lilianna asked Tatiana after their hug ended.

"I've seen how you look at Torenia, and I know you admire her. And if you're anything like you were when we were children, you used to always copy me. The way I did my hair, the outfits I selected...you even had crushes on the same boys as me, Lili. I see how you're doing the same thing with Torenia. Next time I see you, you'll be wearing sleek gowns that will blow men away and have your lips painted red; I'm sure of it."

"Where will you go?"

Tatiana shrugged. "Wherever the winds take me."

16

TORENIA

Torenia knew what she needed to do. Alina was gone, her distrust taken somewhere far, far away. She was certain that when the young witch returned home and saw it thriving, she would certainly forgive her. The distance between them would begin to mend that wound—the way Alina saw Red in Torenia would lessen. Being so close to where the massacre happened, this shift would take time, but she was confident that this would work in her favor.

Next on her list was Tatiana—the girl did not belong in the Blood Queen's castle, but her role was not to walk away. To cast her out without purpose would lead her down a dangerous path, one Torenia walked long ago. No, she needed purpose and a connection to her little sister. While Torenia still loathed Aster, she felt something tingle in her cold, black heart when she saw the loving sisters. It was something she had never experienced, and she did not want it to be destroyed when Tatiana left.

The Blood Queen knew where to put her, but she had to confirm the plan with her advisor first. Rising from her steaming bath, Torenia studied herself in the mirror—how many years had she been alive? Over a century, she knew, but the exact number was lost to her now. There was not a single wrinkle in her pale skin, the veins underneath her flesh ever so slightly noticeable. Her hair still shone with health and vitality. But how long could she go about bathing in blood? One might think Torenia bathed less often in the blood of virgins because of guilt, but that was not it. She aged slightly before and during the Dark Years, when her position was threatened. In light of that, Torenia allowed herself to age a little more, feeling she looked more mature with her features filled out. The earth gave her the powers that frightened man—the abilities that allowed her to look this young, to live this long.

Donning leather trousers and a red blouse that cinched tight around her figure, Torenia approached the council. The table was the same as it was the first time she had sat there nearly a hundred years ago, and she had seen multiple plays for political power since then. She ran her finger along one of the rings, wondering how old that tree was when it was cut for this purpose.

Zaina entered, bowing her head. "Good evening, *Koroleva*. I hope you are well."

"Yes, thank you. Things have been looking up," she admitted. She trusted very few people, especially after the Dark Years, but Zaina was one of them. "I've made moves in the south, beyond our borders. I am confident they will remain discreet and play a vital role in winning this war with the Old Bloods."

"May I ask why you called me here?" Zaina asked, reaching for a chair.

"Don't bother sitting—this won't take long," Torenia told her. Just then, Alexei entered as well, leaning against the wall silently. His massive frame and dark eyes would be intimidating had Torenia not known him for years. "I have sent Alina to assist with the wolves, but I need someone inside the Old Blood house."

"Now that is a bold move, *Koroleva*," Zaina said.

"In war, bold moves win."

"Or get people killed," Alexei chimed.

"People get killed in war regardless. People get killed when there is no war. Death is inevitable."

"Not for you," her advisor spoke daringly.

Torenia raised a sharp black eyebrow. "My time will come. I'm not naïve."

Both Zaina and Alexi tensed. Looking Torenia in the eye, Alexei asked, "Who will you send? Not one of your little experiments, I hope?"

"The coven is no experiment, Alexei," Torenia snapped. One strand of hair fell over her eyes, and she hastily brushed it back. Turning, she looked out the window to compose herself. Frost filled the pane, the cold seeping into the room only to be snuffed out by the warmth of the fire. "They are all powerful. They all have purpose."

She turned and narrowed her eyes at Alexei. "Tatiana Floarea is mature far beyond her seventeen years. I know that she will be the right person for the role. Timid, yet brave. Soft, yet hardened. She needs a purpose beyond protecting her sister, a task she has had to do for too long. However, her maternal instincts do not go unnoticed, either. The girl is perfectly suited to be the young duchess's governess.

"With a familiar, the girl can send us information only a governess can get. She will be a wallflower, not seen as important enough to hide information from." Torenia thought of Anja, then tucked away the pain of her loss. "Words are carelessly tossed when someone deemed of unimportance is lingering. They go unnoticed. She will be perfect, trust me."

"But the Old Bloods have Maksim. He is a warlock, a sorcerer. Do you think he will be blind to a familiar? He surely has his own." Zaina presented this new worry.

Torenia already thought of this. "His is a bat. But Tatiana's will not be something noticeable. No cat, no raven, no rodent... It will be something discreet. At first, I thought a spider would do the trick, but no, I need something that can fly. The thought of a bat crossed my mind, but Maksim would definitely notice. But he would never suspect a moth."

Her advisor considered this, then nodded half-heartedly. "Insect familiars are very difficult. They do not—"

"Accept the Craft well, I am aware. But Tatiana's care for things may work superbly for this. Besides, there is no shortage of moths in the world to try again and again."

Zaina's face crinkled. "I know it is just a moth, nothing more than a mere insect... Yet the thought of using so many is disturbing."

Torenia shrugged. "I've done worse."

"Yes," Zaina agreed.

A tiny knock interrupted them. Glancing at Zaina, Torenia turned toward the door and opened it to find Lilianna. Lilianna's eyes landed on Alexei, and she stiffened. She was, for the first time, quiet and shy. Torenia knew Alexei's brooding presence was to blame.

"Come in, love," Torenia said. The crackling fire made the shadows weave and warp along the walls. "Don't mind him. Everything you say to me can be said with him here. I trust him with my life, and so can you."

Lilianna walked in tentatively, looking around at the large room. Torenia did not blame her for her reaction. Though she was impressed by the story of Tatiana taking matters into her own hands, she wished she had been there to make their father suffer a little longer. Harm done to a daughter was unforgivable—she knew that too well.

"What brings you here tonight?" Torenia asked.

Lilianna smiled sheepishly. "My sister, she wishes to leave and..."

"You wish to go with her?" Torenia asked.

"Oh!" Lilianna brightened. "No! No, M-Torenia. I want to become like you once...once she is gone."

"Like me?"

"A vampire. Tati said I could."

Just like Sorin said—wrapped around her finger. She smiled with a devilishly sweet grin.

"Oh, Lilianna, that is a request I would be happy to fulfill." Torenia flashed her teeth. "I would love nothing more. However, I have one task I need you and your sister to accomplish first. Do you think you're up to it?"

Lilianna nodded with vigor, always eager to please her. After Torenia had excused her advisor and counselor, she emerged from the room. Lilianna was right beside her, trying hard to keep up with her. She could feel Lilianna's eyes on her, trying to mimic her every move, even her gait.

They found Tatiana with her nose in a book, seated by the window in their shared bedroom. It was a mess—clothing was scattered all over the floor, and platters of days-old food were on the tables. Vera had complained that each time she tried to go in and clean up after them, there was some wicked trap waiting for her. A perfectly placed spider-web, or the spider itself hiding in the teacups. Nothing that could be blamed on Lilianna, but most certainly persuaded by her magic to frustrate Vera.

Tatiana put the book down when she noticed the intruders. A hard look flashed across her face, but she quickly smoothed it with a soft smile. Torenia wondered if Lilianna had lied about getting Tatiana's permission or if she had given it to keep the waters calm between them before she left. If she planned on going, which suited Torenia just fine, then Lilianna would be free to do what she pleased.

"It has come to my attention, Tatiana, that you are unhappy here," Torenia said. She closed the door behind her to seal any words spoken within the four walls.

"Not unhappy," Tatiana said, then pursed her lips. "Unfulfilled, perhaps, is the more accurate word."

Torenia crossed the room, carefully navigating the clutter on the floor. She sat down on the chaise at the end of the bed and crossed her legs. "What if I could guide you somewhere that you may find fulfillment and still assist with my cause?"

Tatiana looked between Torenia and Lilianna. A hard look knitted itself onto Tatiana's normally placid face. "I won't hurt anyone."

"Of course not," Torenia said. Though she knew what Tatiana was capable of doing in order to protect herself and her sister, she suspected she would never proactively harm another being. "I simply need you to be my eyes and ears."

"How?"

"Are you versed with familiars and their conception?"

"Somewhat," Tatiana admitted. "Every living creature has a consciousness that comes from the earth, just like our power. Through it, they have their instinct—their ability to survive what humans no longer can. When man separated from animals, they lost their instinct, their connection to the earth. This is why so few of us have the ability to perform the Craft. Very few of us still feel that connection. Any animal can become a familiar, but not every man can create one."

"Only a witch," Torenia added, "who has not lost their instinct."

"I want a bunny," Lilianna exclaimed. Her love for all things precious clashed with her hardened shell that made her immune to death and bloodshed.

"I have something better," Torenia said. "You'll find it in the library, along with an important book. If you create your familiars together, they too will be bonded, as you are. Tatiana, I know that you are to be leaving us soon, but I will not allow you to go without a strong bond with your sister. I don't want you to separate until then."

Lilianna grabbed Tatiana's hand and pulled her along, clearly eager to get to work. Tatiana looked like she was about to protest, but quickly forced herself to follow. They raced out of the room. Torenia smiled, rising to her feet and dusting herself off. She slowly followed the trail of laughter.

By the time Torenia made her way to the library, a slew of candles lit the room. The shadows they cast on the walls danced, and Torenia felt the flames beckoning her as they did witches throughout history. To dance so close to the flames that burned so many of them, to be on the cusp of danger and death... The lure of fire was strong yet inexplicable.

Torenia lingered in the shelves of the library and watched—not hiding, yet not entirely in plain sight. On the table was a bell jar with two beautiful moths fluttering inside. They were the size of small birds, and their wings were a blend of black, white, and gray. Perfectly symmetrical on one side to the other and indistinguishable from each other. Their fat, sectional bodies were layered in soft fuzz. Lilianna lifted the bell jar, and the insects flew about freely. They swirled around each other, trying to decide which light to go to, but were disoriented by the many flames. One fluttered over to Torenia, who lifted her hand and urged it back with a gentle blow of air.

The two sisters had not yet noticed Torenia.

Tatiana picked up the book. "Look here, Lili, the chant."

"It looks like Torenia wrote in it." Lili pointed and read out loud, *"A stronger connection builds for a stronger familiar."*

"There is no stronger connection than that of sisters," Tatiana said with a soft smile. Torenia felt her heart lurch. "I wonder why she chose moths."

"I wanted a bunny." Lili sighed.

"No one will notice a moth," Tatiana said. "It's brilliant. Come on, Lili, read this here. We have to do this right."

Together, the sisters read through the words, learning the incantation by heart. Already the night was at its darkest, and by the time they had everything sorted out, the candles were dwindling to their last inch of wax, hardly any wick left to burn. They recaptured the moths and put them under the jar, then sat on either side. Connecting their hands for a stronger bond, they began to sway rhythmically together.

"Animam meam do vobis: Ego tibi dabo vos ad me," they chanted together, just as the book said. The words flowed off their tongues. The window rattled, the glass shook in the wooden frames, and a *presence* filled the space, as though the earth breathed into the room. A crack formed in the bell jar, snaking up to the top before the entire thing broke in half. The glass fell to each side, perfectly equal. One fell toward Tatiana, the other to Lilianna.

They finished the chant. *"Te vivere, ut ministrent mihi, et ego ad te defendat."*

Both the girls felt that breath of earth inside them—a slender hand slithering into their cores, removing a piece of them. Tatiana could feel it rising within her—a white orb coming out of her mouth—as she watched it happen to her sister. Both white orbs broke into two, and each went to a different moth, entering their fat bodies.

There was no bond stronger than that between sisters.

A tear glistened on Tatiana's cheek. She wiped it away, and as her hand streaked across her cheek, her familiar landed on her finger.

They spoke together:

"Hello, Moloch," Lilianna said.

"Hello, Faust," said Tatiana.

17

LILIANNA

Moloch fluttered around Lilianna's loose brown hair, close enough that she felt his wings occasionally brush against a stray strand. Faust was nestled on Tatiana's shoulder, sitting calmly. But Lilianna wasn't paying attention to either familiar. Her eyes filled with tears.

"This is not the end, sister," Tatiana said softly. "We will cross paths again."

Lilianna could only nod. All this time spent fawning over Torenia and winning her affection left little time for her final moments with her own sister. Though she had known weeks ago that Tatiana would be leaving, it only hit her now. With a bag over her shoulder and a horse laden with satchels of food, coin, and everything else she would need for her journey, Tatiana was truly exiting Lilianna's life.

Alina's departure had been much easier, and Lilianna wondered why she thought Tatiana's might be similar. It was not the same at all.

"What if we don't?" Lilianna's voice came out with a distinct crack. "Cross paths...I mean."

"We will," Tati reiterated. "Should you ever need me, just send Faust. I will not be too far—I will be just outside Osleka, in Krovberg."

"But Torenia says Osleka is the biggest country in the *world*," Lilianna exclaimed.

"Yes," Tati said with a nod, holding her sister's hand in hers. With her other hand, she tucked a stray strand of hair behind Lili's ear. "You must remember to brush your hair. And to wash your face at least once every few days, you understand?"

"Yes," Lili said, a gentle laugh filling the gap between her and her sister. "I'm sixteen now, Tati."

Tati sighed. "Promise me you will make good choices and that you will always be kind."

"I won't stop my tricks," Lilianna whispered, though playing pranks on Vera didn't seem like fun anymore. Perhaps to make sure Torenia would love her like a daughter, she would have to act her age. She knew Torenia already loved her, but without Tatiana around, she would have to ensure it stayed that way forever.

"I would expect nothing less," Tatiana said with a grin—the same grin she used to give her when they decided to steal a pie from a window, or encourage the spiders to make their webs across doorways. She kissed Lilianna's cheeks—one, then the other. "I love you, little sister."

"I love you, too..." Lilianna started to cry. She could feel someone watching her and knew Torenia or Rahella was there, somewhere up high, witnessing this moment. Shame spread through her, but she bit it back as she embraced her sister for the last time. She had never been without her sister before. Not once in her entire existence had she been more than a stone's throw away.

She stood shivering on the castle's steps until Tatiana was out of sight. The cold seeped in, but she didn't notice until Moloch landed on her hair. His antennae brushed against her cheek, and she turned on her heel, returning to the castle that felt emptier now.

Torenia stood atop the landing, leaning over the railing. Her long black hair cascaded over, framing her perfect features. Her blue eyes followed Lilianna as she ascended the steps.

"She will be safe, right?" Lilianna inquired. She wrung her cold hands together in the skirt of her dress.

"Yes," Torenia said with unwavering confidence. "Her task is simple, yet pivotal for my cause. Keeping her discreet and safe is vital not just for the war but for my integrity. I promise you that no harm will come to her."

Lilianna nodded. She trusted Torenia like she trusted her own mother. "Is it time, then?"

"Are you certain you wish to do this?" Torenia asked. "It will only make your life more complicated."

"I don't think so," Lilianna said, then quickly clarified. "It will make things easier, I think."

"You will not lead a normal life," Torenia warned, her hands on the banister. Her rings were large and decadent—onyx gems with silver woven around them.

"I have never led a normal life." She looked up at the Blood Queen with admiration for all she had accomplished. She was a woman who took back her own life, just like Red had done before she died. Tatiana had been the one to kill their father, and Lilianna had done nothing but cry. It was her turn to do something, to take back control.

"It will hurt," Torenia said.

"I haven't felt much of anything in a long time," Lilianna whispered.

Torenia approached her to wrap her arms around her petite frame and pulled her close. In the shelter of her arms, she felt so safe. This was a woman who defied death time and time again, never submitting to it. She had so much to offer and teach Lilianna. Both of them had come from the same town, and both had suffered at the hands of frightened men. Soon, they both would be nightwalkers, and they could live for eternity.

No matter the cost.

Lilianna couldn't live without Torenia.

"You will," Torenia said, walking along with Lilianna still tucked against her. They maneuvered with ease through the winding hallways. When they reached the bedrooms, Lilianna fell silent. Not because she was frightened of what was to come, but because she did not want to do this in the room she and Tatiana once shared. It seemed too sacred a place to tarnish with this change. She nodded toward one of the untouched rooms, and Torenia silently obeyed.

With a flicker of Torenia's hand, the candles in the room lit. The curtains were shut tight, and Moloch fluttered over to them, landing, then circling until he settled. Lilianna climbed onto the untouched bed —the softness of beds always surprised her.

"Remember, after this, you will never see sunlight again. You will never taste food. You will be forced to hunt, and in return, be hunted for what you are. This life is not glamorous, Lilianna. You will not only be a woman in the world but a witch and a nightwalker. It is an ugly world out there."

Lilianna leaned against the plush red velvet headboard. She turned her head toward Torenia. "Why did you do it?"

"I was promised the very things my heart desired." Her voice had a cold edge to it.

"Did you get them?"

"Yes," she said with a nod. "But not because I was a nightwalker. Power, yes, as the Brotherhood was not to be run by anyone but a nightwalker. Everything else I was promised came from the Craft and my ability as a witch. It came from poring over books and scripts, learning from every previous witch's experiences. So I ask, Lilianna, why are *you* doing this?"

Lilianna thought for a moment, her eyebrows knitting together. Tucking her legs underneath her, she cocked her head to the side, her mousey brown hair falling in waves. Briefly, she thought of what Tatiana had said about brushing her hair. "I want to punish those who hurt people like me. I want them all to feel the pain I felt. I want to help every other girl like me...until there are no more girls like me."

And she wanted a mother.

Once Torenia turned Lilianna, she would truly be her mother. As close to it as she could be.

"You are kind," Torenia said, once again making Lilianna think about what Tatiana had said. Silence passed between them, and Torenia nodded to give her the signal. It was time. No more questions, no more preparation. Lilianna leaned back in the bed and watched Torenia lean in. She could feel her warm breath and body heat even though they were not touching. Lilianna kept her eyes open even as Torenia's fangs sank into the soft flesh of her neck.

The pain was bearable.

Lilianna thought perhaps she suffered enough, that now nothing would hurt quite as much as the past. Her big eyes flickered to Torenia, seeking answers. Then she gasped, her air catching in her throat as it closed with agony. Her gasp became a shriek as she fell back on the bed, writhing. Her blood turned to ice and fire, both burning and chilling her. Her vision blurred, and everything disappeared.

There was no way to know how much time had passed when Lilianna felt the pain seep out of her. It emerged from her fingertips, her toes, and the top of her skull. Even her eyes hurt, and something told her that opening them would bring another shockwave of torture.

Her whimpers turned to shaky breaths.

"You may open your eyes, Lilianna," Torenia whispered, though the words sounded louder, as if Lilianna was more in tune to sound. She could hear the fluttering of Moloch's dusty wings.

A gentle blow of air told Lilianna the candles were out, and the throbbing red agony behind her eyes dwindled. Slowly, cautiously, she opened them. Adjusting to the dark quicker than ever before, Lilianna realized that she could see quite well, despite the darkness.

She opened her mouth to speak, but instantly her teeth felt wrong. Too sharp and jagged. Her tongue darted to them, feeling these new protrusions.

"Drink this," Torenia said, handing Lilianna a goblet.

She could smell the blood, but she shook her head. "No. I want...I want to hunt."

Torenia's red lips curved into a smile—a smile only a mother could give a daughter. Warmth spread over her, making her forget about every ounce of pain she endured. Now she could truly say Torenia was her mother.

She would never say the words out loud, but she knew it in her heart.

"I apologize for how much it hurt." Torenia's voice was velvet, yet it filled the room with its power.

"I have been through worse," Lilianna said. Physically she hadn't, but compared to the life she lived before all this, it was nothing. If that were the price to pay to be saved from the evil of this world, she would pay it again and again.

"Regretfully," Torenia added. "I'm going to light some candles. It may hurt your eyes at first. Your eyesight is excellent in the dark. Things in the light will be painful until you've grown used to it."

Lilianna nodded, knowing Torenia's hawk-like eyes saw her. The Blood Queen waved her hand, a gentle wisp of wind from her palm brushing Lilianna's sensitive skin, and the candles flared up one by one. Each one made Lilianna see more clearly than ever before; her eyesight was so much better in the dark now, and even more so in the light. Things she never noticed before astounded her, such as how each ripple in the curtain could be spotted, counted even—and every strand of hair stood alone, rather than one single mass. Lilianna had never realized how poor her eyesight was until she could see clearly.

"You can hear it, can't you?" Torenia asked.

Lilianna did not know what she was talking about at first, but then she heard it. The pulse of blood.

"Good. I brought you someone—you will do this the correct way."

Lilianna flashed her wicked, sharp fangs. "Who is he?"

Torenia placed her hand on Lilianna's flushed face. Then she slipped her hand into Lilianna's to help her to her feet. The girl followed the woman she secretly held as her mother in her heart as the memory of her own mother dwindled, like a candle being blown out. The scent and smoke lingered for a time before they disappeared forever.

Once they arrived at the next room, Torenia opened the door.

Lilianna wore an undeniably evil smile on her lips, one that only a man would think was seductive. This one most certainly did. He clutched his hat in his hands, wringing it nervously. His smattering of curly blond hair was messy, but he was otherwise very clean-cut. Nice clothing, shaven face—or perhaps he was too young to grow a beard.

"He wants you for one thing and one thing only," Torenia told Lilianna.

Lilianna cackled. "And I want him for one thing, and one thing only."

"Go, love," Torenia said with a smile in her voice.

Lilianna's heart swelled with joy at hearing Torenia speak to her that way, to have that tone caress her ears. However good it felt, though, it did not feel as good as the desire for that pulsing sound.

The *thump-thump-thump* of his heart coaxed her. As she walked deeper into the room, his heart rate grew faster. *Thump-thump-thump.* Lilianna's head cocked to the side, like a predator studying her prey.

She did not know if this young man intended to harm her, but her hunger grew too much to care who he was or what he might have done. She lunged with surprising speed, the muscles in her legs springing her forward. Her hands grabbed his face, pushing his head back. Up close, with her flesh on his, she could feel his stubble. She clamped her teeth onto his neck.

He writhed and fought, but Lilianna remained latched to him. Collapsing to the floor, he took her with him—she stumbled, falling over. He used the opportunity to shove her aside, and she growled. With a viciousness she did not know she had, she clawed at his cheek, drawing blood. But he did not cease his struggle.

Lilianna felt Torenia's eyes on her and knew she would not intervene. If she could not do this, she would be a liability. She would be a disappointment. With new determination, she placed her bony knee on his chest and grabbed his head with both hands, then slammed it down against the floor. Dazed, his lids lowered, and Lilianna struck again, lifting his head and slamming it back down. Then, with blood spilling from his scalp, she clamped back down on his neck and finished the job. He had more blood than she needed—he was much larger than she was—so when she threw her head back, full to the brim, blood dribbled out of her mouth. It spilled onto his pale face.

Getting up with a drunken sort of stumble, Lilianna smiled at her mother.

Torenia.

"What a mess," Torenia said, but she was smiling. A real smile. A motherly smile. "You're everything I wanted her to be."

"Who?"

"Hmm?" Torenia said, darkness clouding her features. It was as though two people were in her—the old Torenia and the Blood Queen. They battled for dominance within her.

"Wanted who to be?" Lilianna asked quietly, wiping the last of the blood away with the back of her hand. She might have felt loopy and drunk, but she did not misunderstand what Torenia said.

But Torenia had an answer, and even though Lilianna knew she was not telling the absolute truth, she chose to believe her. "Everything I wanted my right hand to be."

A strange jealousy radiated through her. She wanted to be this other "her" Torenia mentioned. She did not wish to be someone else in the Blood Queen's eyes. No, Lilianna wanted to be her daughter. Nothing more.

18

TATIANA

War took years to begin, so Tatiana was in no rush to bring herself to the Old Bloods. If what Torenia said was correct, she understood the need to remove them. She witnessed the assassin who tried to kill Torenia. However, Tatiana could not find it within herself to urge war on. Perhaps if she took long enough to infiltrate—assuming she was capable of doing it—the war would be over.

Leaving behind Lilianna left a vacant place in her heart, though. While she also wasn't rushing to fill it, she knew the sooner the war was over, the sooner she could move on from that loss. She was still connected to her sister through Torenia and their familiars, Faust and Moloch.

Given no timeline, Tatiana explored each and every place she passed through. The first leg of the journey was the hardest part. Snow still lingered, forcing her to detour. The harsh terrain and weather battered her and her steed. Nevertheless, she continued on until she found civilization, mostly small towns and villages no more significant than the one in which she was born and raised. Though they were wary of her at first, they quickly welcomed her. To keep coin in her pocket and her and her horse sheltered and fed, she tended to the sick and wounded along her journey.

As she went further west, the villages turned into a city, something

Tatiana had never seen before. She believed she had seen it all before she reached Krovberg. After she sold her horse and located a boarding house for young women, she began to wonder how big the world really was.

As she penned a letter to Lilianna, careful not to give away any details, she wondered how she was to find the Old Bloods. When Torenia told her to come to this city, this place of wondrous buildings greater than even the Blood Queen's castle, she must have forgotten that Tatiana was from Silvania—a tiny dot on the map of the vast expanse that was Earth.

Bringing her quill to the parchment, she wondered how to ask. Certainly, any mail would be intercepted and deciphered, even if she could write in code. She could use Faust, but the thought of sending him away before she even reached her final destination didn't sit well with her.

Momentarily defeated, she placed the quill back in the pot of ink and sighed. At least she could be certain her sister was happy, though the decisions she made were not the ones Tatiana would have chosen; they were Lilianna's alone to make. And she could rest easily when she thought of Alina's choice to return to Silvania.

Tatiana got up from her wooden desk and decided to embrace the warm weather. Winter had long since ended—spring was here, and the world warmed in its embrace. Not quite so far north as she was with Torenia, these other places were much more inviting. She tucked her hair into a warm hat and donned her new attire—a rich green, tight-laced dress with large shoulders, making Tatiana feel more like a bird than a woman. But she fit right in once she began purchasing some finer, more suitable clothing. She was no longer the scrappy girl fighting for her life and playing tricks on the neighbors. She was supposed to present herself as a governess to the Lebedev family when she finally found them.

The sun warmed her as she went for a walk. In the past few weeks, she had sought out the library time and time again. She felt safe there with endless knowledge at her fingertips. The smell of old books and dust brought a smile to her face, not that she believed she would find the Old Bloods through the library.

A few hours came and went, and only when Tatiana's eyes began to burn from lack of blinking did she know it was time to head back. As she stood up and returned one of the tomes she had been reading, someone approached her. The library alleys were small, hardly big enough for two people. She quickly pushed the book into its designated spot and hurried out.

"Were you reading this?" the man asked, his voice youthful. His accent was different from Torenia's—more robust and rich.

She turned to look at him. He had chocolate brown hair and full lips, a light shade of pink. "No, I simply like to take books off the shelves for hours, then put them back."

His pink lips tugged upwards on the right side. Faint creases appeared at the corners of his eyes. "A lady who jests. What will they come up with next?"

She eyed him carefully. "I pull a mean prank, as well."

His laugh warmed the whole library. "I bet you do. May I ask your name?"

"You may ask, yes..." She tried not to smile. "But I'm afraid I'm not certain you're worthy of hearing it."

His grin never left his angular face. His nose was a tad too big, but this did not make him any less comely. He reminded Tatiana of a crow or raven if one took human form. His dark attire added to this illusion. "You're quite right. My good looks and charming demeanor are certainly not enough to judge."

"They are a good start, though."

"Would I be deemed worthy if I said I was looking for the very book you've just returned?" he asked, raising a dark eyebrow.

"It depends on why you are looking for it," Tatiana threw back playfully. "There are many dark things in that book."

His expression tightened. "Something tells me that you were looking at the dark things. And I'll tell you a secret... That is exactly what I'll be looking at as well."

She cracked at last. "Then you've earned my name. It is Tatiana."

He swooned, hand to his chest with dramatic flair. "There is no finer name."

Tatiana rolled her eyes. "Flattery won't get you far."

"Cut the flattery; keep the charm. Understood, Tatiana," he said with a wink. "My name is Valentin Chernov."

Tatiana sifted through her brain—why did the name sound so familiar?

"Pleasure to meet you, Valentin," she said, more stoically than intended. Then it clicked, but it couldn't be so easy, could it?

"May I ask one more thing?"

She nodded. It seemed too good to be true—certainly there were plenty of Chernovs in the city. Before seeing the city, she thought it might be easy to find Maksim Chernov or the Lebedev family. Still, once she was deeply integrated into its vastness, the task became overwhelming. But if she was right, she may have just accidentally introduced herself to someone related to the warlock employed by the family Torenia sent her to work for.

"I..." he laughed lightly. "Forgive me, this is such a strange request... Are you seeking employment?"

Tatiana blinked at him dumbly, then cocked her head to the side. "In fact, I am."

His face brightened at this new prospect. "Have you ever worked with children?"

"I have never worked," she admitted and immediately regretted it. "But my mother died, and I took care of my sister for many years. She was—is—close to my age, but our mother's death was hard on her. It was as though she stayed a child."

"Where is your sister now?"

"With her... A new mother of sorts," Tatiana said. "Carving her own path."

"I think..." he cocked his head to the side. "I think you would be just right."

"For what?"

He smiled, somewhat apologetically. His eyes were brimming with sympathy, though Tatiana wasn't sure why. "My employers are seeking someone well-equipped to deal with their children. They have many, and they are...unwell. Very sickly—cannot go out in the daylight. My uncle, Maksim, summoned me to ensure they have constant medical attention. Born that way—a true tragedy. Tatiana, I have one final question."

"Go on," she said softly, no louder than turning a page in a book.

"What do you know about vampires?"

19

SORIN

Sorin was the only one who dined anymore. More often than not, she ate in her room or the library. Sometimes, though, she found herself talking with the few people who worked in the castle. Vera was not overly friendly, but they got along well enough to chat occasionally. It was obvious in the way Vera softened when Sorin was around that she understood they wanted the same thing. They were both there to help Torenia build a better future for witches and women.

Supping that evening, Sorin buttered the hard end of a loaf of bread. There were hot loaves cooling, but Sorin had always preferred the heel. She tossed it on a plate along with some fruit and turned toward the exit. There was much more to find in the tomes within the library, and what Torenia requested of her after the Old Bloods sent an assassin... The work would not do itself.

Vera came through the door just as Sorin was about to leave.

"Oh, good evening, Sorin, I did not see you there," Vera said, shoulders dropping as she let her guard down.

Sorin flashed a fraction of a smile. "My apologies."

"There is nothing for you to be sorry about," Vera said. "You're always welcome here."

"I must get to the library," she told Vera, hoping her tone conveyed some reluctance. She knew that pretending she wished for Vera's company would continue to soften her. Though Sorin supported Torenia, there were always things to learn from those who worked for her. It was best to stay informed of everything at all times.

"You've spent so much time in that dusty room. Surely you must've read every book in there by now."

"Only Torenia would have enough time in the world to do that," Sorin said, somewhat dreamily. She did not wish to live forever, but if she did, it would be to absorb all the knowledge in the world. "Speaking of Torenia—please tell me if I overstep when I ask."

Vera's smile became somewhat pinched. A bead of sweat appeared beneath the cap she wore to cover her graying hair. The scars on her face seemed to pulsate in the heat of the kitchen.

"What happened to—to the rest of the Sisterhood?"

Now, Vera's smile was gone. "I wasn't here for that. I came after."

"I understand." Sorin looked at her plate of food and the smudge of butter grease on her thumb. She wedged past Vera, disappointed that she didn't know more, couldn't offer more. As she navigated the slender hall, this one undecorated, she heard Vera softly call her back.

"Sorin..."

She paused, turning. The hallway was dimly lit, and the lanterns cast fluttering shadows along the narrow corridor. "Yes, Vera?"

"I came after something happened to Torenia. She will not speak of it, and you will not find it in any of those books you read. Something made her begin a reign of terror..."

"What could possibly have sparked that?" Sorin asked quietly. The light fluttering made her wonder if perhaps a moth was lingering nearby, listening. Her face warmed as she worried about what Torenia might do if she knew she was talking about this. Sorin was indispensable, but Vera would be easy to replace. She didn't want anything to happen to her.

Vera shook her head. "I'm afraid I do not know. It's best not to stick our noses in pasts that, if brought up, might recur."

Sorin swallowed this information, turning to hurry toward the library.

After a few hours, Lilianna entered the library, flaunting her new self as she often did. Barely sixteen years old, yet dressing like Torenia with tight-fitting gowns that didn't quite fit her short stature, clumpy in the leg area, and flat in the chest area. But Sorin said nothing about Lilianna's new appearance, for she looked like she was plucked off the street. Wearing the same boring garb daily, Sorin cared nothing for her appearance for the time being.

"Do you miss them?" Lilianna asked, sitting atop a stack of books and making Sorin bat at her until she moved. She flopped onto the floor, the dress stretching unnaturally around her knobby knees. That dress was made for sitting on a throne, not sitting on a dirty library floor.

"In some ways, but we are better off this way," Sorin declared. "Alina is where she wants to be."

"I miss Tati a lot," Lilianna admitted. "I don't think she would have really supported what I've decided, though. Even though she told me it was okay...I'm not so sure. So, I guess I'm glad she is gone so that I—"

"Can have Torenia all for yourself?" Sorin quipped, quickly nudging Lilianna so that she knew it was playful. Then, she said seriously, "I will not be going anywhere."

"Good," Lilianna said with a grin, showing off her fangs. "Torenia said you are helping her with something very important."

"Yes." Sorin dared not say more. She was the only one who knew of Torenia's plans, for she was the one who was doing all the research to get it right the first time. They could not test it on someone else, for fear of creating something that could not be undone. Lilianna was young, and though she adored the Blood Queen, Sorin did not trust her to keep her mouth shut. She did not believe Lilianna would ever betray Torenia, but she could let information slip to the wrong person at any given time.

Lilianna sensed Sorin's hesitation to tell her anything and to hide her disappointment, she sucked her teeth and changed the subject. "Tati has made it to the Old Blood home—the Lebedevs. She sent Faust with word. Moloch told me she's been hired, and not only do the children fawn over her, so does their sorcerer."

"Sorcerer?" Sorin asked, then recalled Torenia wanting this level of protection she was asking of her because of a man named Maksim. "Maksim Chernov? The warlock?"

"Mhm—apparently some wise man-witch who was plucked off the street to try and save the beastly children. Like all the Old Bloods, they are sickly. I wonder if Tati can help them…" Lilianna laughed. "But no, she wouldn't. That would be silly, wouldn't it? To help them get better when the plan is to kill them all?"

Chills skittered up Sorin's spine. This was not the same Lilianna from Silvania. Though she understood, to some extent, that the Old Bloods were an incestual breed of vampire and needed to be snuffed out, the thought of murdering children did not sit well with her. She would not play a direct hand in it; she could turn a blind eye to it. If it meant Torenia would be victorious and the worlds would balance out, Sorin would go along with it.

She knew that Tatiana would never lay her hand on a child.

Not when she had been that child.

"I need to focus on my work. Begone, Lilianna," Sorin said with a wave of her hand. She needed to be alone. Focusing on the Craft kept her sane. The politics of vampires and werewolves—none of it mattered to her. All Sorin wanted was to be protected, and the top of the food chain was the safest place. If helping Torenia through her political warfare meant that she and all other witches would be safe for another century, so be it. Casualties were unavoidable in war.

Lilianna sighed. "You cannot give me a hint about what you're helping Torenia with?"

"No," Sorin hissed. "Now go."

20

ALINA

In the weeks of traveling from Osleka to Silvania, Alina gained a sort of family with Helga and Gyda. Though it was a far cry from her parents and the coven she once had, it was better than what remained for her in the Sisterhood. False promises were all that the place offered. They camped when there were stretches without inns, and they splurged on hot meals when there were taverns to do so.

However, it was her connection to Helga that grew the strongest. Every day as they rode to Silvania, Helga taught her how to use her hands to communicate. Benefits were abundant to this; as they journeyed, she learned that the wolves often lost their ability to speak after they transitioned over the full moon. Many who had been lycans for years entirely lost their speech. She would use this skill while living in Silvania, should she remain there.

Fear filled her every night, the closer they got, and she woke dripping with sweat despite the cold. Gyda would stir, but it was Helga who patted her hand, tucked her back in, and made her feel like it would be okay.

The atmosphere of the town was different now. Once, a dark cloud loomed over this place, but now, though something dangerous was still permeating the thick woods, there was an air of something else.

Unity.

The town's border was just as clear as before, though not for the same reasons. The border was once there to keep the Wolf out. Now, it has been revealed that wolves would enter those borders. A man and a woman stood at the perimeter, on either side of the path. Both of them had the same wolfish features that Alina had seen on Daciana—hair that was braided and messy, as though they had been running through the trees for days on end.

The woman's lip curled into what could only be described as a snarl, her teeth bared. The man, whose mane-like hair could not be separated from his facial hair, put his hand out in front of the woman. Just that simple touch, and she backed down, but not before snapping her head to the side in a vicious glare. They seemed to speak without words, their eyes and twitching features saying everything and more, yet no one on the outside of the pack could possibly understand it.

Helga was the first to communicate. Alina watched her hands, concentrating hard. *Daciana has been sent word of our arrival. She and Torenia have been corresponding.*

"That...one...?" The man croaked out the words, gesturing with a wicked fast jut of his chin toward Alina.

"She's lived on these lands longer than you. She is returning to be with her family," Gyda said, then swung her leg over the horse and dropped to the ground. The warmer weather down south meant the paths were riddled with mud and gunk, and even the horses struggled to get through. Her boots squelched loudly when she landed.

Helga signed, *Where is Daciana?*

Rest, the man signed back.

"Ah, yes, the full moon was naught but a day ago. We will pass through and settle in. Alina will return to her parents, and Helga and I will rest at the inn. Tomorrow, we will meet with Daciana."

"No...trouble," the female growled.

"None," Gyda swore.

The patrols let them through.

Gyda hopped back up on her horse, and they crossed the border.

Alina recalled every tree, their roots reaching deep into the earth, giving her power. Here, she gained every ounce of what made her who she was. All she was now was a witch. She could no longer call herself a daughter, lover, or friend—not even part of a coven. All she was came from this place, despite its horrors. She owed everything to this town, which had always been haunted by a Wolf and was now infested by many.

"How does it feel to be back?" Gyda asked.

"Different, but the same. Yet not quite right either," Alina replied softly. She wondered—would she simply waltz home and be greeted with warm hugs and love? Or would she be cast out for what she brought upon the town? It was her fault that Red was dead—she led her down the path of witchcraft, which sparked her desire to use the Wolf—Blaez—to help carry out the slaughter of her own family. Ultimately, she knew, opening those doors to Red brought Torenia back. Torenia let a pack of werewolves take over like a plague.

"Where do your parents live?"

They reached the first house, noticing a faint glow across a field where horses were scattered about. A young spring foal was learning to run on its lanky legs, and Alina was reminded of life. There was nothing but death at the Blood Queen's castle—a hierarchy built on bones and blood. Here, the town thrived with the birth of animals, and without the curse looming over the town, perhaps even children were born into happy families. Maybe now people were free to love whomever they wished.

It all depended on how the wolves ran Silvania.

"Not far, but..." Alina trailed off, the words stuck in her throat.

"You do not wish to see them yet," Gyda finished knowingly.

Alina nodded. "I'd like to see for myself how this place is before I let them know I'm alive. Perhaps they are glad I left without a trace. It may be better this way."

"No parent can live not knowing."

Alina glanced at Gyda, brushing her blonde hair back to see her hardened expression.

"I lost a child—he was unattended for no more than a few moments. Just like that, he was gone. I hope every single day some young man will show up at my door and say 'Mother, I've missed you.'"

"Tomorrow," Alina whispered. "I'll find them tomorrow. After Daciana."

Gyda smiled, but it was not real. Her lips curled up at the edges, but her eyes remained filled with sorrow—age-old sorrow, the kind you can mask but that will never truly go away. Alina had never lost a child, of course, but the thought of Red made her heart constrict. Some nights, she appeared in Alina's dreams, and Alina always woke up feeling worse. She wished she could forget about her.

The town came into sight, and with it, the shriek of a child. Alina jerked her head around to spot the harmed child, expecting some terrible wolf to appear with one between its jaws. But instead, she saw a woman with the same hair all the wolves seemed to have—forest hair, she thought of it now, chasing after a young child. Giggles erupted from the boy as the woman caught him in her arms and threw him up in the air, catching him gracefully. Her muscular arms rippled as she grabbed the boy, who seemed too old to be a toddler and had to weigh three stones.

Other children swarmed her—some Alina faintly recognized as the neighbor's children, but others were fresh faces. They all worked together to weigh her down, clinging to her arms and legs. The woman, clearly able to break free of their chubby arms, pretended to collapse under the weight. The children enveloped her, and she was lost from sight other than her feet and a single arm. Sensing the newcomers, the children one by one began to back off, and the woman on the ground sat up, legs splayed before her. She ran one hand through the blonde hair, fingers getting caught up in the tangles, and then huffed. She playfully snarled at the children, and they scurried away, all but one.

"Welcome." She spoke more clearly than the others. "Alina, Gyda, Helga... Birgitte." She tapped her chest with two fingers to introduce herself.

As she rose to her full height, Alina and Gyda hopped down. Gyda towered over all of them. Alina was acutely aware of her own tiny frame and felt a dash of envy for the other woman.

"So, you...witch who returns."

"Yes," Alina confirmed. "The Nastaca family... Are they still here?"

Birgitte stepped close, too close to Alina, who couldn't withhold her obvious flinch. The woman smelled her deeply, an inhalation that sounded oddly like realization. Moving away now, Birgitte nodded. "Here."

Alina nodded a silent thanks.

"We are going to rest at the inn, and tomorrow we will explore and meet with Daciana. We have much to discuss, much…" Her trail of thought seemed to wisp away like breath in the cold air.

"Much," Birgitte agreed.

As Alina walked into the inn—the largest building in the town—she found it full of singing, music, and laughter. The cheer was undeniable, and it was not the women who worked there faking their smiles and feigning their giggles. No, it was real laughter, real cheer that Alina had never felt before in this town.

Perhaps the curse had been lifted, and the wolves who moved in made it a safer place.

A happier place.

Retiring to a room alone, she flopped down on the small bed. It creaked and groaned, reminding her she had given up a bed that would fit five of her across when she left Osleka. But there was nothing more comfortable than being home. After so many weeks of travel, Alina felt the weight of it crush her, forcing her deeper into the bed as though someone was laying boulders on top of her.

The desire for sleep began to overwhelm her until she remembered the book Gyda gave her. She felt for her bag and rifled through it blindly until she found it. The smoothness of the thin leather cover, stained yellow from years of use, brushed against her fingertips. She pulled it out and looked at the front of it.

A Brief History of Witches,
as told by various voices

It was time to read about the Dark Years.

A BRIEF HISTORY OF WITCHES
AN EXCERPT

~

The Year of Blood

Decades ago, Torenia created the Sisterhood—a place where witches, women, vampires, and folk of all creeds could feel safe. For years, there was strength—even peace. Even I cannot deny that she created a place of equality for all. But we could not overlook the heinous crimes she committed and the atrocities she still commits. We cannot claim safety and equality when she still bathes in the blood of innocents. Those who challenge her do not live to see another day.

Torenia Luca's power grows rampant. For years, she has resided in the darkest recesses of the North, impossible to reach within a castle that has only been successfully taken once. We cannot access her, we cannot challenge her.

Instead, I have been given the task of infiltrating the castle. To earn her trust. It will take years, and I must remain brave and strong—succumbing to her charm would be my downfall.

While the others seek out what remains of the watered-down Luca line elsewhere—outcasts, distant relatives, vagabonds—and oust them, it is my task that is the most daunting.

~

The Year of Disgrace

It is with the heaviest of hearts that I do what must be done. Forgive me, Sisters, for the crime I am to commit.

This will be what breaks Torenia, what makes her vulnerable and weak. It is now we must strike, while the world rests in a comfortable balance.

21

TATIANA

Getting inside the Lebedev home was too easy—so easy that Tatiana half-suspected they knew who she was and what she was doing there. After Valentin, Maksim Chernov's nephew, informed her all he could about the vampires and their history, Tatiana had feigned shock. She scoffed at him, acting as though there were no such thing as vampires. So, he showed her.

He informed her that he could not bring her the Lebedevs as a potential governess if she did not have an understanding of them. He'd walked her home to the boarding house and told her he would return by nightfall.

The boarding house, however, was locked up by dark.

Tatiana heard the rocks hitting the second-story window. She made her way to the thick pane of glass in no hurry—she would rush for no one. If she played it just right, she could make sure Valentin knew nothing of her time with or connection to the Blood Queen. If her upbringing in Silvania and her time spent at the Sisterhood taught her anything, it was to be aware of everything and never to show her desire for anything. It was easiest to be safe when she kept everything buttoned up.

She couldn't deny the way her heart beat a little bit faster when

Valentin was near, though. For the first time, she was free to explore more than protecting herself and her sister.

When Tatiana opened the window, she looked down at his face. The glow of the moon lit his pale features, darkening the circles around his eyes and hiding the richness of his smile.

"You're going to get me kicked out of here," she told him.

"Then you'll have to come work for my employer," he said, flashing a smile she couldn't help but return. "Come down."

"How on earth do you think I will manage that?" She balked, gesturing towards the gap between the window and the road below. There were no bushes to slow her fall, and she would not leap into a man's arms if the building were on fire—she had more dignity than that.

"You seem like a person with great problem-solving skills," he retorted.

Tatiana laughed quickly. No sense in waking the matron of the boarding house. She glanced back out the window. "Close your eyes. I won't be having you looking up my skirt."

"I wouldn't dream of it," he said as he turned away.

No one else was on the street, so Tatianna sat on the window's ledge and flipped onto her belly. The rough edges of the window frame dug into her ribs, and she gritted her teeth. She lowered herself down as far as she could with all her strength, then dropped. The ground came hard and fast, and she stumbled, reaching for something to keep her balance before falling on her backside.

"So much for not waking anyone," Valentin said, offering her his hand. The lanterns in the lower level flickered to life, and locks rattled. "Let's go—quickly."

Hand in hand, they hurried down the street until they were safely out of sight. It was then that Tatiana realized she was alone in the dark of night in an unfamiliar city, with a man. Her hands began to sweat. She pulled away from him, keeping a short distance between them as they walked down the street. With a furtive glance back, Tatiana wondered what she was walking into. Seeing Faust perched comfortably on a lantern told her it would be okay.

"Where are we going?" she asked after a few moments of quiet.

Valentin had continued to give her space after she jerked away from him and hadn't questioned her once about why.

"I've told you everything I know about vampires, but no one really believes in them until they see them. A long time ago, a few brothers started a fighting ring up north. People from all walks of life fight there. Men would fight for glory, but when they lost, they would be feasted upon by the brothers—nightwalkers."

Tatiana shuddered. It seemed every place had its ghost stories. Silvania had the Wolf: the tales parents told their children, their daughters, were always ghastly. And so incorrect, she learned. She wondered how true Valentin's story was.

"You are taking me to a fighting pit?" She stopped walking, waiting for his response.

He turned and cast a sheepish expression, running his fingers through his dark hair. "Perhaps..."

"Is there no other way?" she asked. "I have seen enough bloodshed."

Valentin cocked his head to the side. "A pretty thing like you?"

She shook her head. "Don't call me that."

"Sorry." He shrank, almost melting away. "Tatiana, if I've said some-·thing to upset you..."

"It's alright," she muttered, crossing her arms over her chest.

"There is another way I can show you," he said, his voice quiet. "I've not told anyone about this, but I—it's easier to show you, Tatiana."

He extended his hand, but she didn't take it. Instead, she fell into stride with him, trusting that he would not do her any harm. A comfortable quiet settled around them as they walked the rest of the way—hopefully toward something less grim than vampires fighting men, Tatiana hoped. He brought her down a quaint alley to a small door. Valentin withdrew a key and unlocked the door, fumbling in the dark to bring forth some light. When a warm glow painted the walls, Tatiana followed him in.

The room was smaller than her bedroom back in Silvania, and it was filled with stuff. The table held a leather case, sitting open with metal devices hanging out of it. The walls were stacked to the ceiling with books—some dusty and most without covers as they had fallen off after years of use. The room smelled of parchment, with a metallic scent lingering beneath it all.

She knew that smell.

Blood.

"It's alright," Valentin said, sensing her discomfort. "I'm training to be a doctor. I work with them—nightwalkers, I mean—so I realized the epidemic at hand. There are so many here, but many of them are incapable of doing what...what they're meant to do. So they come here, where man and vampire meet for a mutual purpose. They donate blood and get something in return."

"What do they get?" Tatiana asked, willing herself to relax.

"Some want money. Many want sex." Valentin paused. "But most just want to keep the two populations happy. The family I work for is different. They have an uncontrollable thirst for blood. They are the last of their kind, but they can take out a city in a matter of days, should they want to. They don't even drink for sustenance after their first kill each night. They go into a blood frenzy after that."

Tatiana's heart skipped several beats. "How could you work for them?"

"The people here donate blood for that cause, as well."

She wanted to tell him about Torenia's plan. It seemed to her that Valentin did not like his employers. How could he? If he were human, he was also food. The thought of being a governess to these children who might go into a blood frenzy should she get a paper cut made her hands clammy.

"Come." Valentin urged her along, into the back of the tiny room.

He lifted a trap door to reveal a room underneath. It was cold down there—she could feel the chill reaching for her. It smelled clean, to her surprise.

In the subterranean room, she was faced with six people and lanterns glowing along the wall. The four people on the right were hooked up to a tube that led to a jar collecting their blood. The two people on the left were pallid and hungry, eyeing the blood.

"One human body contains enough blood to sustain a vampire for a few days—what these people are doing is sustaining them just enough so they do not need to kill," Valentin said. He walked over to his patients and talked to them in quiet whispers. Though Tatiana couldn't hear him, she could feel the tone of his voice—soothing and comforting. When he handed a jar to each vampire, they drank greedily. The four donors were detached from their tubes and given something to eat and some money for their donation.

Back in the small room, the lower level now cleared of vampires and men, Valentin sat at the table and folded his slender fingers. "So, now that you've seen what I do..."

"I must reiterate my earlier question," Tatiana said sternly. "How can you work for them?"

He smiled wanly. "If I do not help them, they will wreak havoc upon the city."

His reason resonated. It settled inside of her like a seed. They wanted the same thing, but unlike Torenia, he wanted to reach a solution without death. Tatiana was so tired of death, so with Valentin's encouragement, she agreed to apply for the position as governess for the Lebedevs. She watched as Faust wriggled out of the cracked window at the door and wondered how long it would be before she saw her familiar again.

22

ALINA

The words in the book still haunted her.

It held over four hundred years of words within its pages, though the timelines were spotty, and big gaps in time festered like an open wound. Alina needed those missing pages—she needed to know everything about the Luca family and the havoc they wreaked over the continent. Her thoughts of Red were tarnished, and she forced the thoughts of the young woman whose death shattered her heart from her mind. There was no need to dwell over the dead.

A knock sounded at her door, and Alina looked up through blood-shot eyes, dark circles underneath them certain never to go away. She sat cross-legged on the bed. "Come in," she croaked, her voice tired from being up all night.

It was Gyda. She tossed an apple towards Alina, who surprised herself by catching it.

"Don't tell me you stayed up all night reading," Gyda said, nodding toward the book on the bed.

She nodded sheepishly. "It was enlightening."

"Go on," Gyda encouraged, sitting beside her. Her voice was cautious. Giving Alina the book opened a new dialogue between them. She trusted that once Alina read it, she would understand the plan. But if she disagreed, what would happen then?

"You're the newest voice, aren't you?"

Gyda nodded. "Yes, the book was passed on to me from a distant relative—my family has been working against Torenia for years. From what I believe, Torenia has no idea."

"If she does suspect, she would never show it."

"Her predecessor, Roman, was always three steps ahead. If she suspects, we will have no chance at stopping her. This is why we need Daciana."

Only a few months ago, Alina thought the only wars were between vampires—Pure and Half and Old—all the politics and bloodlines meaning nothing to her. Now, she understood that it was more than that. The witches of the world would not be spared from this war, which is why Torenia had so many across the globe.

"Which ones can we trust?" Alina asked, meaning the witches.

Gyda inhaled deeply. "The few I am sure of are still working on finding others. Right now, my focus is the wolves."

"How are you going to convince them? Look at this place." Alina gestured around them. "There is joy here—people are happy! I never would have thought such a thing possible, Gyda. Daciana has succeeded in bringing that here. Why would she step into a war and risk losing what she has?"

Gyda smiled. "Daciana has this town because of the Blood Queen. You never want to owe a debt to someone like Torenia, for if you do not pay it, well... They'd lose more than happiness. Torenia sent you to ask her to pay that debt and side with her in the war."

"What do you mean Daciana has the town because of her?" Alina asked.

"She killed the Wolf, clearing the way for Daciana's pack to take over the land that was their territory eons ago."

Alina's lip raised into a snarl. "Is that what she told you?" Gyda scarcely had a chance to nod before Alina laughed darkly. "It was I who did it. It was I who lost *everything* to do it."

"What are you saying?"

"Torenia spun you a web of lies, Gyda. We...we tried to use Red to put an end to his curse. She died during the process, but..." Alina looked up with tears in her eyes. "I had been accidentally blood-bonded with her, so I was able to finish it."

Gyda's face was rock hard. "Are you saying you have Luca blood running through your veins?"

Alina nodded. She began to tug at the end of her sleeve, a loose thread between her fingertips.

Gyda sensed her nervousness and placed her hand on Alina's shoulder. "This changes everything. Alina...you will be the one who sees the outcome of this war. I would like you to be the next voice in the book."

"You mean—" Alina nodded towards the book she had spent the whole night reading. It contained hundreds of years of history following the Lucas and the Wolf, written by generations of witches who wished to end the Luca bloodline and used the Wolf to slaughter anyone who opposed them.

Now, there was only one left. One Luca.

How hard could it be to kill the Blood Queen? No one had succeeded in 125 years. Alina felt the request, though not spoken outright, weighing down on her already. She wanted it. She wanted to be the one who ended the Blood Queen. She continued the hatred within the Luca line when she slaughtered her sister and her children. It was her fault Red died.

It was easier to blame Torenia than herself. Deep down, she knew she had invited Red to the coven and given her a first glimpse of power. Had she not been under the protection spell, she would have been sacrificed to the Wolf. The kind man beneath the fur would have sent Red away with enough to survive, enough to get by. Maybe she would have avoided death, or perhaps she would have found her way to her great aunt and fallen prey to an evil fate.

"Let us not dwell on it now—you can give me an answer at a later time. We must meet with Daciana." Gyda extended her hand as she unfolded her tired legs. Her knees protested. "Let me ask the questions. But if she asks you something directly, answer honestly."

Alina nodded and took her hand. They walked to the lower level of the tavern, where various tables and chairs were scattered throughout. A fire burned low but hot in the massive hearth in the room. It was much quieter than when they arrived the night before, the clients and women now sleeping off their late nights of drink and sex in the rooms above.

Daciana sat at one of the tables, a steaming cup of tea in her hands. Her trouser-clad legs were spread, making Alina blush. Helga was also there, and for the first time, Alina noticed a snake with her. It was a familiar kept hidden for the entire trip from Osleka to here. Alina felt a swell of trust—a witch only revealed the existence of her familiar as a show of power or when she truly trusted someone.

Gyda pulled out a chair and flopped down, immediately placing her elbows on the table and tenting her fingers. Alina sat modestly with her hands in her lap, nodding gently towards Helga.

"Remember...you," Daciana said to Alina. "Scent."

"Yes. I left some time ago, but this place has always been my home, so I returned," Alina replied. She was shocked. Daciana recalled her scent even though they had never been face-to-face before. "I can understand if you sign, if that is better for your...voice."

Daciana nodded, then turned to Gyda. She signed: *She suspects?*

"No, not as far as I or any of my confidants believe," Gyda confirmed. "But we cannot afford to slip up."

"Trust...her?" Daciana spoke this time, flicking a scarred hand toward Alina.

"Absolutely," Gyda said. "Torenia sent her in her stead to parlay with the wolves. She wants her favor returned."

Daciana cracked her neck, lips twitching. Composing herself quickly, she let out a low growl. Alina was starting to learn that this was just how werewolves acted, as though the wolf inside them fought their humanity. She understood how that felt.

"Torenia does not trust me," Alina said. "She sent me away because she doesn't trust me, and I do not trust her. She sent me back home to keep me away from her and her plans—I am certain of this. However, she still saw me as useful here, hoping I could convince you to fight for her. Perhaps as a reminder that...that you owe her a favor, but I am here to correct that."

Daciana cocked her head to the side.

She explained to them what she had told Gyda. "Torenia had nothing to do with Blaez's death. She took that from me, from...Red."

Torenia does not know that the wolves have this knowledge, Helga signed. *We must keep it this way.*

"You're right. She may suspect it would come up in time, with

Alina knowing the truth. We must keep an eye out for that possibility," Gyda said, steepling her fingers. "We will join her for this fight—we all want the Old Bloods gone. Then, when she believes she has won, we must act. We all agree that Torenia Luca must be stopped?"

Helga signed, *Yes.*

Daciana nodded in agreement. She looked at Alina again and signed: *You are a witch?*

Alina nodded.

"Moon Ma...gic," Daciana croaked. "Eclipse."

Gyda perked up, nodding in agreement. Reaching over, she offered her hand to Daciana. The wolfish woman grasped Gyda's wrist, and they shook once and parted. Gyda rose, and Alina quickly followed. They stepped outside the tavern and embraced the fresh air.

"What happened in there?" Alina asked.

"We're going to have to perform some very, very strong magic. And you're going to be a key ingredient," Gyda said. "Blood Magic and Moon Magic will have to come together. Only then can we ensure the death of the Blood Queen."

Raising her pale hand to the door, Alina realized how strange it was to be back here. Standing on the doorstep of her childhood home, knocking rather than waltzing in as she used to. Her knuckles rapped against the wood twice, and she stepped back to wait. A strange nervousness twisted inside her—would her parents want her back? Would they be happy to see that she returned?

She wrung her hands together. Footsteps came from the small two-bedroom home, and her father opened the door. His wispy blond hair was nearly gone, but his eyes lit up at the sight of his daughter. He swept her into a back-breaking hug, his warmth enveloping her frame until she was half-gasping for air. She didn't realize until he released her that she was shaking with tears.

"Papa," she said through her sobs.

"My child," he whispered weakly, pushing her hair out of her face. His hands cupped her cheeks. She smiled up at him, and he hugged her again, gently. "You've come home."

"I am so sorry I left," Alina croaked.

"I'm sorry too," he replied.

"It wasn't your fault," she informed him. "My hand was forced, my options limited. I had to flee for a time, and it's my fault. It was all my fault."

"If by fault you mean the death of the Luca girl and freeing of the town, then yes, you are to blame. Things got much better after that day, as though darkness had lifted. The only gray was that you were gone."

"Where is Mama?" Alina asked to change the thoughts in her head.

Her father sighed. "She fell ill not long after you left. I'm sorry, Alina. She did not survive the winter."

There was so much death left in her wake. So much blood on her hands. Her father appeared to sense this and quickly swept her into the living room, where he had a pot of water for tea over the fire. He did his best to cheer her, to remind her that this place would always be her home. She would have to protect it if it were to be her home.

There would be a time when Torenia came to collect her dues.

After a long silence between them, Alina asked, "The lycans who took over—they treat the townsfolk well?"

He nodded. "Yes, they do, even in their beastly forms. Some leave for the three days of the full moon, as they are young and have less control. The rest are fine." He chuckled momentarily. "I never thought I would be saying good things about creatures I did not know existed a year ago... But I have learned never to judge a person for what they are, but what they do."

Alina stared at the swirling leaves in her tea, letting her father's words resonate inside her. "Papa, I...I was so afraid before. I still am. But I understand now what I must do to overcome these fears. I cannot lie about who I am anymore. I loved Red, Papa."

Their gazes met, and he nodded softly, understanding. An unspoken agreement between them—he would love her for what she did, who she was.

"I could not protect her, nor the others. I know now what I can do to protect the people I love. And so...I must do it, right?"

He understood what she was asking. "I trust you will always do what you believe is right."

23

TORENIA

The Blood Queen looked at the chessboard. Her slender fingers with their sharp, pointed nails hovered over a pawn, contemplating. All her pawns were in their places. Alina, Gyda, and Helga with the wolves. Tatiana in Krovberg with the Lebedevs, quietly submerging herself into their world, learning their secrets. Lilianna was kept close to ensure Tatiana stayed where she was supposed to be. Sorin, with her knowledge of the Craft here, kept close, where she would be of most use for Torenia. But Sorin was not really a pawn—she was far more important than that.

In chess, the goal was to protect the King at all costs. But the most important player on the board was the Queen. Without her, the chances of winning were practically nonexistent.

Torenia sneered at the board, flicking the King over. It toppled with a heavy thud off the board. She rose, grabbing her goblet to take a sip of the warm blood.

Lucien, Sorin's familiar, scurried into the room and sat upright. He gazed at Torenia with his beady black eyes, his whiskers twitching. Sorin entered moments later.

"I am ready," Sorin announced. "Are you?"

Torenia cast a rueful smile. "I have been ready for this for a very long time. After all I've endured...I have no use for it any longer."

"So be it," Sorin said with a dip of her head. They exited the study and walked through the quiet halls. Lilianna had taken to hunting and was not here. Though she had her uses, Torenia did not need the young girl to know about this. She would not be intentionally disloyal, but Torenia suspected she might have loose lips.

Near midnight, they reached the cellar below the castle, where Torenia spent time during her integration with the Brotherhood. A smudge of black blood made the place smell faintly toxic. A wooden gurney outfitted with leather straps stood in the center of the large room. She never thought she would be on the table where she claimed so many Siren lives, but she tried not to dwell on it.

Beside that table was a smaller one covered in medical tools, silver, and clean. Next to that was a box of her own design—black with no filigree or adornments. There was no need for this particular box to be glamorous. A brass keyhole was the only color, and it matched the key that sat in front of it.

"I have not done anything like this before," Sorin told Torenia again. Torenia did not doubt her skill to accomplish this task. Sorin was the only person she trusted with it.

"No one has," Torenia said. "Only in legends of pirates in other worlds. Worlds, Sorin, of which you are familiar."

Sorin nodded. "Stories, legends, myths."

"All of which have truth to them. The legend of the Wolf revealed itself to be true."

"You may die."

Torenia laughed. "I plan on living for a very long time. With the war looming, involving the wolves and using Alina as my voice there, I cannot trust that she will not betray me. I suspect she may have already. The only person I trust not to betray me is you, Sorin, because you see the world as I do, with all its ugly imperfections, its flaws. You and I see a world that needs changing. I cannot do that if I am deceased."

Sorin looked bashful, as though the words of trust and praise surprised her. After years of power, Torenia knew what people wanted to hear. Roman had taught her that, as had Ivan. To this day, she wondered how much of Ivan's words had been genuine and how many lies Roman had told him to say.

"Let's begin," Sorin said. She gestured to the table, and Torenia gracefully lifted herself onto it. With her legs dangling, she began to unlace her top. Once she had removed it, Sorin took it from her and hung it on a hook. She glanced at Torenia and studied her for the briefest of seconds, eyes lingering on the scar below Torenia's navel.

Neither of them acknowledged it beyond that.

Leaning back so that her head rested on the leather headrest, Torenia pulled out a small tonic from her pocket. It was murky white with flecks of gray and pink. She quickly downed the liquid and grimaced at the taste. She wiped her mouth. "A little something to take the edge off."

Sorin asked, "You won't be able to feel?"

"It will be dulled, but I've added something to stay conscious and avoid the fogginess that usually accompanies opium. I would very much like to witness this moment in history."

"What can possibly allow you to stay awake for this procedure?" Sorin inquired.

"A touch of gray matter and a drop of adrenal fluid," she said.

Sorin processed this silently, then reached for the scalpel. With one more cautious glance at Torenia, Sorin began to work. The sharp blade dug into Torenia's flesh, and she felt a tugging sensation. She kept her head leaned back to keep her torso straight while Sorin worked. The scent of blood filled her nostrils—it had been a long time since she smelled her own blood.

Sorin replaced the scalpel on the tray as plasma spilled down Torenia's slender sides to stain the table. The rib spreader was next—only now did Torenia see the gentle shake in Sorin's hands.

Torenia spoke, her words garbled as though there was blood in her mouth. "You're doing great."

Sorin continued without pausing again. The device was so cold that Torenia could feel it, even with her dulled senses. Sorin began to turn the hand crank. The gears turned around and around, and her chest ballooned outward before her eyes.

Sorin glanced into the cavity, squinting. It was as if she was searching for something—perhaps she did not know the setup of the human body. Forgivable, as she had likely never desecrated a corpse.

However, Torenia had ensured she did all the necessary readings on the human body.

Something was wrong.

"What is it?" Torenia asked, her voice garbled. She was dizzy.

In answer, Sorin plunged her hand into Torenia's chest. The Blood Queen gasped. Sorin continued to work, using clamps to pinch off blood vessels within her chest. Then she pulled out Torenia Luca's heart.

She studied it for a few seconds, silence building up like pressure, ready to burst.

Inside Sorin Nabita's hand was a blackened thing that had once been a heart.

Torenia locked eyes with Sorin. "Oops."

"It's…"

"Expected, I suppose," Torenia mumbled as her head began to swim. It flopped lazily to the side, and she heard Sorin moving fast. Vessels, muscle, and sinew were tugged and stitched, pieced back together with one important piece missing—or rather, replaced with a fresh, new heart. With enough power from the Craft, Torenia could live forever without her own heart, and if her physical body were to die, part of her would carry on so long as that heart remained. Rahella would live on until she found a body suited for it.

"Torenia," Sorin said softly. Her eyes fluttered open—she did not know how much time had passed. "You must drink this."

Torenia opened her mouth and allowed the flask to be brought to her lips. The blood filled her, but she could scarcely taste it. It would sustain her until she could bathe again in the blood of youth. With a few enchantments, her body would recover from this.

Then, she would be unstoppable.

24

TATIANA

Sunny skies were once something Tatiana loved, but the children were sick on days like this. Forced to handle them, to help them with everyday things, and clean up after them, she quickly felt exhausted all the time. On days when the sun would shine, the children would not sleep. Instead, they moaned and cried about their aches and pains. After only a few weeks she grew tired of it; after a few months, she was ready to pull her hair out. At that particular dawn, the children looked as though they were about to devour her, so she stepped out to let them have their tantrum without becoming a casualty to it.

Valentin joined her in the immaculate hallway outside the children's bedrooms a few minutes later. His raven black hair looked silky smooth, even when it was in disarray. His dark eyes were always curious, like he knew a secret no one else did. It reminded Tatiana of all the times she and Lilianna played tricks on the other families back in Silvania. Of all the people in the castle, she only took a liking to him.

"Winter cannot come soon enough," he said to her.

She agreed, pushing her stray hairs back underneath her cap. "I miss the days when sunshine meant things would be a little bit easier. I suppose, in this world I live in now, daylight and sunshine will always be the enemy."

"I do not think your final destination is here, Tatiana." His voice was gravelly, with a sharp edge. A unique trait Tatiana had never noticed in anyone else.

"Where, then, do you think I will end up?"

"Somewhere that the sun never sets."

"You mustn't mock me." She shied away, tightening her hands together where they were latched on her skirts.

"Mock you? Tatiana, no." He let out a gentle, breathy chuckle that made her stomach lurch. "I mean it. The night might suit some, but not you. I can see it wearing you down."

"I think the children might have something to do with that," she replied in a whisper. She dared not speak ill of the children, lest anyone be listening in. She learned early on that those who said anything about the children that was not praise of their kindness and beauty, of which they had little, would earn a lashing from their mother, Katrin. Tatiana learned quickly to respond with only kind words when asked how they were each day.

But Valentin chuckled. "Such an undertaking. It's no surprise they summoned me for help."

"Is there much that can be done for them?" Tatiana asked. She asked the question, a deep sense reminding her that this information was for Torenia. She wondered what would happen if she didn't tell Torenia. When she sent Faust to communicate with Moloch, she told them that all was well, the children were healthy, and Lebedev had his pawns aligned. What if she lied to Torenia? A sudden realization hit her, one that made the idea of lying to the Blood Queen wither to ash.

She had Lilianna. One wrong move, and Torenia could remove Lilianna from the world.

Valentin sighed, leaning back against the wall. His knee bumped against Tatiana's skirt, but he did not move away. She did not either, and a warm feeling filled her, making her forget about her sister. "Let's take a walk, shall we? The children have had their blood and opium—they will sleep through the day now."

Walking around in the daytime was safe with a castle filled with vampires. The moment they stepped into the sunlight, they were protected. Tatiana felt life flood back into her, as if living inside that castle meant she became a vampire, too. Her skin lit up, rosy and warm. Arm in arm with Valentin, she felt at ease. Above them, the blue skies were dressed in streaks of white clouds like a painting.

"We are not supposed to discuss that their blood diseases are caused by their lineage. The family considers it blasphemous. However, that is the truth. I must admit, and I only admit it to you, Tatiana—I do not believe they should continue breeding. The lineage must branch out, but they will not speak of it. They're the last Old Blood family left, meaning the children..."

"Don't speak it," Tatiana said, shivers running down her spine. It reminded her too much of her father. "I...I do not wish for that to happen to them."

"The thing about the Old Bloods, what's left of them, is that it is what they want."

"They're raised to believe it is what they want. That does not mean it is what they feel in their hearts," Tatiana snapped.

"I agree with you, Tati." Valentin was the only person other than Lilianna that she allowed to use the nickname. He stopped walking and turned to face her.

She felt as if bugs crawled on her skin after Valentin's discussion of how more Old Bloods would be made. He was right that they needed to die out. And yet, here they both were, working day and night to ensure their survival. "What if none of them make it?"

"Then nature will have spoken. However, I have sworn to do my best to ease their pain, keep them alive, and ensure they make it to adulthood," Valentin reminded Tatiana. "And you have sworn to watch over them as a mother. So, don't be getting any thoughts."

"Of course not," Tatiana said. "They are children, and I would never lay a hand on a child or let them come to harm. Regardless of what lineage they come from, they are innocent."

"I am pleased to hear you say that," Valentin said, and they walked in silence, soaking in the sunshine before they would be forced to sleep.

Up all night, but wanting to experience the daylight, was a battle within Tatiana that never seemed to cease. Like the war around her, she was unsure what side she was on. She had yet to meet the children's father, even though she had worked there for months. The mother was hardly there, too. She was constantly exhausted and hiding in the depths of the castle.

All she had heard about the war were murmurs in the kitchens, whispers from the maids. The Old Bloods had partnered with Man, who had the most enormous army on the continent. She heard mentions of their inability to be defeated and how they would succeed because they could attack in the daylight. That they planned to attack in the summer when the Polar Days hit.

After making their way around the castle, Valentin escorted Tatiana back to her room. It was nothing much. She had a cot to sleep on, a dresser for her clothing, and an oil lamp.

"Good day, Tatiana. I wish for you to rest well."

"And you," she replied bashfully. A blush spread over her cheeks as he brought her hand to his lips, kissing the back of it. The tip of his long nose grazed her skin.

When she was alone with the warmth from the sunshine as well as whatever was blooming between her and Valentin, she flopped down onto her cot. Not a moment later, the thud of a fat insect hitting her window made her sigh. Her work was not done—she had to report to the Blood Queen.

Playing two sides of a game of chess was tiresome work.

25

LILIANNA

"It's not fair," Lilianna said to the empty room. Or perhaps she spoke to Moloch, who fluttered about aimlessly. She sometimes thought her familiar was a stupid creature. Flitting about and doing nothing useful. All he did was wait for Faust to come with news, and then she shared that news with Torenia. She told her everything, gave her everything, and Torenia still kept secrets from her. She and Sorin shared secrets, keeping them hidden from Lilianna.

It was not fair—not at all.

The sky was the sort of twilight that appeared as night turned to morning, just before the sun came out. Enough time for her to wander outside, but only with urgency and the awareness that death approached with the sunrise. The quiet moments prior to dawn were when the castle was still. Lilianna found use for Moloch, sending him to survey the halls and follow Sorin through the castle.

Moloch's dusty wings left a trail only Lilianna could see. She followed him down corridors, through boring hallways with paintings she didn't care about, until he led her to a door not unlike the one that brought her to the harvest. A rich, dark colored wooden door with metal straps across the top, middle, and bottom. There was an old brass handle, and while it was locked, Lilianna had stolen the key from Vera hours before.

It was easy to locate the right key, for its heaviness was different from the rest. She hurried down the steps, the smell of blood drawing her like a beckoning hand. When she reached the room at the bottom of the stairs, she discovered it was a laboratory. Tools were scattered across the blood-stained table, and there was more blood on the floor. Lilianna's mouth watered.

A bean-shaped bowl filled with bloody rags drew her attention. Lilianna picked up the bowl and sniffed. It was blood, but there was something different about it. It was not man.

It was nightwalker blood.

A shudder consumed her, and she lost her grip on the bowl. Gathering her wits, she hugged it close to herself before it could topple free. This was Torenia's blood—she knew it deep in her heart because she and Torenia were connected. They were connected on every level, and each fiber of her body was also part of Torenia. She brought the rag to her lips and sucked some of the cold, coagulated blood out of it.

Lilianna choked, sputtering and spitting it out.

It was putrid.

She tried again, desperate to absorb Torenia into her, but she could not stomach it.

Cannibal.

"No," she responded. She needed to leave this place, so she kept the bowl clutched to her chest and hurried out of the laboratory. What had Sorin and Torenia done? Why was it kept secret from Lili, who just wanted to love and be loved by Torenia?

You want to be Torenia.

She wanted to deny it, but found herself incapable of responding to the voice in her head. Lilianna hurried to her bedroom unseen. In the safety of her lonely room, her mess piling higher and higher, she clambered through the heaps of clothing to the large wardrobe. It was the perfect place to hide the blood. She yanked it open, placing the bowl in the far corner. She haphazardly shoved piles of clothing to hide it, then latched the wardrobe shut.

No one would find it in here—no one came in here.

No one ever came to visit Lilianna.

Lilianna watched in a daze as Moloch and Faust did their aerial dance, bumping their fat bodies and scattering dust below them. It had been a week since she had her first taste of Torenia's blood—it had been wretched then. Now it was thick like gelatin. She no longer tasted it when she brought it to her mouth and devoured a small portion of it.

Moloch landed on her cheek and crawled to her ear, sealing their bond. His soft whispers in her ear told her the secrets of the Lebedevs, all the things Tatiana had learned in her time with them. Lilianna forgot how long it had been since her sister left. Months? Or had it been a year now? Living at night made time pass strangely.

When Moloch finished, he pushed off of her and went back to Faust. They were more connected than Lili and Tati were. She sneered at her familiar, feeling the threads that connected them tightening.

She looked down at her gown, drowning in yards of fabric. It dragged on the dirty floor as she trampled to the door. The hem was torn and covered in filth, but she didn't care. Her feet were bare as she walked toward the council room. The place where wars started. She had something to contribute now, something that would earn her a place at that big wooden table with the adults.

Her tiny fist banged on the door, the sound hollow, as though nothing she could do would cause a ripple in this place. She held her head high as Zaina opened the door, revealing Torenia and Alexei seated at the table.

Torenia beamed lovingly at Lilianna, making her heart skip a beat. Every doubt that filled her when she was alone disappeared when Torenia looked at her like that. Like she was her daughter. She walked around the table, choosing the side opposite Alexei, her eyes on Torenia the entire time. When she reached her side, Torenia wrapped Lilianna in a warm embrace. "You've come with news, haven't you?"

"Yes," Lilianna said.

"What have you brought me, Lilianna?" Torenia urged.

"The Old Bloods will attack in the Polar Days," Lili told them, eyes flickering toward Alexei and Zaina for a split second before looking back at Torenia. "They mean to catch you at your most vulnerable since your armies are made up of Pure and Half-Bloods."

Torenia pressed her lips tight, a flicker of rage in her brilliant blue eyes. She snarled, "So Lebedev thinks he can attack me while I'm stuck inside... Well, then, I think the only course of action is to bring the fight to him."

"*Koroleva*, we are strongest here. This castle has only been breached once, by an army larger than Lebedev's," Zaina countered.

"We will not be strongest here during the forty days in which none of my army can go outside," she snapped back. "This information is invaluable. Thank you, Lilianna."

Torenia turned back to Alexei and Zaina again. "We are competing against man, but we have the bulk of the nightwalkers and the witches. We will have the wolves, though I do not trust them." Torenia looked at Lilianna. "I think it is time I visit your old friend Alina."

Lilianna's head cocked to the side. It would be quite pleasant to see Alina again. "I would like that. Just us?"

"Lilianna, I require your services here. Who else will keep the castle safe in my absence?" Before Lilianna could respond, Torenia continued. "I need you to protect this place and listen for your sister's familiar. Would that be something I could trust you with?"

Lilianna nibbled her lip—she didn't want Sorin hogging Torenia, but she wanted to please Torenia. She nodded her consent and earned a warm smile from Torenia.

26

ALINA

The nearly forgotten warmth of spring brought something deep inside Alina Nastaca back to life. The part of her heart that had cleaved in two was stitching itself back together. She could feel the warmth of the town—one that had never existed in the past.

She rose from the bed and walked barefoot through her one-bedroom home. The floorboards were quiet. Built within the last year, it had no leaks in the roof, nor crooked door frames that were sinking. She approached the small woodstove and added another log, watching the fire grow. When it was roaring, she shut the door and closed her eyes.

Smoke wafted into her senses, the sacrifice of the woods for the warmth of the house, for the shelter the home offered. Alina gave a quick acknowledgement to the way the forest gave back to her.

Two strong arms wrapped themselves around Alina, and she melted into the sturdy frame of the woman behind her. Birgitte's smell was that of the woods—old forest growth, the essence of smoke, and the crispness of a clear night. The stitches of her heart tightened, the gap growing smaller day by day.

"The full moon is tonight," Birgitte whispered, her voice like honey and gravel. It made Alina's core flip. Birgitte's dirty blonde hair mixed with hers as she leaned down and kissed her neck. "Come back to bed."

Alina slowly accepted that there was room inside her heart to love again. Though she was somewhat reserved with Birgitte in ways she hadn't been with Red, there were things she did with Birgitte that she and Red never got to experience. In some ways, her love for Birgitte was much stronger, having been given the chance to grow rather than being ripped from them after a fortnight.

Something about Birgitte's boldness and how different it was from Red's shyness allowed Alina to let her in. Birgitte occupied a different part of Alina—the part that allowed her to breathe. She was free to love Birgitte as she had not been allowed to do so with Red. That alone made all the difference in the world.

Turning to face Birgitte, Alina looked up at the tall woman. Her eyes were an amber color that, when she turned into a wolf for three days and nights, reflected the moonlight. Right now, they were not wolfish—they were hungry. Alina kissed her, realizing that she only wore the sheet from their bed. Her hands slipped underneath the thin piece of fabric to touch the warm flesh of her body. She was sturdy like the trees in the forest, and like the trees, she gave Alina strength.

Alina caressed Birgitte's muscular body, feeling her ripples of pleasure as she knelt between her thighs. Her fingertips traced the definition of her calves, moving around the perfection that was her body. The softness of her hair. There were scars along her legs, though they were not as defined as the ones on her arms and back. Still, Alina kissed each one. Birgitte moaned softly, her hands running through Alina's blonde locks.

Alina, though smaller, overpowered Birgitte with her newly developed strength. Wrapping her arms underneath her thighs, she caressed Birgitte's stomach and began to devour the woman with steady strokes. Their bodies moved in graceful sync—writhing, moaning, cresting. Only when Birgitte found her release did she shift from her position underneath Alina.

The werewolf flipped around, Alina's legs around her hips now, and stood. She held Alina with ease, bringing her back against the wall. The rounded log wall scraped against Alina's spine in a painfully delicious way. Birgitte used her strength to hold Alina up with one hand while she slipped the other between her legs. Gentle fingers combined with growls and bites, the gentle drag of her tongue against Alina's neck—it was her undoing.

Birgitte carried Alina back to the bed, carefully lowering her and joining her.

Breathless, Alina said, "I love it when you do that."

"I know," Birgitte replied with a hearty laugh.

"I never thought...before this, before you, I never thought I would experience that." Alina rolled onto her side and draped her arm around Birgitte. "When I met Red, I never imagined it could be like this."

"The pack understands lust and love. What our bodies want is not questioned—it is embraced. Though I have been part of the pack, living a very different type of life, I understand the difficulties of being like us."

"The pack always accepted you?"

"The pack always accepted me, yes," she said. "And they will accept you, Alina. Have you decided?"

She nodded, then kissed Birgitte's collarbone. "It's one of the few things in life I have been sure about."

"Mm," Birgitte moaned. "What else?"

Alina slid her hand down Birgitte's body, fingers skating across her most sensitive places. "This. Us."

The woods were filled with the sounds of drums on the cusp of the first night of the full moon. The sun had not yet set, and sheltered from the gentle wind, Alina was warm. Despite this, she felt goosebumps prickle over her arms. The drums beat in a rhythm she had never heard before. Deep, throaty words filled the spaces the drums could not.

Clad in nothing more than a white shift—the same style she often wore with the coven—she walked. There was no path, but an undeniable strength pulled her the right way. Just as the craft came from the earth, the wolves were controlled by the pull of the moon. The tides it created rose not just in the oceans but within her as well.

She walked alone, as she had for most of her life, in the same forest where she burned pig's hearts and bound herself to Rose Luca. The same forest that she asked for protection from love, only to learn it was impossible. She was surrounded by love. The love of her father, the love of Birgitte, the love of the wolves that took over her town and made it a place where love could flourish.

Alina glanced up at the sky. She could feel the pull of the moon, but she had not yet shown her face. The earth beneath her feet kissed her with each step, giving her a drop of power with every footfall. She could sense the pack up ahead, but it had not yet shifted. As she entered the small clearing, she saw Daciana on the other side, Birgitte beside her. The Alpha and the Beta.

The animals in the trees were lively, she noted. No creatures had stirred when they had gone searching for Red and the Wolf. Now, they were alive with the rhythm—they too felt the earth and the moon dancing together in the fateful twilight.

Walking through the line of lycans on either side of her, all of them watching her stride barefoot towards their leader, she felt empowered rather than threatened. When she arrived, stopping a meter away, she dropped down to her knees before them.

"Alina Nas...taca," Daciana said in broken speech. "Give up...days."

"Three days a month, I will lose," she recited. "I shall hunt with the pack, fall in line with the pack, learn from the pack, protect the pack, and in time, learn to control my mind during those three days."

Daciana nodded approvingly. "Dis...obey..."

"I will be torn apart by the pack," she said shakily.

"Usurp..."

"I will be torn apart by the pack," Alina repeated. She had been taught these lines when she made her choice. Though all the wolves could challenge the Alpha for leadership, it was to be done forthright and with honor.

"Mm," Daciana growled. Soon, the moon would appear in the sky; Alina could already feel it. The ripples of power through the air, like static.

Gyda appeared, and she said to Alina, "Your connection to the moon, and your connection to the earth... The power you will inherit and learn will allow us to defeat our common enemy. Your sacrifice is the key to the beginning of the end."

Alina wondered how her choice to become a lycan was a sacrifice, but she supposed to some people, it would be unimaginable to lose control for three days. She was looking forward to it, though she admitted it to no one. In her research, she learned a lone werewolf could never control himself, could never fight back the urges. However, as a pack, they could use a hive-mind type mentality, and their combined humanity formed a lucidity. This allowed them to have control over their actions when in their wolf form.

But it was a hard-learned skill.

"Do... Not... Move." Daciana said as the moon came out, full and bright. The shift rippled through them. All around Alina, the sound of bones cracking and cries of pain echoed—she wished to cover her ears, but she knew not to move. When Daciana, in wolf-form, walked around her, tongue lolling and saliva dripping, she shivered.

The slight movement was enough to make a younger wolf yip excitedly. A few of them began to pant hungrily, growling around her. They circled her, three concentric circles of wolves, all padding around. Scattered growls came from all directions, but she remained still. Her instincts screamed to run, but she knew, even with control, the pack might rip her to shreds.

Running from wolves was not an option.

Daciana growled, nearly too low for Alina to hear. The wolves were silent and stopped moving. Having been told what to do earlier that day, she slowly raised her hands out before her. She flipped one so it was palm up, and with the other, she held a small blade. She sliced across the scar on her palm. Blood bubbled up over the wound, and the wolves around her reacted.

Daciana silenced them with another growl. She dragged her wolfish tongue over the wound, lapping it up. One by one, the other wolves followed her actions. By the time all twenty wolves had licked the wound, it no longer bled. Now they all knew her, and when she made the shift into a lycan, she would be accepted into the pack immediately.

All that was left was the bite. Alina expected Daciana to do it, but it was Birgitte who delivered the near-fatal bite to her shoulder. She cried out in pain, scrambling to get away from the wolf whose long canines clamped into her flesh. It tore when she fell away, muscle and sinew shredding. The other wolves barricaded Birgitte from doing further harm—it was said to be very difficult to stop a wolf from finishing their kill, which made turning man into lycan difficult.

Crawling, Alina reached her good hand before her and clawed at the earth. She could feel its power coursing through her and the power of the moon pulling her back. They battled within her, and when Alina reached her hand out again, she saw her nails shifting into claws as her bones cracked before her.

Everything began to fade when Alina's eyes sharpened briefly, allowing her to see the sleek black raven perched in the tree, watching eagerly as the witch writhed and shifted into a beast.

27

TORENIA

The wedge had been driven deeper now. Torenia watched through Rahella's eyes as Alina shifted into a creature. No longer human, no longer just a harmless girl, but an unpredictable werewolf. Vulnerable as she was when she left, Torenia knew how easy it was for Alina to grasp onto a pack. Cults worked their magic on the most vulnerable—this was proof. Alina needed someone to latch onto, someone to make decisions for her, something to validate her.

Torenia raised her lip in distaste and pulled away from her familiar's vision. A growl came from her, as though she were a werewolf. Tearing herself away from her seat before the fire, Torenia felt the ache in her chest where the stitches were still tender. Her new wound was more troublesome than she wished to admit. Not only was it unfashionable, forcing her to cover more of herself than she would prefer, but also, even the simplest movements tired her.

She had recovered from worse.

Torenia knew she needed to get answers to her questions. There was nothing that could be done about Alina now, but she was still in Torenia's clutches. Wolves were not at the top of the food chain. Torenia had questions for Sorin, her strongest link to the coven she'd spread out across borders to work on her behalf.

Finding her exactly where she expected her to be, Torenia made her worries clear to the only person she trusted. "Your friend has joined the pack."

She watched through narrowed blue eyes as Sorin pondered her statement. The woman nodded as though it was no surprise to her.

"She always needed a pack. It's the reason she formed a coven," Sorin responded, then rose to her feet.

Some people lowered their heads in Torenia's presence, but Sorin never did. The woman knew she was her equal, and Torenia appreciated not just the bravery but the honesty in the action. Knowing Sorin felt the way she intended let her know she was doing something right. No one person knew everything about Torenia's past. People knew parts of it—her blood bathing, the massacre of her own family, the Dark Years. What came before the Dark Years.

"Have you ever transferred your consciousness?" Torenia asked, forcing herself from her reverie.

Sorin cocked her head to the side curiously. "Only with Lucien."

"I'm going to teach you how you can be in any place at any time." Torenia reached out her hand, and Sorin took it. She channeled her energy through to the other witch, pulsing surges to show her exactly how to accomplish it. It simply could not be explained through words, only through connection and touch.

"Do you feel that?" Torenia asked.

Sorin nodded, her eyes shut, lips slightly parted. "It feels as though I could be everywhere and nowhere."

"Precisely. Practice this. We must visit your old friend," Torenia told her.

"The best practice is doing," Sorin said. She picked up on it immediately, just as Torenia trusted she would.

"It is unpleasant, and Silvania is very far away." Torenia frowned. "Let's try somewhere nearer first. I cannot risk losing you to a transference disaster. People have been torn apart doing this unprepared."

"Give me a few days, and I will have mastered it."

Not three days later, the two witches transferred from creature to creature, from insect to insect. Their minds flew down south across the borders of Osleka, into Silvania. When they reached their destination, Torenia transferred back into physical matter and waited as Sorin figured out how to manipulate the matter just right; it was always harder the longer the journey. A few moments passed, and Torenia grew weary and glanced around. If she could locate Sorin's consciousness, she could pull her out of whatever animal she currently inhabited. Then she felt a warm figure appear beside her as Sorin gasped.

"That was incredible," she breathed.

Torenia smiled. "Now, let's go pay your friend a visit."

They walked right up to the border and the patrol. Werewolves always struggled with humanity the day after the shift, and even worse, the night after. Torenia used this to her advantage.

They growled at her, trying to barricade her by blocking the path with their bodies. They could easily overpower her—she knew what they were capable of. However, Torenia did not have a death wish, so she said, "I must speak with your Alpha."

"Three...days..." one of the patrols said, barely a whisper.

"No, tonight will do," she said, her voice hard. "Tonight, or I bring him back."

The two glanced at each other, using a combination of hand movements, growling, and facial movements to discuss. Torenia knew they were discussing whether she was capable of bringing back Blaez from the dead. She was not, but they did not know this. Anything was possible when it came to witchcraft, but bringing back someone who had died was something Torenia had tried and failed.

She pushed away the memory and waited to be let in.

"I can poison your waters, prevent crops from growing, bring a plague of locusts to your doorsteps—do not doubt my ability to bring back the dead," she warned them.

"One...hour."

Within the town again, Torenia wrinkled her nose. It no longer reeked of spite and hatred, yet now she felt as though it was heavily lacking in those very things. Perhaps due to how she was raised, it felt wrong to feel so...normal.

They were quickly met by Daciana, Birgitte, and Alina.

"You're looking well, Alina," Torenia said and meant it. The young woman had filled out as though becoming a lycan was the best thing for her health. Her muscles were sinewy and visible now, whereas before, she'd been incredibly lithe and lean. She still carried a haunted look in her eyes, though.

"Home was...good for me," she replied. Her voice was hoarse, as they all were when coming down from a shift. It took years before werewolves lost their ability to speak in human form, but it was an inevitable outcome for all of them. Just like the desire for blood can consume rational thinking in a vampire, in a lycan, the animal eventually takes over. They all learned to speak in other ways.

Alina looked at Sorin. "How are...Lilianna...Tatiana?"

"Well," Sorin replied. "Lilianna has never felt more secure than she does now. She is thriving."

"Tati?"

"She is finding her way in the world." This answer seemed to please Alina, whose smile flickered briefly.

Torenia turned her attention to Daciana. "We won't stay long—we have a war to plan. I came to congratulate you on your newest member. She will be good for your pack, I am certain. I hope this shows the strength of our bond."

Daciana eyed her—a challenge.

Torenia stared her down just as viciously, reminding herself that the animal inside Daciana did not appreciate another strong leader in her presence. She added, "I do hope this confirms that you will come when I call to arms."

Daciana bared her teeth. Slowly, she nodded. "Yes."

"Very well," Torenia replied with a clap of her hands. She glanced around the town, its brightly lit homes and camaraderie making her shudder with distaste. "I sent Gyda and Helga with you, Alina. I expected to see them here. Where are they?"

There was a shift. Alina tensed, as did Daciana. Only the blonde who stood close to Alina didn't react. So, they didn't want to tell her where they were or what they were up to. Torenia wondered if the witches she trusted were playing both sides. The kind of people who waited to see who was winning, then sided with whoever offered them the most significant outcome. It sickened Torenia to know that there was no integrity among witches anymore. Perhaps there never was.

Despite the unanimous dislike of man by all others—witches, vampires, werewolves, seers—they were all human on some level.

And there was no integrity among men.

Daciana answered Torenia's question. "Left."

"Of course. They have important matters to attend to, I'm sure. I shall send Rahella to find them." Torenia looked up to where her raven was perched. "Surely they mentioned where they were going?"

Daciana shook her head, her one eye narrowed into a slit. "Not...Ask."

Torenia pulled her lips into a tight smile. She turned to Sorin. "We must race home. There is much to prepare. Oh, Daciana. I forgot to mention my other reason for coming." She turned back to the Alpha. "The Old Bloods intend to attack during the Polar Days. We will draw them out before, then meet them with a swift knife when they least expect it. I would like to conclude this war before summer arrives. Will your Omega be ready? We wouldn't want any casualties on the field."

Birgitte snarled at Torenia, stepping in front of Alina protectively.

Daciana put her arm out to shield the two. With a nod, she confirmed that Torenia could count on them.

"That concludes my business here," she muttered. "Love what you've done with the place—it's disgustingly pleasant. Come, Sorin, we must return. I believe our hour is up."

28

SORIN

After visiting the wolves, Torenia called a meeting with Sorin, Alexei, and Zaina. There was much to be discussed. It was no throne, but sitting on the left-hand side of the Blood Queen at the massive table in the meeting room was throne enough for Sorin. She had reached such heights considering where she came from... Some of the ascent felt as though she was being forced to climb the rungs of a ladder with her hands tied behind her back—each gruelling step meaning she was close to tumbling backward. But she prevailed, and now the steps were easier, more like stairs than rungs.

Sorin was not foolish enough to believe that her climb was over, but she was comfortable where she sat now. Across from her, to Torenia's right, was Zaina, with Alexei beside her. News arrived from Tatiana, and for the first time, Sorin was invited to listen. Now, she played a vital role in the war, one so key it could change everything if anyone found out. She held Torenia's heart—only she knew where it would be hidden.

The nights were quickly growing warmer; Sorin felt comfortable without layers. Summer approached, and so did war.

"A few powerful families of Man have agreed to side with you," Alexei said. "Though they have no interest in vampire or witch politics, they have other interests."

"My enemy's enemy is my friend," Torenia suggested.

"In this case, yes. But they want something in return," he continued.

"Men always want more. Simply joining together for a cause means nothing to them—they must have more." Torenia revealed a wicked, sharp fang as she grimaced. "What is their request?"

"An agreement. Their families will earn eternal protection from being fodder."

She pursed her lips and tented her fingers together. "An easy request—there is no shortage of food."

"This is true, but…"

"Spit out what you wish to say, Alexei."

"They want protection from *all* nightwalkers. They say if you are a true queen, you will have the power to control the others, and your protection over them will be the rule."

"And if we help them, tell them what they wish to hear, what happens when another rogue vampire takes them out? That cannot be my fault. They are asking for the impossible. No ruler has full control over everyone. They wish to see me fail."

"It's hard to say," he replied with a grumble, but then looked confidently at Torenia. "I do not think you need more enemies. Not when you have the wolves dangerously close to flipping sides. I believe they are asking the impossible of you, so they have a reason to target you next."

"So, you do not wish for me to agree to their terms? If I do not, I am short many good fighting men." She added in a whisper to Sorin, "The only thing Man is good at."

"I think you can rally them another way. You have the wolves, at least as far as we know. You have every coven in the far reaches, and one witch is worth five men."

"Six," Torenia whispered to Sorin. Sorin gave a curt, sharp laugh, earning a grin.

"There is one other way to ensure your army is large enough."

Torenia turned back to Alexei with a marble expression. "If you dare to suggest what I think you might, do not waste your breath or my time."

"Roman had—"

"Roman lied to thousands. Half of whom did not die, discovered his deceit, and turned against him. For years, he fought back not just the Pure Bloods but some of the Half Bloods he lied to, as well. I will not be Roman. For too long, I wanted to be just like him. Now, I wish only to be better than him."

"Who is Roman?" Sorin asked. She had heard the name before, but getting Torenia to open up about her past was not easy.

Torenia waved her hand as though she could brush the question away. "Someone I both admired and hated."

It did not answer Sorin's question, but she wondered who felt this way about Torenia. Alina, perhaps. Tatiana, maybe. How many others?

"You have made your opinion clear, *Koroleva*," Zaina said.

"And you've given me nothing of substance," Torenia growled as she rose. Towering over all of them, she declared, "We will take out Maksim Chernov and the Lebedev family. Whether it be through brutish warfare and the ways of men or by the wicked, cunning ways of women, we will accomplish this. Everyone will remember my name, and they will shake with fear again. They will not rise against me when I have won. All I need is for one task within the Lebedev home to be committed, and they will come to my door."

"And you think the girl you sent will be capable?"

"Sorin?" Torenia redirected the question to her. "Tatiana was part of your coven."

Sorin wondered if Torenia was using her as the scapegoat to pass off the blame later if Tatiana were to fail. No, she decided, not when she had her heart in her hands, literally.

"Yes, she will be capable when the time comes," Sorin confirmed. "You must remember, you have her sister."

The room fell quiet as brief, uncomfortable glances were exchanged. Everyone knew that Lilianna loved Torenia like her mother. But no one really knew Torenia's feelings for the girl. Did she see her as her daughter? Was the Blood Queen capable of feeling anything of the sort? Sorin wondered if her statement opened up a gaping wound, the one that she saw on Torenia's stomach when she removed her heart.

Torenia grinned her signature wicked smile. "Oh Sorin, you have the mind of a true ruler."

Sorin dipped her head down, both to humble herself and to hide her smile.

"It is true that I have Tatiana's little sister. It is true that I *could* use her for leverage should I need to. However, I have no desire to harm the girl. Perhaps, though, planting that thought in Tatiana's mind when the time is right... It may douse any doubts she has. When I command it, Tatiana will be the swift hand that delivers quiet justice. She is the key to balancing the scales. If she succeeds, the war will be over much quicker."

Sorin sighed in relief. No one turned to look, but she knew Torenia noticed. Nothing went unnoticed by the Blood Queen. Though Sorin suggested that Lilianna could be used as leverage, she wished nothing of the sort. To know Torenia wished her no harm would help her sleep at night.

"I think we've come to an excellent conclusion here. Tatiana will be given one final task. The war will come to our door sooner, but less collectedly and cohesively. We will be ready, and we will finish it," Torenia said with a clap of her hands. "Now, Sorin, I believe it's time. You know what to do."

With such a delicate task at hand, Sorin took every precaution she could. When daytime arrived and the castle grew quiet, she carried the box containing Torenia's black heart to the throne room. Glancing at the smashed thrones, she thought about what had happened here. She had heard there was once a Sisterhood—a blood cult run by Torenia, a woman on either side of her throne. Equal in all ways. Now, the Sisterhood was a formality, not a reality.

What happened to make her destroy it all?

This task, Sorin wondered—would it earn her a place beside Torenia officially? Would the thrones be rebuilt, a new Sisterhood rising from the ashes of the old? Was there such a fine wire to walk with Torenia that one wrong action could cause her to tear apart everything she had built?

The questions scratched at her as she left the castle. Sunlight poured over her, and she soaked it in, shedding her light coat. She placed it on a bench, planning on picking it up when she returned. Pausing to concentrate, Sorin used her new ability to transfer her consciousness through the wildlife. With a jerk and a jolt, she flew through the country, not knowing exactly where to go, instead letting the Craft guide her. It took much of her energy, but she hopped through bird and bug, mammal and amphibian.

Then she arrived in Ocleau.

The place of Azalea Luca's birth and death.

The forest around her was familiar, like the forests in Silvania. A great power was here—she felt it immediately. Deep, rumbling vibrations rippled beneath her feet. The animals were silent but watching. Sorin knelt and placed her hands on the dirt, feeling it between her fingers. The moment her flesh touched it, she gasped. So much death happened in this soil, so much betrayal. Letting it consume her inch by inch, Sorin was ripped apart by the emotions of this place.

Forcing open her eyes, Sorin allowed a few tears to fall as she ripped her hands free. All around her, the earth was unsettled, and the trees leaned in, their roots reaching for her. Nothing had changed, but everything changed in that moment. She knew this place was one of horrors, but also one of the birth of power. This was where Azalea Luca sacrificed her daughter to create the curse that lasted four centuries. This was where Azalea Luca had been burned alive.

This was where she would bury Torenia's heart.

Sorin used her hands, soaking in that unfathomable power with each grain of dirt under her nails and each sharp rock that ripped through her tough skin. It was not until she found the corpse that she realized she had dug so deep. It was night, and mountains of earth and mud were all around her. She knew when she touched the bones that this was where they left Azalea Luca after they burned her. After they doused her inflamed body, they ripped her down unceremoniously and left her on the ground to be consumed. She was never buried, but the earth took her back. Just as the earth gave her power, it took it back until it was ready to be found again.

Sorin contemplated taking Azalea's skull for Torenia but decided against it, for it might tell Torenia where her heart was hidden. The

Blood Queen didn't want to know, so she couldn't be tortured into revealing the information. Sorin didn't think about the danger she was in by being the sole person who knew where Torenia Luca's heart was buried.

She pocketed a few small bones for herself and placed the box with Torenia Luca's gently pulsating heart inside Azalea Luca's ribcage.

29

TATIANA

Spring was in full bloom. With each passing day, as sunlight devoured more of the night, the Lebedev family grew increasingly vicious. Tatiana was tending to a bruise, covering it with powder, when a soft knock came at her door. Her eyes flicked to the wood separating her from whoever was on the other side. She quickly covered the bruise and opened the door, finding a red-faced Valentin on the other side—the only person in the castle she looked forward to seeing.

"May I come in?" he asked.

She wanted to say yes. She wanted to take his hands inside of hers, usher him into the room, and shut that door. But fear held her back, so she shook her head.

"Outside, then?" he inquired, never questioning why Tatiana never let herself be alone with him, not since that first night. Though he had proven himself to be someone she could trust and possibly even love, being alone with him in her bedroom was too much.

"Very well," she agreed, following him. When they were outside, she looked up at him, admiring his features and the way he seemed to glow in the sunshine. Brilliant flowers were blossoming all around them, the scents reminding Tatiana that she was a witch. That the flowers grown from the earth were just like her, given power from Mother Nature. There were night-blooming flowers, too, just as some witches preferred to harness the power of the moon. She smiled, thinking of Lilianna.

"I heard the children lashed out at you," he said.

She nodded softly. "Yes."

"But they did not break the flesh?"

"Of course not." She looked up at him. "We both know I would be in much worse shape if I'd bled before them."

"It's... I should never have brought you here, Tatiana." He stopped, looking at the ground below them. "It's too dangerous for you."

Now, Tatiana offered a soft laugh. "Oh, Valentin, I appreciate your concern. There has never been a time in my life when I wasn't in danger."

He ran a hand over his sharp features, tugging at his skin. "All the more reason to get you out of here. It was wrong of me to bring you here, to put you in danger. You cannot have a life here."

His thoughtfulness touched Tatiana's heart. No one had ever cared about her like this. The coven had tried to protect her, but it wasn't the same as the way Valentin protected her.

"It was I who brought you here, and it is my duty to ensure you get away from this place," he concluded as though he had recited this many times in his bedroom before this moment.

Another smile crept onto Tatiana's face, but it withered as quickly as it showed up. She could not leave, not without risking Lilianna's safety, and she could not tell Valentin that. Her compromise for even this much freedom was to do Torenia's bidding. Soon, the war would be over, and Tatiana would be free.

Or would she?

Would Torenia release her? What if one day Faust fluttered in with another request, sent by Torenia through Lili's familiar, Moloch?

"Tati?" Valentin asked.

She snapped back to the present. "Give me time to think about it. We cannot abandon our duties here."

"We?" he asked.

Tatiana blanched. "I—I simply mean, if you help me, they might terminate your position here, as well."

He cracked a smile. "If you wanted me to leave with you, I would. You need only to say the word."

Valentin offered her the chance at a normal life, a life where she wasn't always in danger. But what would she lose to achieve it? Could she make that sacrifice after all she had been through to save her sister?

She returned to her chambers, her thoughts spinning. Sinking down onto her bed, she forced herself to breathe, collecting her thoughts into a pile where she could sort through them and weigh her options—but was interrupted by the fat bodies of two fluttering moths on either side of the window.

A new task from the Blood Queen.

Tatiana's heart sank. She opened the window to listen to the new order. Until now, it had been only questions Torenia needed answers to, ones Tati was to listen for, to gently pry from the loose lips of those in the castle. Her gut told her that this was not about information—this was an act of war.

She bonded with her familiar, her eyes rolling back into her skull. She and Faust froze, the consciousness transferring from him to her. She experienced what he experienced.

A phial of Siren blood to ease them from this world. Find it in the garden where the roses grow white. A toxin to nightwalkers, Pure and Half, Old and Young.

"Tati?" A firm hand shaking her shoulder jostled her.

She snapped out of her bond with Faust, a cry leaving her throat as the moth fell to the floor. He writhed in agony for a moment before shaking dust from his wings and crawling under the bed. The pain of being ripped from the bond before it was over felt like knives inside her eyes, and Tatiana knew Faust felt it too.

She stared at Valentin, rising to her feet and staggering back against the far wall. The door behind him was closed. Tatiana began to tremble.

"You're a witch…"

There was no use in lying, so she nodded.

His face was pinched. Shutting his dark eyes, he sighed. "You work for her, don't you? The Blood Queen?"

She snapped her head up, watching him drift further away from her. Part of her wanted to reach out and grasp his hands, but she was afraid of what he would do if she touched him.

"She has my sister," she whispered.

His demeanor changed.

"I don't want to hurt anyone. I just gave her information...until..."
Her body tensed.

"What did she ask of you?"

She looked at the window where the dust of the moths settled.
"I'm not sure... She said something about Siren's blood. She had it
placed in the garden where the roses grow white."

Valentin took a deep breath, then stepped towards Tatiana and
reached for her hand. She took it. He kissed her on the forehead and
whispered into her skin. "We will leave tomorrow at dawn."

"But my sister..." she said, though her voice lacked conviction. She
thought of the words Torenia chose. Old and young. Lilianna was the
youngest of them all, and she was certain this was what Torenia
intended for Tatiana to take away from her cryptic message.

"Pack your things and write your sister a letter. I will come to fetch
you at dawn. I promise everything will be okay."

Valentin left her, and Tatiana fell back against the wall, placing her
hand over her mouth and inhaling deeply through her nose. Faust
crawled out from under the bed and clambered up her body to perch
on her shoulder, all sticky legs and dusty wings. Calm washed over her,
and she guided herself to her small desk. Pulling out the parchment
she kept on the underside of the desk and the ink she kept hidden
behind her bed, she penned her letter to Lilianna.

Lilianna,

I trust you are doing well, my sweet sister. I
hope you are being treated well, given everything your
heart desires, everything you deserve in this life and
more. You've been through too much to be granted
anything less.

I urge you to make the best choices and do
what you know in your heart is the right thing. This
is what I have to do. I must make the right

choice, the choice my heart tells me is just. What Torenia has asked of me is not something I can do. We were children in Silvania, Lili. We were not given a fair chance at life. Torenia's demand is vile. They are children, and they have not been given a fair life. My heart is telling me to leave while I still can.

If you love Torenia as a mother, I can only hope she loves you like a daughter.

We are no longer the children who hid eggs to rot in the neighbor's cupboards, but I hope one day we might enjoy a time where we feel as free as we did then before Mama died.

I love you with all my heart,
Tatiana

She then packed her meager belongings into a bag and hid it underneath her bed.

Tatiana spent the rest of the night tending to the children, fearing for her life. Though it was foolish—it was as though they could sense her fear. The night drew on for what felt like a lifetime, and when they were safely put to bed in their windowless rooms, she hurried back to her small bedroom.

Not long after she arrived in her room, Valentin came in. His clothes were wrinkled, and there was something as black as a starless night sky on his sleeve. His eyes were wild and crazed. Tatiana had never seen him in such disarray, and it frightened her.

"We must hurry," he said, and reached out his hand.

Tatiana took it, and they rushed through the halls with quiet steps. A few maids chattered, so they darted down another hallway, hiding until they passed.

"Valentin..."

"Shh."

"You look half mad," she whispered.

"Not now, Tati," he urged.

"What did you do?"

The firm look on his face gave away nothing. The hallways cleared, and he pulled her through them with urgency. Outside the Lebedev home, the sun rose, and it awoke something inside Tatiana—fear and calm all at once. Leaving meant Lilianna might be hurt or worse. Leaving also meant Tatiana could find something meaningful in her life, something that was hers. She wanted to grow something, nurture something.

"What did you do?" she asked again when the castle was behind them.

"What I had to do," he said, not looking at her, "to keep your sister safe."

"Valentin..." Tatiana gripped his arm. "The children?"

"It's the only way your sister could survive, and the Blood Queen is right—they cannot go on forever." Tatiana stopped moving, and Valentin stumbled. He recovered quickly and turned to face her, gripping her shoulders. "Tati, listen to me," he moved his hands to her cheeks, holding her face gently. Tatiana could see the tears in his eyes. "It was a mercy. You know what would become of them when they reached maturity."

"I—" Tatiana had no words. She knew he was right. She was shocked that the idea of the children lying dead in their rooms, poisoned with Siren blood, didn't make her crumble. Instead, it lifted a weight off her shoulders. She hated that she felt what Valentin did was right. "It was supposed to be me who did it."

"I couldn't let it be you."

30

ALINA

Alina felt the animal inside her creeping up into her throat, as though scratching with its sharp claws to get out. There was an eclipse coming, and the wolf within her yipped and stretched inside her human body. Never before had she felt power of this magnitude—a pack was much stronger than a coven in many ways, and not just physically. The connection between them was an unbreakable bond. She quickly picked up on social cues—even a flinch was enough to convey immediately what previously would have taken a conversation.

The pack understood her.

The pack would die for her.

And she would die for the pack.

Helga and Gyda entered the Nastaca house, bringing Birgitte with them. The mute witch carried a bowl, the werewolf carried an unlit candle, and Gyda carried a small leather satchel. Alina sat before the fireplace, her hands resting on the brick hearth, palms down.

She thought of Red and how the firelight drew her to the coven— the beginning of the end for Rose Luca. Their love, their infatuation, burned bright and fast. The pain taught Alina so much about herself and helped her understand how she loved. Now, she had a quiet, slow-burning flame with Birgitte, who taught her that love could be soft and gentle. Not all fires burned the same.

"Fire manipulation is very difficult," Gyda said, cutting off Alina's concentration. "But after you have been imbued with Blood and Moon Magic, you will find you may be open enough to accomplish it."

"Mastering flame after so many of us have been burned," Alina said quietly.

"It can be done," Gyda said, "with a powerful enough witch."

Alina felt the tug of more power. It tasted like iron on her tongue. She wanted it all—she wanted the power of the Craft and the power of the pack. She wanted to absorb every last drop of it so she could defeat Torenia. Having read about the Dark Years, she knew it had to be done—she wished to be the hand that delivered justice to the world.

Rising slowly, Alina turned towards the two women. Her eyes lingered a moment on Birgitte. Though she was quite a bit older than Alina, they were a good pair. Her heart would never heal where Red had torn it open, but that did not mean she could not love again. It was mutual between them. Their bodies seemed to gyrate inside when they were this close.

Birgitte produced a flask from the pocket in her leather vest. Unscrewing the cap, she drank from it, then brought her lips to Alina's, trading it off the way a mother would to a child in the days of old. The shared liquid quickly made her head swim in a foggy sort of way. Her legs turned to air, as if they were barely connected to her. Being out of control was not something she ever allowed, but she felt safe with the pack surrounding her.

She trusted them as they guided her. Birgitte had taken a smaller dosage, or perhaps she had a tolerance to the liquid that was now making Alina dizzy. The outdoors provided a feeling of strength, her bare feet able to touch the earth and draw up her power, and Alina sobered up just enough to walk on her own. Into the forest they went, leaving the essence of civilization behind them and entering the wild.

As the ritual site came into view, it looked scarcely different from when Alina turned. Birgitte had done the deed, and for that, they were forever bound. Now, there was nothing to light the way. Alina could see it all, sense every tree and root, every rock and grain of dirt. As she maneuvered to the front where Gyda stood, briefly wondering how she got there, she stopped before the wooden bowl. It was filled with something red.

Iron prickled on her taste buds, telling her what was in the bowl.

"When the moon eclipses, prick thy finger—
A drop of blood, from one and one—
Bonded in spirit, bonded together,
A drop of blood, from one and one"

Alina spoke the words. She had never heard them before, yet she knew what was to be spoken. They rolled off her tongue as though she had studied them for years. The rest came as the moon eclipsed. Alina raised her hand over the wooden bowl, holding a fine blade against the tip of her finger. One prick—just enough to draw blood—was all she needed. She did not even feel it.

Gyda handed Alina the leather satchel. Opening it, Alina saw the crushed bone, blended with that which she loved, blended with that which Torenia loved. With a careful tilt, she spilled the contents into the blood. The mixture fizzed before turning placid once more. Kneeling, she gripped the bowl and swirled the liquid inside.

How will this stop Torenia? Alina had asked, but she had received no answer.

One did not question Blood Magic. One did not question Moon Magic. And no one had ever done them together like this. No one knew—only the speculation that if all the magic came together, one could defeat the Blood Queen. Raising the bowl of blood and skull ground so fine it was like rock flour, Alina drank the contents. The width of the bowl made some of the liquid spill over the sides of her mouth. The iron flavor filled her mouth, but she did not stop until the bowl was empty. The mixture sloshing inside her was uncomfortable, but whatever Birgitte had given her eased the discomfort.

The vibrations of the earth reverberated through her. Every bone in her body shook. A pulsing sound raged through her skull, making her drop the bowl. She curled into fetal form, her hands clutching the dirt, begging the earth to give her strength. The moon overhead eclipsed and pulled her away. She felt fire inside of her, as though the moon and the earth were battling.

A chant echoed around her, filling the air. She forced her eyes open and saw the pack had come together. They circled her, holding hands in an unbroken circle—like the earth, like the moon. Their combined strength shielded her as the blood and moon fought inside her body, slowly settling, and with it, the urge to vomit faded.

When Alina passed out, all she could think of was what she had ingested.

Her blood. Torenia's blood.

Fragments of that which she loved—Red.

Fragments of what Torenia loved—her child.

A BRIEF HISTORY OF WITCHES
AN EXCERPT

For ten years, I have been running from my mistake.

For ten years, Torenia Luca's reign of terror has been brought upon this world, but I have been the one to blame. How much blood has been shed for my mistakes? Oceans of it. My hands are red. My dreams are red.

I know now that had I left the child alive, Torenia may have been capable of change. The blood bathing had ebbed, and there was peace between vampires, peace between the covens of witches around the world. But I had my task —to rid the world of every Luca.

Including the child.

I should have seen it—that Torenia Luca would slaughter every person within her castle. Vampire, witch, man. None

were safe. And then none were safe outside the walls.
Not when she sent her army to find the killer.

Me.

She killed so many innocents because I was too afraid to
own up to my mistake.

The murder of her child.

Now more than ever, the Blood Queen must be stopped.
We must combine all forces of our power to do so…

31

LILIANNA

"No, no, no!" Lili shrieked as she reached her arms into the back of the wardrobe. With an aggravated growl, she yanked the dresses out of it. Smooth silks and soft cottons tore as she ripped them free, and when the closet was empty save for one dress and two pinafores that escaped the onslaught, Lili cried out again. There was nothing. The bucket of Torenia's blood she had foolishly kept was gone. It congealed weeks ago, thick and putrid, but Lili hid it there to keep it safe.

She had failed Torenia.

Crawling inside the wardrobe, she shut the doors behind her. If she closed her eyes and focused only on her scent, she could smell its essence. How long had it been missing? Hours? A few days? When was the last time she checked? Had it been Vera, finally braving the filthy room to clean because she simply couldn't stand the thought of leaving it be?

Lilianna's eyes snapped open as she thought back. Her dry lips parted. "Where *is* Vera?"

When was the last time she had seen the maid? Her brows furrowed. Shortly after Torenia and Sorin left to visit Alina in Silvania, Gyda and Helga, two of the witches from the Witches' Feast, arrived. Torenia had left her in charge of the castle, and...

Lili blanched, bringing her knuckles to her teeth. Her sharp fangs broke the flesh, and blood dribbled. She lapped at it absentmindedly.

"I let them in," Lili mumbled. "I let them in."

They had only asked if Torenia was present to speak to them. Lili had informed them that she was not. Being hospitable, she offered them to freshen up and have something to eat. The journey to the castle was difficult. They must have encountered Vera. Of course, they had—she would have prepared them food.

Lili groaned, clambering out of the wardrobe and pushing her way through her torn dresses. She barreled out of the room, winding down the halls and steps until she reached Vera's quarters. The door was unlatched. It was cold in here, as though it had been empty for some time. Days? She threw the bed linens aside, finding nothing, then went through the chest on the floor. Clothes, shoes—all simple and boring. There was nothing else in the room.

She collapsed to the floor in a heap, a whine escaping her. Torenia was always busy with the war. Sorin was always at her side, doing her sneaky tasks and corrupting Torenia into loving her more than Lilianna. Tatiana was gone; Alina was gone.

No one loved her as much as she loved them.

A lump beneath the bed caught her attention, and she quickly scurried under the bed and snatched it. A small book—leatherbound. It was a journal of some sort, latched with a metal buckle on the front. She frowned, turning it over to study it. As she went to open the latch, she heard voices.

Scurrying from the room with the book tucked in her skirts, she avoided getting caught. Lilianna headed towards the kitchens and ducked into the pantry, yanking an apple from the shelves. She flopped onto the ground and bit into it as footsteps approached.

"Lilianna," Sorin called. "Lilianna, I know you're down here."

The pantry door opened, and Sorin appeared, Lucien in her pocket. Her hair was unkempt, and Lilianna smiled, remembering the many times they snuck out into the forest and practiced curses and spells—a time when things were simpler, but they were also much worse.

"A letter has come for you from your sister," Sorin said, pulling the parchment from her pocket and handing it to Lilianna.

She snatched it, shaking with excitement. Part of her dared not open this in front of Sorin. Until now, Tatiana had always sent Faust to speak with Moloch. What reason could Tatiana have for sending a letter that could be read by someone not meant to see the words?

"Well?" Sorin asked. "Aren't you going to open it?"

"I'm eating," Lilianna said.

"You don't eat food," Sorin muttered, "But nice try."

Lilianna frowned. She sighed, tossing the bitten apple to the ground with a growl. "I'd like some privacy, please."

"I have not told Torenia about the letter," Sorin said, her hand on the doorframe. She paused, mid-step, then looked over her shoulder. "If that letter says what I think it might..."

"Torenia wouldn't hurt Tati," she said, wondering if it was true the moment she spoke the words aloud.

"It's not Tatiana I fear for." Sorin shut the door, secluding Lilianna in the darkness of the pantry.

She tore open the letter, doing a quick scan for Lucien before she unfolded it to reveal the words—Tati's familiar, elegant handwriting, but clearly written in haste. Her heart pounded, as if the traitorous thing wanted to escape her body.

As she read, Lilianna felt more abandoned than she ever had.

Tatiana was going somewhere Lilianna did not know, without leaving an inkling of how to find her. And she expressed fear—fear that Torenia would harm her because Tatiana failed to complete her task.

Tears leaked from her eyes, and she tore the letter to shreds. As she did, she placed each small fragment of parchment into her mouth. Her saliva softened the pieces, and she swallowed them. The words were too much for her to understand right now, so she ate them, devoured them, keeping them all to herself.

She fell asleep in that pantry and was only awoken when the castle grounds shook with the footsteps of a thousand soldiers and the drums of war. Torenia's army was ready.

Disoriented, Lilianna shakily got to her feet. Her stomach twisted —was it hunger? Or were they the secrets inside of her trying to get out? The book in her skirts fell to the ground with a thud, and she remembered—Vera's journal.

She tore it open.

Lili dropped the book and began to heave. She threw up on the floor between the sacks of flour and rice, regurgitating a few strange-looking paper pieces and a bit of old plasma. She needed to warn Torenia before it was too late. As she gripped the door handle, she found that the door would not budge. Her stomach lurched, and her heart sank. Shoving again, she heard something squeak against the door. Wood against wood.

"Don't fight," a familiar voice said through the door. "You will be safer in here."

"Zaina?" Lilianna asked, her voice scratchy with desperation. "Please. Let me out..."

"It's for your own protection," Zaina said through the door. "The war is here—you'll be safe in here. When Torenia finds out what you have done, she won't be able to find you here."

Lilianna listened to Zaina's retreating footsteps and crumpled into a heap. Her new mother was going to get hurt, and it was all her fault.

32

TORENIA

A knock sounded on her bathroom door.

"Enter," Torenia exclaimed, holding Rose Luca's skull, filled with blood. She brought it to her stained lips and sipped. She could feel her great-niece's power filling her.

It was Alexei, and in his hand was a letter. "The children are all dead."

Torenia's lips twitched, and she hid her excitement behind another sip, the macabre goblet obscuring her features. Her blue eyes were locked on Alexei's, urging him to continue.

"Found deceased a fortnight ago, all with black froth on their lips," he told her. "You were right about the girl."

All five Lebedev children were deceased.

She hadn't thought Tatiana had the guts.

Surrounded by candlelight, she basked in the warm blood. Though she bathed in it so irregularly now, there were moments when she knew she must. Before a battle was the ideal time to find as much strength as possible, to adorn herself in youthfulness.

"They are on their way, I presume?"

"Scouts say they will be here by dusk," he said. "They are likely to wait until sunrise, but the castle will not be breached."

"Will they lay siege?" Torenia asked. Alexei's nonchalance with her nakedness and her blood bathing reminded her of Ivan. Roman grew distraught whenever she exposed herself like this, but Ivan would have done anything to have such an opportunity. She briefly wondered why she never bedded Alexei—on the eve of battle was the ideal time to explore such urges.

She let her thoughts fade with the candle smoke. She would never lie with a man again. Adam had disappointed her, Ivan couldn't be bested in bed, and the last one left her with a world of pain.

"No. They came in haste and are ill-prepared. They will not have the means to remain here long. This battle will be short-lived. It is Maksim you should be concerned with."

"Yes," she agreed. "He will prove himself a worthy opponent. And the two remaining Old Bloods—what of them? If their children are dead, surely they will not be in attendance?"

"Our sources say no. After burying their children, there has been no sight of them."

"I will not fight this battle without being certain they will be dead by the end of it." Torenia sat up, placing the goblet on a small table a bit too harshly. It teetered, spilling blood onto the marble floor. "Do your sources say where they are hiding? Cooped up in the castle, alone?"

He nodded. "Yes."

She grinned. "So, I can transfer my consciousness there, slaughter them without interference, and return here in time to enjoy the battle?"

Alexei's lips quirked up. "And if they suspect you are capable of this level of witchcraft?"

"Well, they would be fools if they didn't suspect it," she said with a hint of annoyance. Her fingers drummed against the rim of the bathtub. "I will go with Sorin."

"Good choice," he agreed, handing her a towel.

She gracefully wrapped it around her body and stepped out of the basin. With a bloodied hand, she patted him on the cheek. "You've been nothing but good to me, Alexei. I do hope you survive."

"As do I, *Koroleva*."

"Let Zaina know the plan," she said, leaving the room.

"I've not seen her today," Alexei said. "But I will see to it."

She wore black, as though it were a funeral. Perhaps it was. Practical boots hugged her calves, her bodice was laced up tight, and a long-sleeve blouse shimmered red in the proper lighting. Sorin wore a simple dress that didn't fit tightly, allowing plenty of movement.

Before them was the castle on the outskirts of Krovberg. Smog from the train filled the air, and the dim light from the lanterns gave it a gloomy feeling as a gentle rain began to fall. Torenia looked up at the sky with a smile. The rain hid their footsteps as they neared the Old Blood castle. Very few guards patrolled—likely the ones unfit for traveling.

Rahella landed on the roof up ahead of them. Torenia crept along the edges of the plant-lined path. She slid a dagger from her boot and crept closer to the guard. Sorin mimicked her on the other side, where another one slowly patrolled. When Rahella let out a quork, they acted. Stepping out from her hiding spot, she wrapped her arm around the guard's neck and slit his throat from ear to ear with a quick jerk of her hand.

The rich scent of blood and fear made Torenia's mouth water as she continued up the steps to the front door of the castle. Death didn't come knocking—it came waltzing in. She pushed open the doors and closed her eyes, listening to the sounds around her—distant footsteps, no panic, the gentle rhythm of a heartbeat pumping blood through veins. Opening her eyes, she saw Sorin standing beside her.

"What now?" Sorin asked.

"We kill them all," Torenia replied, a grin creeping up onto her lips. She vibrated with excitement—it had been such a long time since she felt this way. Not since she murdered most of her family. She briefly wondered if Aster felt like this when she killed their parents.

No, she thought, she wouldn't have. She poisoned them like a coward.

"I'd...I'd like to stay here, to keep guard," Sorin stammered.

Torenia withheld a snarl at the younger witch's weakness. She still needed Sorin, and if she was too green to handle a good old-fashioned slaughter, she had to accept that. Not everyone was as immune to it as she was. So many years of bloodshed had numbed Torenia. In reality, she became numb to it the moment her father killed Madame Scarlett. She had to be—she was forced into this life, even if she was built for it.

The world didn't need another Torenia Luca, another Blood Queen. She smiled at Sorin. "That is exactly what I was thinking. Send Lucien if you need me. Rahella will watch over you."

Sorin touched her forearm. "Be careful."

Her concern surprised Torenia. When was the last time someone worried about her well-being?

Blinking, she nodded. "No one has succeeded in killing me yet."

She headed deeper into the mouth of the castle. It was quiet—too quiet. Most of the Lebedev forces were marching on her castle in the north, but some would have remained here to protect the last Old Bloods. With her hand on the railing, she ascended higher into the building. There were no windows here, and she felt safer knowing that daylight could come at any time, and she would not need to worry.

The walls were bare—no art, cobwebs, portraits, or dust. She turned a corner and felt something sharp hit her cheek. With a growl, she recoiled from the attack, her hand darting to her face. Blood dribbled down her cheek. She wiped it away and scowled.

She heard padded footsteps in the hall as a flutter of batwings whipped by her head—Maksim's familiar.

"Torenia Luca," a deep voice filled the empty halls. "You have become predictable."

She licked her lips. The warlock in the flesh.

"Maksim Chernov. Did your mother not teach you how to treat a queen?"

"I was taught to be loyal to those I support. You are not *my* queen."

Torenia withdrew her blade and stepped into the line of fire once again. Makism stood at the end of the hall. He donned all black, and his long black hair blended into his coat. His rich eyes narrowed into slits as he glared right through her. A lesser person might have shuddered from fear.

Torenia shivered in delight.

"I will not allow you to harm them," Maksim stated, flipping a blade in his hand. It glinted in the lamplight.

"I do not wish to harm them," she corrected. "I wish to kill them.

To rid the world of the atrocities they are. I've already succeeded in eliminating their young."

"And for that, you will burn." He stopped flipping the blade and advanced toward her. The lantern went out with a gust, submerging them in total darkness. His footsteps were silent, but Torenia could hear his blood and breath. As he closed in, he lunged for her. She ducked under his arm, evading the blade with ease, and used her own to slice into the back of his thigh, tearing through the leather he wore and drawing blood.

"Perhaps you forgot, Maksim," Torenia growled. "I am a nightwalker."

"And they are Old Bloods," he retorted, humor in his voice.

Torenia's temporary heart skipped a beat as though Sorin's intricate stitches were too tight. Two pairs of feet padded toward her, and she turned just in time to see the last remaining Old Bloods charging. Their hungry mouths opened, revealing their jagged teeth and their beastly faces. They knocked her to the ground, clawing at her viciously. There was no method to their onslaught, just chaos. She felt teeth bite into her shoulder, her arms, and her wrists.

She bucked, but they were too heavy.

They were feeding on her.

She refused to lose her perfectly good, reliable husk to them. Reaching for her blade, she felt the hilt and gripped it tight. With great effort, she plunged the dagger into the side of one of them. A guttural groan filled her ears. These pallid, cave-dwelling monsters were not immune to death, no more than any other nightwalker.

She stabbed the blade into the side of the monster until he retreated. The other backed off, pulling him away from her. As Torenia rose to a crouch, Maksim wrapped his arm around her neck and began pulling her away from the Old Bloods. She gasped and choked, each second drawing in less air. She dug her sharp nails into his arm, but the leather protected him.

She waved her hand with all her strength, calling to the moon to give her power. The lanterns reignited and set the hallways aglow. The two monsters shrieked and shielded their eyes. Torenia, less affected by the light, could now see better. She saw the male Old Blood on the floor, bleeding and twitching, still trying to protect himself from the firelight, which grew brighter by the second. The female cowered, sheltering the dying male.

Maksim dropped Torenia, and she fell back against the hard floor with a thud. The remaining air left her lungs, and she struggled to right herself. Staggering to her feet before she could be attacked again, she backed herself against the wall and listened as the blood flowing through the male Old Blood faded and stopped. A wail from the female filled the room.

"The fate of the Old Bloods is determined. It cannot be changed now," Torenia mocked, spitting blood onto the floor. She withdrew another blade from the inside of her coat. "I could disappear now, and the Old Bloods would eventually die."

"But she is with child," Maksim said as he stepped back to protect the female. "I will not let you harm her."

Torenia scowled. "I will burn this entire *city* down to stop you."

"Go ahead. I will make certain you will burn too—" Maksim turned, hearing something she did not. He looked down at the ground; Lucien came into sight, scurrying across the floor. Maksim cocked his head to the side, then gasped, staggering backward. He clutched at his gut before slowly pulling out a small dagger.

Sorin stepped into the light, another blade in her hands and her eyes on Maksim.

Torenia took control, stepping behind Maksim and growling into his ear as she struck the killing blow. "You've been bested by the Blood Queen—the last mistake you'll ever make was thinking I came here alone."

Blood from his carotid artery sprayed, and he collapsed in a writhing heap, face first. The female Old Blood jerked her head up at the scent, saliva dripping from her mouth. Torenia thought she would go for the dying warlock, but the Old Blood's instincts wanted live prey. She turned, reaching for Sorin.

"No!" Torenia shrieked, stepping over Maksim's body and shoving Sorin hard. The other witch went soaring backward into the wall while the Old Blood grappled with Torenia. Her beastly strength was too much for Torenia—weaponless now, it was all she could do to hold back the gnashing jaws.

A familiar quork filled the small space, and Rahella emerged from the darkness that surrounded them. She went for the Old Blood's face, her talons clawing out the eyes first. Torenia reached her hand up and gripped the torch on the wall, wrestling it from its holder, and swung it in a wide arc into the side of the Old Blood's head. The monster fell to her side, landing atop her dead lover.

She let out a shrill war cry, dropping the torch to the ground. The Old Blood's clothing caught fire, but Torenia wasn't finished. She found her dagger on the floor, blood glittering in the firelight, and plunged it into the female. As she withdrew it, she felt the Old Blood give up. She collapsed into the pile of bodies again, short breaths fluttering in and out of her body.

Torenia stood tall and watched her take her final breath.

"It's done," Torenia said in a whisper. She took a shaky step towards Sorin and helped her stand. The other witch winced, pain filling her eyes. "You'll be alright, Sorin."

Sorin placed a hand on Torenia's shoulder. "Thank you."

"The world will be a much better place without these monsters."

33

ALINA

Her return to the Sisterhood left a sour taste in Alina's mouth. So did fighting a war for Torenia Luca, the Blood Queen.

As they traveled through the mountain ranges, the moon waxed, its pull on the wolves strong, guiding them night and day. They would arrive at the castle by twilight, though the nights were shorter as summer drew near, Alina wished it were the Polar Days so she would not have to see Torenia. She could hole up in her castle while they fought the war for her. It would be better for everyone if she weren't there.

"You look like you're plotting a murder," Birgitte said, sidling up next to her.

"Perhaps I am," Alina responded, a lightness to her voice for Birgitte alone. She smiled fondly at the woman. Her face was far more worn than Alina's, giving her a more mature appearance. It would not be long before the shifts and the moon's pull did the same to her. She longed for it—to appear older, to look stronger. With every passing day, she felt her bones grow stronger. Becoming a witch had given her access to power, but becoming a lycan had given her strength.

Torenia's pathetic excuse of a Sisterhood held no candle to the pack.

Her stoniness did not affect Birgitte, who grinned broadly. She slipped her arm around Alina's shoulders and bumped her head against hers. A throaty growl hummed from her, and Alina found herself reciprocating it. They kept close until Daciana called for them to make camp for the night. Tomorrow, they would be at the Blood Queen's doorstep.

A mountainous cavern housed them for the night, and no glimmer of the oncoming full moon pierced the den. The pack was vast—over forty of them—and all were squashed into the earthen space, warming it with their bodies and the fire flickering in the middle. Some slept soundly, while others were restless as the full moon was so near. There had been a handful of new pack members since Alina, and each of them struggled more than she did with the shift. Perhaps it was her understanding that the world would always be a brutal place that allowed her to accept the pain and lack of control, to submit to it.

"Your thoughts are dark," Birgitte said, gray-blue eyes so different from Red's—not as warm, but less vicious. Despite Birgitte being a lycan, she had never given Alina that power-hungry look that Red once had. It only confirmed her thoughts and fears of the Lucas.

"The eve of war should not be a time for anything else," Alina said quietly. The wolves near her could hear her, but none of them paid any mind. The two women were leaning against the side of the cave, shadows of the other pack members cast upon the walls, flickering in the fire. A reminder of how protected they were.

Birgitte pulled her close, so she was partially on the woman's lap, her back against Birgitte's chest. Their bodies melted into one another, and Alina relaxed. Brigette's hands slipped around her middle, and she rested her chin on her shoulder. Her nose brushed against her ear as she said, "When it is over, we may rest. And you will smile."

"What if..." Alina began, her thoughts trailing off. The words frightened her. She looked to the fire—how many witches had been burned? Would she be next?

"What if...I do this." Birgitte kissed Alina's jaw. "What if...when it is all over, you will be healed."

Alina inhaled the forest scent of her lover. She did not know if Birgitte was right, but she hoped so.

～

198

Alina Nastaca stood under the dying last light of the late spring day. It was warm, but her skin was covered in goosebumps. The moon would rise full tonight, and for three days and nights, they would remain in their wolfish forms. Behind the pack were hundreds of armed soldiers —some vampire, some man—and behind the soldiers stood the dark castle—Torenia's home. It was a place where Torenia had created something good, something to fight for equality of all people—man, woman, witch, vampire. It had once been a place of justice. But a Luca would always be a Luca, and Torenia's desire to be ruthless, to bathe in the blood of innocents, was the bane of her existence.

The bane of her child's.

The castle was a place where Torenia was so destroyed because of a single act; she tore it to shreds and for years became the same unstoppable, blood-thirsty monster she was so desperate to stop.

She was no different from the Old Bloods she hated.

The moon, pale during the day, finally had her time to shine. As the sun finally set, groans of pain rippled through the pack. Daciana was the first to transform, and her kin followed. Every lycan shifted into their beastly form, their cries of pain turning into howls of strength and unity.

The other army approached, their uniformed footfalls now heard by Alina's more powerful ears. Through her paws on the earth, she could feel them marching. But it was one person coming up behind them who made Alina restless. Her hair rose, and her jaws parted, revealing rows of dagger-sharp teeth.

Torenia Luca made her way through the vanguard, where she placed the lycans for their strength, carrying something with her. Alina could smell the stench before she saw it. The coagulated, iron-rich blood.

She stood before all of them, surveying her supporters.

"My friends," she called out to the army, her voice strong and carrying with the winds. "The Old Bloods are dead."

She held up the heads she carried, and the ensuing cheers and uproar were jarring to Alina's sensitive ears.

"Maksim Chernov is dead. But their ignorant armies, who failed to protect them, still march. We could end it quickly, but they must be taught a lesson. Anyone who *dares* support elitists, anyone who *dares* suggest we hide in the shadows because the power we wield is too terrifying for their fragility, must be stopped. Fight this battle with me —stand by me—and I promise the injustice will be stopped. Once their lesson is learned, the world will know of us. Of witches. Of night-walkers. Of lycans."

She waited until the cheers of support died down with a smug look on her face, one so often present. "For so long, they have been afraid of what lurks in the dark, but only as legends. Myths. Slowly, they forget about us. They tear apart the earth so there is no more darkness for us to hide in, no more power for us to draw from. I refuse to be forgotten, cast away as a tale used to frighten children into behaving. I refuse to be pushed into the shadows and become nothing more than lore.

"We will finish this fight, and then we will make sure the entire world knows who we are and what we can do. I will not hand over my power to man." She was breathing hard. "Will you?"

The words crawled beneath Alina's fur and flesh, igniting a fire there. No, she did not wish to watch the earth be taken from her, and she did not wish to be reduced to nothing more than a bedtime story like Blaez had been. But she would not stand behind Torenia Luca, not when she could snap and kill anyone on a whim.

The soldiers cheered, boots stomping, and some of the pack howled.

Then light came over the horizon—the flames of the encroaching army.

34

TORENIA

Torenia walked with the wolves prowling a few yards behind her, a head in each hand. The opposing vanguard appeared—a man on horseback galloping toward her. Two of the wolves—she did not know which—lunged ahead until they were in line with her. They stalked forward on either side of her, growls emerging from their throats.

The soldier, a pawn of the Old Bloods and of Man, approached. He was small and shrouded in well-fitted attire that revealed his slenderness. He had no facial hair, just like the boy they sent to murder Torenia. The young soldier eyed them with distrust.

"For good reason," Torenia muttered to herself, cocking her head to the side and looking up at the soldier. "Those whom you fight for are already dead," she said, throwing the two heads on the ground between them.

The young soldier looked down and jerked back, his horse taking a few steps back, then. He looked back at her with shock and horror. When she offered him nothing more than a wicked smile, he reared back on his horse and galloped toward the army. When he blew his horn, they picked up speed.

"Go for their knees and thighs—they bleed out faster that way," Torenia commanded.

The wolves bounded ahead. Torenia withdrew two curved blades.

Rahella flew nearby—they would fight to the end together, but she did not think this was the end. Two soldiers came for her, their blades raised. Using the Craft to manipulate the earth to uproot them, both soldiers fell to the ground.

As the men tried to stand, Torenia whipped her blade against the throat of the one. The second one looked at her, wide-eyed. There was no time for taunting. She gripped his shoulder, pulled him to her, and clamped her teeth into his throat. When she pulled back, his flesh between her teeth, she smiled and left him to bleed out.

It was not time to feed, but her greatest weapon was what she was. Ruthless. Just like Roman taught her to be.

The battle lasted mere hours before Man's retreat began. The horns blew in frantic, tired breaths. Torenia knew they would not make it far. Though it was nearly the summer, the mountains were brutal any time of year when you were wounded. They would drop like flies, their bones picked clean by the animals who lived there.

A handful of wolves pursued the retreaters, but most pulled together and nudged heads, mourning their fallen.

Torenia stepped over a body she recognized as Alexei. If she had a heart, it would have ached for him. There were other corpses strewn along the earth with chunks of flesh missing and limbs askew. Her taste buds danced, urging her to feed. She was famished, but the sun would rise soon. The safest course of action would be to go back to her castle and feed from the harvest.

Slowly, with the dead pulled aside and the wounded carried with care, Torenia's pawns made their way to the castle toward the promise of warmth, medical attention, and food. She stood at the steps of the Sisterhood.

When she turned, she noticed the witches and the wolves alike waited at the bottom, not following her. Unrest swirled in the air, vibrating through the stone steps. Torenia surveyed the crowd, seeking out Sorin. When she spotted the witch, she beckoned her. Sorin climbed the steps toward the Blood Queen.

Something was wrong, but so long as she could trust Sorin, she would be okay, no matter what happened today. Sorin held her heart, after all, somewhere even Torenia knew not. The woman stood beside her, hands clasped before her, head cocked to the side as she listened, also sensing that something was incredibly wrong.

"Torenia Luca," a voice called, deep and rich. A familiar voice—a Sister. Though her physical form was not visible, her voice echoed through the air. Torenia noticed the shift of the sea of faces. People who fought alongside her only moments ago now stood stony-faced, hatred dripping from their features. "*Koroleva* of the long-destroyed Sisterhood, murderer of children, murderer of kin..."

Gyda's voice came again, this time more solid. "Too long have you reigned with terror over the masses. Today, you stand trial for your crimes."

"Crimes?" Torenia scoffed, searching for Gyda with fire in her eyes. "How have my crimes been any different than yours? Did you not play a part in all of this?" She waved her hand, gesturing to the masses of the dead, the torn-up battlefield.

"This battle was a means to an end. One lineage is down, but another must burn tonight." Gyda's voice came closer, but she was still nowhere to be seen, using the wind and the Craft to shift her voice without giving away her position. It did not go unnoticed that no one within the crowd below was willing to reveal the traitor to Torenia.

So they were all traitors. Torenia now understood why Roman killed people on his side of the board so easily at mere whispers of betrayal, even in jest. She scanned the crowd opposite her and spotted Zaina among the blur of faces. It seemed that there was no honor left anymore.

"You hide behind your fighters while I stand here alone to face your wrath. Gyda, show your face. Or are you afraid?"

Gyda stepped out of the shadows, parting the sea of wolves and bloodied witches. Beside her stalked three lycans—Daciana, her one eye focused on Torenia with hunger, and Alina and Birgitte, walking on all fours close together. Their fur bristled against one another. The four walked as though they were queens, with no shame or fear, proving to Torenia that they were not going to back down. This was planned. A game of strategy was played on both sides, down to the last blood-stained pieces.

Torenia breathed slowly, keeping her composure. It was more

important now than ever before. "Will I receive a true trial? Or will I be murdered like my ancestor, Azalea Luca?" she challenged.

The wolves and the witch continued climbing the stone steps towards her. They stopped out of reach, ensuring their physical safety. Daciana growled low and consistent.

"Because of Azalea Luca," Gyda started, speaking for the wolves, "lycans have been hunted for sport by the witches we seek to destroy. They try to replicate what Azalea Luca created with Blaez Kõiv. In the beginning, her crimes and heinousness seemed like a one-time occurrence, the act of a desperate woman. But with each passing generation of Lucas, evil bloomed. Not all of them were tainted, but most were. None of them, however, were like you. Evil filled you as though you were Azalea's child. As you aged, you proved that you were so much worse than her."

"Worse?" Torenia asked, a delicate eyebrow raised. "Or greater?"

"We are sorry for what happened to you in your childhood and throughout your adult life, as you were pushed and persuaded by the Sokolov brothers. But what you have done can not be forgiven or written off as the fault of those who have wronged you."

"Everyone in my life has wronged me," Torenia snarled. She glared pointedly at Zaina behind them. "The few who did not were murdered. Scarlett Răceanu, stoned to death for helping me survive the evils of my father. Lovers poisoned. And..." Torenia stopped, the ache inside of her choking her. Her head tilted; she could not show these monsters that she was weak. A momentary lapse. "And her."

"We are sorry for the loss of your child," Gyda said, the regret in her voice turning Torenia to ice. "That, we agree, was a step too far."

Torenia snapped her head up, baring her teeth. "*What?*"

Gyda opened her mouth to respond, but Torenia closed the space between them and whipped the back of her ringed hand against her face. The slap echoed in the quiet air. Gyda, though larger and stronger than Torenia, stumbled back a step. She thrust her arms out to regain her balance as blood dripped from her cheek.

"*What did you do?*" Torenia hissed, hands shaking as she reached for the blade at her hip.

As she withdrew it and went for Gyda, ill-prepared for an attack, Birgitte lunged, her jaws open wide. Torenia growled back, slashing the dagger. The blade contacted the beast's face, slicing along her snout. Birgitte missed Torenia, landing with a hard crash against the steps and whimpering as blood gushed from her snout.

She was not dead, but her pride was deeply wounded. The other wolves yipped and snarled, their cacophony making Torenia dizzy. She was heavily outnumbered. She whipped her head to Sorin, who stood off to the side, watching the carnage with wide eyes. They locked gazes, and Torenia thrust her hand at Sorin, urging her to leave the scene. Sorin needed to live if Torenia did not make it through this.

The woman backed away, but she didn't have the time to see if she left the confrontation. While the majority of the wolves closed in, Gyda stood face to face with Torenia. Alina tended to her fallen lover, her tongue lapping the wounds.

Disgusting.

Torenia was a feral animal backed into a cage, with nothing to lose. They were giving her no option but to attack.

"You killed my child," Torenia shrieked at Gyda. Her voice went from high to demonically low. Paranoia and panic settled deep into her bones as she wielded her blade, her free hand subconsciously tugging at her once perfect black hair. Now it was tangled and matted. She spent *years* trying to discover her daughter's murderer.

"Torenia!" Gyda shouted over the growls of the wolves. "Torenia, please listen."

"No!" Torenia raised her lip into a scowl. "No, I will not listen to any of you."

"You were out of control."

"I was in control! I have always been in control!" Torenia snapped. "Only when you murdered her did I lose control. And you base my judgment, the punishment for my crimes, on my reaction to you murdering my daughter?"

Gyda did not answer—she did not have the opportunity—as Daciana lunged up the remaining steps. The Alpha of the pack could easily take Torenia, who was blind with rage.

"Torenia!" Sorin shouted from behind her. "GO!"

Torenia, with her hand on the blade, considered the odds. With a grimace, she swiped the blade towards Gyda right as Daciana completed her lunge. She felt the blade slice into flesh. The wolf closed

in on her, and she shut her eyes, disappearing into thin air. She channeled her energy into Rahella, watching from above as Daciana hit the
ground.

Her forearms snapped, bones jutting out of flesh—meat, blood, fur,
marrow all mingled together. The wolves' howls ignited the air, making
Rahella waver. The animals surrounded their whimpering Alpha,
tending to her.

Gyda dropped to her knees, raising her hands to her throat as the
blood seeped through her fingers. A serene look crossed her face
before she fell, bleeding on the steps.

Rahella flew away from the scene.

35

ALINA

Birgitte snarled at her when the Blood Queen disappeared from the battle. Alina, knowing Birgitte would be fine, straightened her legs and looked up at the horizon. The sun was nearer to them now—Torenia would have to go into hiding. If she barricaded herself inside the castle, there was no way they could penetrate its walls. Even without the support of the witches and the pack, Torenia still had tricks up her sleeve and people who supported her inside the walls. The way she evaporated into thin air suggested to Alina that the Blood Queen would not be so easily found.

Knowing that Birgitte's wounds would heal, she approached Daciana. The pack leader was in far worse shape—with her forearms snapped, she was in agony. Alina could smell the pain. Her blood was rich with it. The pack leader, her fur a deep black and one eye darting around madly, lay on her side. Three other wolves circled close, wanting to assist but knowing they could not—Daciana made it clear she wanted to suffer alone. Alina understood that desire, but suffering with someone beside you made the pain easier to bear.

A handful of witches, all from different creeds, walked around the wolves. It was their turn now. Alina watched as they ascended the stairs, torches in their hands. If they could not find Torenia, they could burn her castle to the ground.

When her eyes spotted movement in the bushes alongside the steps, she cocked her head to the side. The scent was familiar, earthen. Walking a few steps closer, she spotted Sorin. Their eyes locked, and Alina's head dipped. Ever since they left Silvania, Sorin's allegiances had been questionable. Now they were clear as day. Sorin sided with the woman who devoured children, bathed in the blood of the innocent, and slaughtered thousands during her reign.

Alina bared her teeth to show her disgust at Sorin's betrayal.

The woman she once called her sister disappeared into the night, using Torenia's cunning tricks to save her skin.

Alina whipped her head around as she sensed a presence behind her, but she relaxed when she saw it was Helga. She bore the expression of someone who carried too much weight. Deep-set lines in her face and a sadness in her eyes revealed her love for Gyda. Her loss was a tremendous one.

She crouched before Alina and moved her hands to speak with her. *You know what you must do?*

She referred to the task placed upon her when she bonded herself by blood with Torenia Luca—a bond strengthened by her bond with Red. A bond that began so long ago that it seemed a distant memory. Alina nodded at Helga, her eyes flickering to Gyda's body. Someone had moved her so that she rested lengthwise on a step, on her back, hands folded over her chest. She would be given a proper funeral.

Alina turned her back on Gyda. It was a crime, witches killing witches. Sisters killing Sisters. Only one more had to die before there would be balance again. Alina knew it in her heart. But what it meant for her—the sacrifice that she had to make to create this balance— took her breath away. She lowered her beastly head and began to pant.

Following the scent of the witches who had ascended earlier, she saw someone had lit the castle on fire. Multiple windows burst, with flames pouring from their gaping maws.

"Down with the Blood Queen!" Someone shouted, echoed by hundreds. The air filled with the words like a chant. Their chant drew the powers of the earth and above them, the retiring moon. With the blood inside of Alina, she harnessed the power of all three forms of the Craft, willing it to do her bidding.

"Down with the Blood Queen," she thought, adding her voice to the chant. Giving it more power.

When the castle was ablaze, Alina knew it was time. The massive building that had stood ominously for so many years, housing some of the world's worst people, was crashing down. The power was stripped away from it, stripped from Torenia, as the people took it back. No longer would they be ruled by her. The world was shifting, and people wanted change. They no longer wanted rulers above them.

But politics and rulers made no difference to her cause. Alina simply agreed with what she once read about bloodlines harboring a power too strong to break from. The Lucas needed to be snuffed out. Though she loved Red, her death was the second-to-last piece.

Torenia's was the last.

The night sky filled with thick, black smoke, obliterating the stars. What would have been a beautiful spring night would be the end of Alina's life. Thankful for its beauty, Alina walked toward the flames. While the others around her were beginning to back up, she persevered.

To say she was not terrified would be a lie.

The crowd noticed her, one by one, and their silence was louder than the castle burning down. As they began to chant, hum, and sing for her, she felt their power extend to her. It gave her courage of sorts to face death, knowing what it meant for those behind her. For all those who came after her.

As she got closer, the heat began to hurt. Not yet within the reach of the flames, she winced as her eyes became dry and pained. How many witches before her died this way—not by choice, but by force? The number was too high to know for certain.

May she be the last.

The massive entrance had not yet fallen, and she entered the flames through the front door, the fire now licking at her, singeing her fur. She yelped, her muscles trying to force her to back out, but she pushed through. With a final leap, she allowed herself to be engulfed in the flames. All she heard as the fire consumed her was the howls of her kin and Birgitte's deep, mournful cry.

She hoped that when she suffered their bonded fate, Torenia would know she betrayed her.

36

TORENIA

Rahella sat atop the grave marker, her head bowed. The familiar watched her witch drop to her knees, digging furiously at the previously upturned earth. She dug even as her nails snapped in half and as her tears soaked through the dirt, staining her face with streaks. She dug as she shrieked in panicked frustration and betrayal. When she reached the small black coffin, she knew. She knew the body had been desecrated in death. How dare they. How dare they be the ones to murder her child, then dig up her body.

A throaty wail ripped free as she tore away at the coffin lid. The skull was gone. Torenia sank into the backs of her calves, her filthy hands staining her trousers and blouse. She let herself sob and heave, releasing emotions built up over many decades. She thought she might never stop. What she presumed to be true was fact, and what she feared would come to pass.

Blood magic.

But who, Torenia wondered as she wiped the tears from her eyes with filthy hands, would have given these traitors her blood? She thought of Vera, her missing maid. She thought of Zaina, who had been on the opposite side of the field. Perhaps they all had a hand in it, waiting until she was vulnerable to blindside her. But only one person had access to these parts of her, only one person knew how to hurt her like this.

"Torenia," Sorin's voice would have once been soothing. Now, it made anger rise up in her chest.

"You!" Torenia shrieked, getting to her feet. She slapped Sorin hard across the cheek. "You betrayed me!"

"I would never," Sorin replied quickly, not holding her cheek or crying out. The wide eyes and shock were not from the slap but the thought of betrayal. Something bent in Torenia. Somehow, she knew Sorin was not lying.

"Did you tell *anyone?*"

"No." Sorin stood stock still, her head high. A mirror of Torenia once.

Not anymore, she reflected sourly. Covered in dirt, reduced to tears, she was no longer *Koroleva*. She was not a queen—or if she still was, she was the queen of nothing.

As she glanced at the smoke and fire in the distance, she felt everything seep out of her. Gone. Everything she had, everything she had worked for and fought for, was gone. Just as Roman's empire fell due to his need to control his brother, Torenia's empire fell due to her need to remain beautiful. But vanity was not her only crime.

"May the choices you make be the right ones, Sorin." Torenia echoed the words Alina once spoke to Sorin. Two ends of the sword— which choices would be the right ones for Sorin? Would she follow Alina's move to end her reign, or would she make the decision to bring her back when this was over?

Torenia would not know until the time came.

"I must ask if this is what you really want." Sorin spoke the words carefully, considering them before they left her lips. She was uncertain—Torenia could taste it. She had seen betrayal before, and it was dancing within Sorin. She did not think she intended to betray her. Was she wondering if the others were right? That the others knew better? Surely, the masses could not be wrong. She was giving Torenia a way out of this. To never live it over again.

Torenia realized she could not trust Sorin. She would be warped by the others, convinced that this was for the best. She would accept that Torenia was dead, leaving the heart hidden somewhere. Or maybe she would dig it up, roll it around in her hands, assess just how black it was, and wonder how it became such charcoal. Then she would crush it or burn it in flames. Sorin, Torenia knew now, would make the choice her friend wished for her.

"Perhaps death would be the best option," Torenia said. A flash of white caught her eye, but she didn't show that she had seen it. Her last chance, she realized, was hiding behind a tree, listening. Torenia raised her voice so the young witch hiding behind the tree could hear her. "You, Sorin, have my heart. Keep it locked away, burn it, revive me... I leave this in your hands."

"My decision is not made."

Torenia smiled, her whole body feeling weak and deflated. "I've had *everything* taken from me, even that which was dearest to me. Perhaps I deserved it, but she didn't. My Lilith didn't. I want you to promise me something, Sorin."

Sorin waited with a stoic expression that made Torenia proud despite the circumstances.

"Take all the information—gather every last drop of it—before you make any decision. Determine facts from lies. Then, Sorin, you make your decision."

"You speak as though you will die tonight," Sorin noted.

Torenia smiled wanly. "I am confident in that fact. Alina has successfully connected the two of us through Blood Magic, which I could have altered if I'd had the time. Enhanced by Moon Magic, I am at her mercy—what happens to her happens to me. We are bound by blood. I do not know how she obtained my blood or how she stole my daughter's bones. Zaina, Vera, Gyda. They knew exactly what to do. Tell me, will your friend do what needs to be done to end it all?"

A sad look crossed Sorin's face, her stoic gone. "Without question."

Then, as if her confirmation was what set it into motion, Torenia felt the warmth. It crept up through her fingers, from her toes up her legs. Her face began to sweat. She cast one last sympathetic smile at Sorin before her body was engulfed in flame. Her screams of pain were nothing compared to her cries while unearthing her child. She dropped to her knees, and she felt peace washing over her. The fire was purifying her, and though she could not stop crying out as she collapsed, she was finally at rest.

Sorin watched it happen, her expression filled with sadness and horror. Torenia had no idea what would become of her.

The white flash in the woods disappeared, and Torenia's last thought was hope that Lilianna would be the one to save her.

37

LILIANNA

Lilianna knew that Torenia spoke these words to her, sheltered in the shadows of the thin trees surrounding the cemetery. Someone had let her out of the pantry, where Zaina had locked her in when the fires were devouring the castle. Now, in the cemetery with smoke blotting out the dawn, the air smelled of freshly disturbed soil —the scent of worms and bugs—with a subtle essence of death. The words were spoken to Sorin, but they were meant for her. Because Torenia knew that Lilianna would not leave her this way.

As she lurked, still hidden in the shadows, her distrust for Sorin grew as Torenia spoke. Lilianna tried to calculate what move to make next. Torenia spoke as though she knew she was going to die. It shredded Lili's insides and took everything in her to not call out to her, to go to her, to nestle in her arms and remind Torenia that she had another child.

Anger bubbled up into her throat then. Torenia lost her child, but a child could be replaced. Children died all the time—at birth, in their first year of life. Lilianna was not enough, but she promised herself she would be. She had to work harder than a *real* daughter. The natural bond between mother and child was strong, so Lilianna had to do more to earn her place. In that moment, she decided to take Torenia's guidance, find the heart she spoke of, wherever it may be, and bring her back. Only then would she be truly worthy of being her daughter. It all made sense now. She had to give Torenia life, just as a child gave a mother a reason to live.

"I am confident in that fact. Alina has successfully connected the two of us through the use of Blood Magic, which I could have altered if I'd had the time. Enhanced by Moon Magic, I am at her mercy—what happens to her happens to me. We are bound by blood. I know not how she obtained my blood or how she stole the bones of that which I loved most. Zaina, Vera, Gyda. They knew exactly what to do. Tell me, will your friend do what needs to be done to end it all?"

Torenia's words sent chills down Lilianna's spine. Guilt ripped through her—the missing blood from her wardrobe. Vera had left the note, and Zaina had confirmed Lili's hand in all this. There was no denying that this was her fault. Lili brought her hands to her mouth, hiding her horror.

The people she once trusted with her life were all back-stabbing liars, yes, but it was she who was Mama's downfall. Lilianna crouched down, her fingers digging into the soft earth.

She wanted to attack Sorin. She wanted to kill anyone who tried to harm Mama.

But before she could do anything, Torenia caught fire. Her terror-filled screams ripped through the spring fog, and the air filled with the scent of burning flesh and charred hair. The grotesque sight of Torenia, a beacon of beauty, burning like that was, despite everything Lilianna had seen, impossible for her brain to process.

The screaming ebbed, and Torenia's body lay smoldering, blackened.

Something in her snapped then. Up until that moment, she was certain Torenia would escape her fate as she had done hundreds of times before. But she accepted it with a cold smile. But Lilianna refused to accept it. She lunged from the trees, tripping over her feet and falling to the dirt. She crawled towards Torenia's body and wept, shrieking so loud that everything else was silent to her.

When Sorin approached, her lips moving but the words not

reaching Lilianna's ears, she slashed at her with filthy fingers. They could do no damage as her nails were chewed down to the quick, but her teeth could. Ferocity filled her, and she threw herself at Sorin—she needed someone to blame for all this. It could not be *all* her fault. It was too heavy a burden to bear.

"Lilianna!" Sorin shouted, shoving her away and recoiling from her fangs. "Lilianna, stop!"

"You killed her!" Lilianna shouted, blinded by rage. "You killed her!"

"I did no such thing." Sorin smacked Lilianna so she stumbled, tripping over Torenia's body and landing in the shallow grave. Sorin stared down at her. "I did not want her to die, Lilianna. Perhaps it is for the best."

"No!" Lilianna shrieked but stayed where she was in Torenia's daughter's grave. She curled up inside of it, tucking in on herself and regressing further. "Not the best. No."

"Come with me, away from all this," Sorin said softly, extending her hand. But Lilianna did not take it. Instead, she shut her eyes, pretending to be dead and awaiting dirt to be tossed onto her body, where it would settle, and the worms and maggots could begin their feast. Their beautiful dance of decay.

Lilianna refused to respond, her body rigid and stiff as she shut out everything around her, and Sorin eventually left. Alone at last with only the cold as a companion, Lilianna wondered if she would die here. It would be poetic. People would write about it when they found Mama's—the Blood Queen's—body, with a child so dedicated to her that she died when Torenia did.

Some time had passed, her muscles stiff and taut, when Lilianna felt a tug inside her—the gentlest of pulls, a wisp that guided her heartstrings. When she opened her eyes, she noticed the lightness of the sky and realized the sun had long since risen, and the smoke was clearing. The smoke from the castle was still clouding the air, making it look like the end of days, but there was no denying the sun was waiting to claim her.

If she died, Torenia would remain dead. So, Lilianna broke from her cocoon and reached a hand out of the grave, pulling her small body from it. She had scarcely the energy to rise to her feet, so she clambered hand over hand towards Torenia. Placing a dirty hand onto Torenia's blackened body, she whispered, "Don't worry, Mama, I'll help you."

She didn't know how to help her. She did not know where she would find the heart hidden somewhere in this big wide world. She had forgotten much of the Craft in recent years, and she was uncertain if she was even still a witch. Leaving the grave behind, leaving the Blood Queen behind, Lilianna staggered through on tired feet, ignoring the sticks and rocks that cut them open, and swiftly sought out shelter. She could not help Torenia if she too were dead, burned to ash.

38

SORIN

Sorin and Lucien watched as the castle turned to ash, just like its last inhabitant. She felt the loss, too, the ache in her heart for having nothing but her familiar. She knew Alina was gone, had watched her wolfish form walk into the fire, and she never got the chance to say goodbye. Never had the opportunity to make up with her friend. In the end, they could not even be considered friends, not with such conflicting choices. Alina had accepted that the Lucas were evil and the bloodline needed to be wiped out, as some strange acceptance of what happened to Red. That it was her blood that made her the way she was—that her death was necessary.

Sorin understood it on a certain level but wondered where it left the rest of them. Influence played a role, too, did it not? Torenia's manipulation worked on Lilianna—perhaps too well—and on Sorin, too. However, she thought she did not see it as manipulation. She sought power, knowledge, and protection. Torenia gave her that.

As she studied the heap of ashes, the broken throne still standing despite the blaze, Sorin realized this was what power led to. In other parts of the world, a new era was beginning—it was the turn of the century. She wondered what new form of power would fill the void that was created. People would always fight for—and against—power. Sorin had washed her hands of that desire.

She had enough power from the earth. Soaking it up whenever she could, she could grab what she needed or let it rest when needed. The Earth and the Moon were always balanced. It was when blood spilled that things became uneven.

She felt eyes on her.

Hearing growls and the yipping of wolves made the hair on the back of her neck stand on end, and goosebumps rose along her arms. Turning, she saw a cluster of them looking at her, padding up the stairs and around her to form a vicious circle of teeth and claws. Sorin was one of the Blood Queen's pawns in their eyes. The wolves did not know what was going on within her, and there was a need for a quiet life after this bloodshed. They did not care, and she knew words would not convince them.

They wanted blood. Every last thread of the Blood Queen's reign had to be cut.

Her fingers curled, untrimmed nails digging into her palm flesh. With Alina gone, there was no one to try to reason with. Sorin did not want to leave on poor terms with the pack. To be better than Torenia, she had to try at least.

"She is gone," Sorin called out loudly, keeping her voice as steady as she could manage. "Let those of us who wish to mourn. I accept what has been done."

A snap of teeth and a collective growl from the wolves told her there was no reasoning with them. She wondered sourly if there would ever be more to this world than fighting and scrambling for power. Would it ever be a peaceful place where there were no wars?

From what she saw through her jarring life, the answer would surely be no.

Before the wolves could rip her apart, Sorin and Lucien disappeared. Never before had she transferred her consciousness with her familiar. She clutched onto him when her physical form disappeared, and she flew through nearby creatures that accepted her consciousness momentarily. With all her might, she kept hold of Lucien, but along the way, she no longer felt him. No longer felt his thoughts and consciousness beside hers. Her mind was being flipped through too rapidly. She did not know where she had lost him, and when she appeared where she needed to be, there was nothing in her hands but blood.

A whimper escaped her lips, and she called for him, despite knowing in her heart that he was gone. Trembling, she fought back the desire to cry, her body quivering violently. Lucien was the only one who stuck with her from the beginning—he was hers. She was supposed to take care of him, as he took care of her. A part of her was severed as she leaned over her bent legs and placed her forehead against the dirt.

Under her breath, she muttered, "*Vale amor.*"

A dense fog filled the air around her over the next hour, and when Sorin finally stretched out from her broken position, she felt its chill on her flesh. The low, white clouds around her were so thick that she could see them swirling all around her when she moved. Rising slowly, Sorin noticed the birch trees around her, the moss growing on them thick and rich with life. Foliage beneath her crunched as she turned and wondered where she was. In her panic about finding Lucien in the transfer, she did not know where she ended up. When she left Osleka behind, she did not know where she was headed; she only knew that she needed to escape.

The fog billowed and opened around her, a path forming through the woods, weaving back and forth. With a broken heart, Sorin wiped Lucien's blood onto her skirts and followed the path.

39

TATIANA

Valentin worked on the house while Tatiana reached out to those in the community, offering her skills in any way possible. She began with simple things like childminding and basic healing without any use of the craft. In a town known for burning one of the most notorious witches on the continent, she was not going to be hasty in revealing what she was. A smart witch tested the waters before diving in.

As she set her roots in Ocleau, letting them spread and grow underneath the surface, Tatiana earned a name for herself. She found herself accepted in this town and began to realize that this place was where she would be grounded. Though she once thought she would want to see the whole world, her ideals changed. She had made a life of her own here.

"If you aren't producing enough, drink this," Tatiana told the woman who was struggling to breastfeed her newborn. Tired and achy from the birth itself, the woman was already having a hard time. This was her first child, and her husband had been missing for two weeks now. All she had were people like Tatiana and other neighbors who brought food and helped with tending to the land and animals.

"And if this young lad doesn't start gaining weight, you'd best let me know. End of the week, if he hasn't fattened up, I'm the first to know, alright?" She held the infant, supporting his head and gauging how heavy he was. Too small for a baby born a month ago. "I'll have to put a spell on him."

"You sound like tales of the old witch who haunts the forest," she said with an out-of-breath chuckle.

Tatiana handed the baby back, then began to pack up her satchel. She took it from Valentin so she could masquerade as a professional midwife rather than a witch posing as one. Over her shoulder, she replied with an airy lie, "I'm unfamiliar with the tale."

"Yes, right, you are new here," she breathed. She shifted the infant from one breast to the other. "Legend says a powerful witch once lived here, and that, though she was put to trial and burned at the stake, her power still lives on. No one goes into the woods alone, and no one goes into them after dark, even if they don't believe such things."

"Perhaps they are not so silly, these cautionary tales. I come from a town where the woods were also haunted, not by witches, but by a Wolf. They all hold some stock, though—these fears. Our fear of the dark or the woods, of snakes or of spiders—they all rise from something." Tatiana thought of her old home, a shudder rippling through her. The monsters were the ones in the town, not the Wolf. Not Blaez.

"You're very strange, Tatiana," the woman uttered, but not unkindly. "But you are good with children, something I know the witch that haunts the woods was not. Rumor has it, she killed her own daughter for some spell."

"Unfathomable," Tatiana concluded, though she knew some parents did not truly love their children. Then, she put on her black cloak and headed to the door, gathering her skirts. "Now, one week, and if he has not put on some weight, you come straight to me."

"Tatiana, I don't know where you live," she said.

She smiled, knowing something on her face was reminiscent of Azalea Luca, Torenia Luca, Rose Luca, and all the witches in between who were drawn to this power inside them that came from the earth. "The old house deep in the woods. I believe the former owner was the very witch who haunts this place."

～

By the time Tatiana made it through the unkempt path towards her home, her feet ached. Her slightly swollen belly already tired her, and she sighed with relief when she saw the house. An unusual fog for this time of year had crept into the nooks and crannies of the forest and left her unsettled. Hands roving to her belly, she cradled it protectively.

Relief flooded through her when she saw Valentin at the door. His hand was gripping the doorknob, but his eyes were on the woods—he was looking out at something frozen where he stood. The crunch of the gravel under Tatiana's feet made him shift ever so slightly, acknowledging her. He nodded his head toward the woods, and Tatiana turned to follow his gaze.

She saw nothing. "What is it?"

Valentin pointed into the forest, but it was black as pitch between the trees now; the fog made it impossible to see anything. Tatiana wondered when it got so dark; it had not been too late when she left the woman's house. When something shifted in the dark, Tatiana swore she saw eyes.

"Tatiana, get in the house," Valentin said, his voice steady, but Tatiana knew he was worried.

There was something familiar about those eyes. "No, it's alright, Valen."

"Tat—"

"Valentin, please go inside."

He obeyed after a brief hesitation, shutting the door to let Tatiana deal with whatever was crawling to their doorstep. It was her job to use whatever power she could to unearth what was coming for them. Tatiana's heart lurched when she saw the movement again. She hoped desperately that her sister had returned home, so she walked down the stairs of the porch and tentatively called, "Lili? Lilianna, is that you?"

Whatever was stirring in the woods ceased moving. With a gust of bravery, fueled by both motherly and sisterly love, Tatiana crossed the short backyard through the gardens and walked to the fringes of the forest. It was hard to see through the fog, and she had to squint just to catch a glimpse again of the shape only a few meters away. Closer now, despite the darkness, Tatiana saw with a sinking heart that it was not Lilianna.

Instead, it was another familiar face. "Sorin..."

The woman who once brought a coven of witches up from nothing taught them that they held magic in the palms of their hands if only they learned how to channel it. The woman who protected them fiercely when she was not obligated to do so. The woman who tried to lead them to a safer place. She once looked so strong and held her head so high, but now she was covered in dirt and scratches, and there was days-old blood caked onto her filthy hands and matted in her hair.

Sorin Nabita was a mess, but Tatiana approached her slowly with her hands extended to show that she meant no harm, like one would approach a skittish stray or a spooked horse. She looked her age now, older than all the others of the once close-knit coven, now torn apart within the short span of a few years.

Reaching her, Tatiana gently grabbed Sorin's hands. She flinched at the touch but then seemed to melt into it. "Come," Tatiana said, guiding her toward the house. "Let's get you cleaned up."

She spoke words that she should, words that were expected of someone taking care of someone broken, someone fragile. But the question hanging on the edges of her closed lips was, "Where is my sister?"

Once Sorin was inside, she seemed to come back to herself. Glancing around at the house, it appeared from the flash of recognition that she knew where she was. Her wide brown eyes bore into Tatiana, asking her the question without speaking the words.

Tatiana nodded. "Something brought me here—I cannot explain it..."

"Yet I understand it." Sorin's first words were low.

Tatiana brought over a kettle of hot water, pouring it into a bowl with a cloth. Wringing out the cloth and grabbing a chunk of soap, she cleaned up her old friend. Sorin accepted this by remaining still, only flinching when Tatiana touched a wound—a scratch from a stray branch or a cut from falling onto sharp rocks. Whatever her journey here, it appeared as though Sorin traveled for a long time on foot without ceasing. When Tatiana reached her feet, removing her tattered boots, she saw how raw they were—calloused in some spots and blistered in others.

Sorin would recover with a few nights of good rest, food in her belly, and a roof over her head. There was more than enough space to house her. Tatiana wondered what would come after and allowed herself to hope that whatever power had drawn them both here would bring her sister home.

Only when Sorin was in new clothes, a blanket draped over her, and a steaming hot cup of tea in her hands did Tatiana realize Valentin was there. She hurried to him. "She is an old friend."

This eased his mind, and he ducked outside to busy himself so Tatiana could catch up with Sorin and hopefully find answers about her sister. Once Valentin was outside, Tatiana sat in front of Sorin and placed her hands in her lap.

Sorin said, "Tati, you're with child."

Tatiana nodded, but it seemed like trivial information compared to whatever Sorin knew. The events that unfolded after Tatiana and Valentin fled. "Tell me everything," Tatiana commanded gently. "Is Lilianna...?"

"I could not convince her to leave with me."

Tatiana bowed her head and withheld a sigh. "Let's start from the beginning of the end. How did you go from Torenia's right hand to...to this? How did you end up here?"

Sorin never met her eyes when she told the story from the moment Tatiana left. She told her everything—the attempted assassination, Lilianna's change, the war, the betrayals, Alina's death, the end of Torenia's reign, her child who was murdered. This particularly made Tatiana wince.

"So she is dead?" Tatiana asked quietly. The tea was cold, and the fire was dying. "And my sister..."

"Torenia is dead, for now. Alina must have bonded with Torenia through powerful magic—her death triggered Torenia's. Your sister was wrought with grief, almost as though she believed herself to be the cause. I tried to get her to come with me, but she refused. I—I don't know what happened to her."

Tatiana had to accept this. But there was one thing that Sorin said that she could not understand. "What do you mean 'for now'?"

Sorin sighed, eyes cast down. "We took out her heart and replaced it so that..."

"So that she could be brought back if she was killed," Tatiana replied with horror.

When the words filled the air, there was a pulse, like a heartbeat of power.

❧

They lit a fire in the woods to commemorate the losses, both those that were known, such as Alina's, and those that were speculated, like Lilianna's. Tatiana always thought she would know the moment her sister died—that she would feel it in her heart—but now she was uncertain. She learned that sometimes, one simply didn't get the answers to certain questions. It bristled uncomfortably under her skin, and though she would never stop hoping for her sister's return, she accepted that she might never know.

She and Sorin had put off this funeral for some time. Getting Sorin settled in the village and Tatiana giving birth set them back. Now, enough time had passed that it was less of a painful moment of grief, but one of moving on. Moving forward.

Odette—Tatiana and Valentin's daughter—was wrapped in a warm blanket and pressed against Tatiana's body. Her brown hair kept her head warm in the November night. A light dusting of snow had fallen the previous night, signaling the approach of the winter solstice.

The carefully constructed pyre burned with crackles and pops, fighting back the creeping cold.

"What became of your familiar?" Sorin asked.

Tatiana looked to the sky, adjusting Odette. "For a long time, I neglected the part of myself that was a witch. For as long as we live, they live. A moth lives just shy of a year. Faust lived many years. Torenia's familiar lived as long as she did—likely ten times its own lifespan. I believe I was not harnessing enough of my power to keep him alive. For that, I am deeply regretful."

Sorin nodded, and Tatiana thought she saw a flicker of anger in her eyes. She knew how Lucien died was heart-wrenching—it was likely Sorin would never fully recover from that. It was like losing a part of oneself.

"I must ask you something, Sorin, and I do hope you will be honest with me." Tatiana paused, but Sorin made no motion to respond, so she carried on. "You helped Torenia become immortal. Have thoughts of reviving her crossed your mind?" She tried to keep her voice neutral, but her worry made itself known with a gentle shake. Tatiana, after all, had a daughter to care for. A daughter she did not want subjected to the horrors that they faced in their lives. And that included the Blood Queen.

Sorin stared into the flames. Was she thinking about who was dead, who the pyre was burning for, because of Torenia Luca?

"At the time, yes. Now? There has been too much blood spilled for her life and for her death. It is better off this way."

Tatiana nodded, pulling Odette closer to her. She believed Sorin's words to be true. They were no longer kids who played at the Craft in the Mørke forest—not that Sorin was a kid when she arrived in Silvania. Despite everything they had gone through—the different sides they stood on, the evil they had done—things were returning to something that could be considered normalcy. A simple life with a hint of the Craft. It was all either of them wanted. The power that surged here was undeniable—the strongest either of them had felt—and it would surely draw others.

"More will come," Sorin said, as though reading Tatiana's thoughts.

"And we shall teach them," Tatiana replied. "I have no doubt my daughter will have it within her. She will not follow the path blindly, but with guidance. Every witch has a voice and a story to tell. So let them flock here; let them gather around this undeniable power. Let us rise together, rather than divide ourselves as the others did. Torenia, Gyda, Helga, Alina, Red... Let all this end with unity."

"How will we guide them?" Sorin inquired.

"We are the ones with history now—we are the ones who can guide." Tatiana shifted Odette, who began to stir. "If what they said about the Luca curse rippling through generations was true, that all of them needed to be wiped out for what was in their blood, then we must raise our children differently. We must raise them with unconditional love for *each other,* not for power. If we let the Craft take control, we will be no different than Azalea, Torenia...Red."

Tatiana shifted Odette and pulled a thick book out of her satchel. "I believe Alina left this for me."

"Alina? But she is dead."

"Yes," Tatiana said, hardly a lie, yet it still felt wrong. "It must have been before the war. She must have known what she would have to do."

Sorin nodded to the book. "What is it?"

"The history of the witches hunting down the Luca family to kill them, believing that it was Azalea Luca's tainted blood that made them evil. Much of it is them trying to have Torenia murdered, but she was too powerful and well-protected in her stronghold. Generations passed, each new one wanting the same thing. After I read it, I asked myself, are they better or worse than her?"

"What are you suggesting?" Sorin said, looking at the book and taking it from Tatiana's hands. She flipped it over, opened it, and studied the words. Tatiana reached for it, and Sorin handed it back. There were pages at the very end that Tatiana swore no one would lay eyes on.

"It makes me wonder... The family was cursed with intergenerational hatred, among other things. When Azalea killed her daughter, it broke something in her, and thus, in everyone who followed after her in that line. But did the hatred of others create evil? Cause and effect —perpetuating evil creates evil? I have asked myself these questions many times," Tatiana said.

"Have you received an answer?"

"No," Tatiana replied with a hint of laughter. "There is no one to answer. I believe my purpose is to ensure it doesn't happen again. That my daughter will be raised with the Craft—should she want to—and see other witches not as the enemy. Never the enemy. Only as those to learn from and grow with."

"You were always meant to be a mother."

"I hope so," Tatiana said.

Quiet, they watched the fire again. Odette was now awake, her green eyes studying the source of the heat. She looked around, curious. And as though she felt the power here too and understood the meaning of the pyre, she remained quiet yet alert. Tatiana knew then that her child was imbued with power like they were.

"Burn it," Sorin said after a few minutes of silence. The sky was dark now, clear and filled with stars.

Tatiana looked down at the book in her hands. *A Brief History of Witches*, as told by various voices. It was an ugly history. Was it best to burn it to shield the new generation from the violence, hatred, and ugliness? To trust in the old ways of storytelling to convey the importance of history? Could it be trusted? Would their words be twisted and changed, and thus, history would repeat itself? She looked down at her daughter as the questions ran through her active mind.

"Burn Torenia's heart, and I will burn the book. Then we will wipe our hands clean of the blood and the ashes of our fallen sisters. We will bring forth a generation that lifts up, not tears down."

"So be it," Sorin agreed.

The heartbeat pulsed faster.

40

LILIANNA

She lived underground. Every time the sun began to rise, she dug herself a grave and buried herself half in dirt and half in foliage. Enough to breathe, enough to be hidden from the sun's vicious, fatal rays. But she was getting closer. Every single night she walked until her feet bled, her muscles shaking violently from the never-ending journey. There was scarcely anything left of her, for she fed on small animals while she traversed the forest's terrain. Her hair was knotted and tangled, filled with filth. Only one thing ran through her mind, over and over like the heartbeat that drew her in.

Mama, mama, mama.

The power grew stronger every night of travel. It lulled her to sleep as she hid in the cold dark earth, like Mama telling her a story. Singing her a song.

She forgot her name.

Weeks went by.

Months.

This time, when the night came and the little crescent of a moon leered down at her like a wicked grin, she knew she would find Mama's heart. It was so near—that pulse, that *thump, thump, thump* that drew her closer every night. Crawling out of her den, she shifted the dirt from her body and hobbled along. Her senses flickered when she heard something nearby, and she froze as though she were prey. But she was a predator, not prey. The critter nearby stopped moving as well, sensing her in return.

Her foot shifted in the dirt; then, she spotted it in the dark. A squirrel clung to the bark of a tree, tail flickering once, twice. She crept toward it and yanked it by its thin body from the tree. The animal writhed in her hands, but she had a firm grip on it, both hands grasping its writhing, frantic torso. She sank her teeth into it, half its body in her mouth as she sucked on its blood. It was mere seconds before it was empty, and she was left with only a taste, a tease that reminded her how empty her stomach was.

What was her name?

Thump, thump, thump.

Crawling now on hands and feet, as though she never learned to walk upright, she launched her body through the woods. Seeking out that heart. She quivered with excitement as it grew so loud that it deafened her to everything else. All she could focus on was that heart, so she followed it for the final time.

Lili.

Lilith.

Yes, that was it.

Freezing when she realized she was right on top of it, she jerked with excitement. Then, just as she had done every night before, as though it was preparing her for this momentous event, she began to dig. Fiercely, she dug with her bare hands. They bled and bled, but that was what you gave for love, right? You bled for those you loved, yes.

She did not notice the two witches and infant child just through the trees in a small clearing. Her grunting and panting were loud but not as loud as the heart. It beat faster now, harder. It was exciting— salvation was so close. As she dug, she found it. Smooth ribcage bones snapped what was left of her nails off when she dug carelessly. The nubs of her fingers were so cold she barely felt the pain. Her mind no longer registered that type of thing.

There it was.

Thumpthumpthump.

She reached her hand in between the ribs and gripped the black heart. She felt it beating inside her gently clasped hand. Raising the heart, she could barely see it with nothing but the starlight. It began to glow orange, as though coming alive. But it already was alive—she felt it beating inside of her hands.

"Oh!" Someone shrieked behind her. "Sorin, take her—that's Lilianna!"

Lilianna.

A shuffle behind her made her turn. Brief recognition crossed her mind, but an irrational thought told her she did not know these people, these strangers who approached her. She growled at them, flashing her fangs. Suddenly, she remembered how *hungry* she was. Her free hand lashed out at the woman approaching her, but her fingernail-less hands were not a threat to anyone.

"Lili, it's me, Tatiana. Your sister," the woman said.

Lies.

Hungry.

"Put it down, okay, Lilianna? Put it down, and we'll get you cleaned up," she told her. Then she turned around and said to the other woman. "Take Odette back home. Valentin will know what to do."

The other woman protested, but the one called Tatiana barked the order in a tone that one dared not question. The woman left with the infant, leaving Tatiana alone with her.

"Do you not remember me?" Tatiana asked, tears in her eyes visible by the torch she held. They glittered orange, shadows dancing on her cheeks. "Lili, I can't believe you're alive. Please...please say you remember me. I'm so sorry I left you."

"Lilith," she growled.

Tatiana's face dropped. She impaled the end of the torch in the soft ground, where it leaned to one side but remained upright. Then, she got down low, approaching her slowly, hands extended.

"So hungry," she growled this time, making Tatiana freeze.

"We can find you something to eat. Just put the heart down, Lili...Lilith."

She looked at the heart in her hands, blinking at it as though just remembering it was there. Her tongue darted out against her dry, chapped lips. Her stomach churned, and she sank her teeth into the heart. Blood filled her mouth and she sucked it in, chewing to make it gush.

Thumpthump.

Thump.

Thu—

"Lilianna, stop!"

She was tackled to the ground, but by then, half her heart was in her belly, thick and spoiled. She kicked furiously at Tatiana to shove her off. She had to finish it. She *had* to eat it. Her nub-fingers shoved what was left into her mouth. She chewed quickly, blood spilling from her lips. Dark blood. Then she swallowed and curled in on herself, as though protecting her belly. Surely, this Tatiana would cut her open and take it out of her. She wanted the heart all for herself.

"Oh, Lili..." Tatiana scurried away backward. "What have you become?"

"Lilith," she growled from her fetal position, then began to rock herself to sleep to the lull of the *thumpthumpthump* inside of her own body.

Mama, mama, mama.

A raven quorked in the trees above her.

A BRIEF HISTORY OF WITCHES
AN EXCERPT

~

Tatiana,

Burn this book when you have finished reading.

I trust only you with this knowledge—the words within these pages show that we were right about them. The Lucas. Their blood was poisoned by Azalea Luca, and it tore through them like a generational disease. I no longer mourn for Red, though I mourn for what she was forced to become. She never had a choice.

I see you have found happiness, someone who loves you and seeks only to protect you. A daughter to care for the way your mother cared for you. I, too, have found happiness, Tatiana. Birgitte and I now lead the pack—Daciana did not survive the journey home to Silvania after the war, and a leader was needed. I never saw myself as a leader until I mastered all forms of the Craft. I invoked the power of the earth, the moon, and blood.

It was more than that, though. I did not believe I would survive the flames. My life had to be taken for Torenia to die. I believe it was my acceptance of death that allowed me to be reborn, unharmed by the flame while Torenia burned to ash.

Do not tell the others—I know Sorin lives with you, and I wonder if Lilianna will be drawn to you as well. The Craft in Ocleau is so strong. As I finish the pages of this history, I ask you to keep my secret, for I am, for the first time, truly happy.

Protecting my heart from love only caused me more pain. So, I embrace it now.

Forever your friend,
Alina Nastaca

ACKNOWLEDGMENTS

It's a scary feeling to give acknowledgements for this book, because at the end of the day, it is also a goodbye to the series. The journey of this process began when I was fourteen, over half my life ago. What was once a ten-chapter story just shy of ten thousand words, turned into a four book fantasy series. So my first thank you is to myself, I couldn't have done it without you.

To the Quill & Crow team, Cassandra, Alma, Stefanie, my wonderful editor, Tiffany. Thank you for taking a chance with The Blood Bound Series, and giving her a home.

To my friends and family who have watched me on this adventure and cheered me along throughout the highs and lows. Thanks for sticking with it, supporting me, showing up to my in-person events to fill the space and give me confidence.

To you, to the readers, who picked up these books and gave them an audience. You came back for more, wanted to see the outcomes of these characters. I wouldn't have this series without an audience.

A special shoutout to Soph, who spoke softly of queer joy over the years. Our conversations changed the outcome of Alina's story, who was not supposed to make it to the end. You reminded me that softness is not a weakness, but a strength. So I channeled that into Alina, gave her the ending she deserved, and the story is better for it.

And to Kate, my oyster. Without this series, I would not have met you, and having you has changed my whole life for the best. You've beta read, listened to me yapping about theories and ideas. You've always given critical feedback, in writing and in life—especially in life. Every twenty-five (let's face it, more like fifty) minute voice note you sent, every ounce of your opinion, matters to me.

INDEX A
THE BLOOD BOUND SERIES TIMELINE

<u>The Year of the Curse</u> (1504) Azalea Luca's time/Blood Coven
<u>The Year of the Pines</u> (1781) Torenia is 7/Ashen Heart
<u>The Year of Ash</u> (1783) Song of the Sea
<u>The Year of the Siren</u> (1785) Song of the Sea
<u>The Year of Gluttony</u> (1786) Song of the Sea
<u>The Year of the Raven</u> (1791) Torenia is 17/Ashen Heart
<u>The Year of the Brothers</u> (1795) Brotherhood is won
<u>The Year of Indulgence</u> (1798) Torenia meets Roman/Ashen Heart
<u>The Year of the Black Tide</u> (1808) Song of the Sea
<u>The Dark Years</u> (10 years time)
<u>The Year of the Moon</u> (1891) Red's time/Blood Coven/Blood Queen

INDEX B
TRIGGER INDEX

This book contains the following:

Blood Drinking
Body Horror
Child Death
Fantasy Violence
Gaslighting
Mentions of Rape
Murder

ABOUT THE AUTHOR

Sabrina Voerman is a West Coaster with a penchant for visiting the numerous cemeteries across Vancouver Island. With a profound love of fairy tales and all things witchy, she draws her inspiration from the nature around her, allowing it to bleed into her storytelling. She is always seeking new adventures and places to explore, either in life or in her writing. When she isn't traversing all Vancouver Island has to offer, she can be found with a cup of coffee either reading a book or writing one.

THANK YOU FOR READING

Thank you for reading *Blood Queen*. We deeply appreciate our readers, and are grateful for everyone who takes the time to leave us a review. If you're interested, please visit our website to find review links. Your reviews help small presses and indie authors thrive, and we appreciate your support.

Other Titles by Sabrina Voerman

Blood Coven

Ashen Heart

Song of the Sea